PRAISE FOR JENNIFER ASHLEY
AND *THE PIR...*

"The heated ve... ...enes keep things spic... ...*imes*

"Readers who re... ...ably tortured heroes and spirited heroines who can give as good as they get will find much to savor in the latest bracing mix of sexy romance and treacherous intrigue from the consistently satisfying Ashley."

—*Booklist*

"The twists and turns within this narrative held me captivated until the final page. This is one tale of passion and adventure you don't want to miss!"

—*Round Table Reviews*

"*The Pirate Hunter* is a wildly exciting adventure story. Smoldering sensuality and intense emotions from the characters make this a nonstop read!"

—*The Best Reviews*

"...with *The Pirate Hunter*, Jennifer Ashley delivers as promised. The action is non-stop.... If you enjoy a good pirate read, don't miss *The Pirate Hunter*!"

—*Romance and Friends*

"...Jennifer Ashley has done it again! *The Pirate Hunter*...is nothing short of brilliant! Whatever you do, don't miss this book!"

—*Romance Reader at Heart*

PRAISE FOR
THE PIRATE NEXT DOOR!

"*The Pirate Next Door* is a wonderful tale full of humor, passion, intrigue, excitement, and non-stop adventure."

—*Romance Reviews Today*

"A witty and splendidly magical romance."

—*Booklist*

"*The Pirate Next Door* is a fast-paced, enjoyable story, one guaranteed to throw a bright spot into a dreary fall evening."

—*The Romance Reader*

"I was teased, tantalized, and enthralled while reading *The Pirate Next Door*! Full of twists and turns, adventure, love and lust, and betrayals, this is a great new addition to the pirate books of romance!"

—*RomanceJunkies.com*

"A delightful treat."

—*All About Romance*

SECOND MEETINGS

"Why are you alive?" Honoria demanded.

"That happy to see me, are you?"

Something had happened to his voice. It had always been deep, with a faintly French accent, but now it had an edge to it, like it had been broken and imperfectly repaired. Gravel on a dry road had a sound like that.

She took several gulps of air. "Happy to see you? Why should I be happy to see you?"

Christopher placed his hands on her shoulders. Heat burned through her silk dressing gown.

"The last time we met, you threw yourself into my arms."

"The last time," she repeated, barely able to breathe. "Why is there a *this* time?"

ACKNOWLEDGMENTS

Special thanks to the members of the Valley of the Sun and Desert Rose chapters of RWA for all their enthusiasm and support, as well as for being a nice bunch of people. Thanks also to the ladies who put together the gatherings called Celebrate Romance, where good books are celebrated. And as always, thanks to my editor, Kate Seaver, for her wonderful encouragement and support of my zany adventure romances.

Other books by Jennifer Ashley:

**THE PIRATE HUNTER
THE PIRATE NEXT DOOR
PERILS OF THE HEART**

The
Care & Feeding of
Pirates

Jennifer Ashley

LEISURE BOOKS   NEW YORK CITY

A LEISURE BOOK®

February 2005

Published by

Dorchester Publishing Co., Inc.
200 Madison Avenue
New York, NY 10016

ISBN 0-8439-5281-4

Visit us on the web at www.dorchesterpub.com.

The
Care & Feeding of
Pirates

Chapter One

June 1813

Honoria Ardmore looked across the dark street and straight into the face of the pirate Christopher Raine.

Mists swirled between her and the apparition, obscuring the pale smudge of his golden hair, the bulk of his tall, rawboned body, and his tanned and handsome face.

Three ladies in opera finery and enormous, wavering headdresses nearly ran her down. One sniffed to her companions, "Well, really."

Honoria craned to see around them, searching the mists, but the apparition had gone.

He'd never been there, of course. Christopher Raine was dead. He'd been hung by the neck in Charleston four years earlier, captured by her brother, James, tried and condemned to death for the crime of being a pirate and liking it.

Sailors afterward spoke of seeing his ghost in a haunted ship with a demon crew, the notorious Captain Raine scouring the world to seek his vengeance. None mentioned him turning up after a deplorable production of *Love's Labor's Lost* at Covent Garden Theatre in the middle of the London Season.

The street teemed with people spilling from the theatre. They flowed past Honoria, never caring that they blocked her view of the shadows of Bow Street. Just as the crowd parted and Honoria could once again see the place she'd spied him, the black bulk of the carriage her sister-in-law had hired rolled in front of her and halted.

The hired footman hopped from his perch and opened the door, looking pleased with his own efficiency. His face fell when Honoria climbed past him, too distracted to give him a tip.

She plopped to the lumpy seat, limbs weak, and peered anxiously through the dusty panes. There was nothing to see, of course.

There never had been. Christopher Raine had been dead for four years. She had finished with him. It bothered her that her imagination had conjured him tonight out of the rather thick air.

Her sister-in-law, Diana, climbed more gracefully in beside her, settled herself on the seat, and gave the footman the nod to close the door. The carriage jerked forward, nearly scraping another. The mists thickened, swallowing the crowds, the street, and ghosts of pirates.

"Are you all right, dearest?" Diana asked her. "I know it's been a rotten day."

Honoria dragged her attention from the window. "Yes, perfectly fine, thank you." She kept her Charleston tones dulcet and moderated, aware of Diana's scrutiny.

Diana was right, this day had been just awful. First, a maid had let Honoria's best pair of gloves fall into the fire, where they'd burned merrily, giving off a lovely stench of roasting silk. When Honoria and Diana had gone to a glove maker's in Oxford Street to replace them, they'd encountered three ladies who'd amused themselves making fun of Honoria's accent.

Diana had grown coldly angry at them, but Honoria had only held her head high. She would never dream of responding to anyone ill-mannered enough to taunt a stranger.

Then Diana's deaf daughter Isabeau had cut the ribbons from all Honoria's slippers because they were the perfect length to finish the rope she'd been weaving. She wanted to swing across the landing, like her step-papa did on his ship. The predictable disaster ensued. Isabeau's bruises had been kissed before she'd been put firmly to bed and Honoria's slippers hastily repaired.

The carriage had been late, it poured rain, the play had been dreadful, and the crowd in the theatre was unruly and rude.

All this paled next to the stunned shock of looking into the fog and seeing Christopher Raine.

Do calm yourself, Honoria, she snapped silently. *You cannot possibly have seen him.*

And she would not, absolutely would not, let herself remember the weight of his body on hers, the

3

cold floor against her back, his wicked smile as he whispered, "That's my Honoria."

No one knew, *and no one would ever know,* she added firmly, Honoria's Secret.

Diana sighed as she leaned back into the hard seat. "I had forgotten how wearying an evening at the theatre could be. Everyone peering at us through quizzing glasses or lorgnettes as though we were fascinating insects. No wonder I ran away from London."

"Then why did we come out?" Honoria asked. She gazed through the window again as they rolled into James Street and made their way to Long Acre. She saw no sign of a blond, gray-eyed, sinfully handsome pirate anywhere.

"I thought it would be a treat for you," Diana answered. "I am sorry." She puckered her brow, then gave a soft laugh. "I am lying. I wanted you to myself tonight. After you marry Rupert, I shan't have the time with you that I've had this past year. It's been a joy to have such a friend."

For one panicked instant, Honoria thought, *Who is Rupert?* before her senses returned. "I should think you'd like me settling down with Mr. Templeton. I'm sure I've been no less than a clinging limpet."

"Well, of course you haven't," Diana exclaimed. "If James has said so, I'll box his ears."

"No, no." Her sister-in-law really would box James Ardmore's ears, or at least throw something at him. He'd throw something back, and then they'd burst into a fine shouting match. Diana and Honoria's brother had a marriage of turbulence that Honoria did not quite understand. She did understand that they were madly in love with each other. Why this should involve very loud arguments and flying objects, she did not know.

But she suddenly remembered Christopher Raine's kiss and his touch on her body, and what it had done to her. Perhaps she understood all too well.

She felt queasy. Diana was staring at her as though she could read her thoughts. Honoria had never confided in Diana, had believed she'd never need to. The only one who'd known of her frightful infatuation with Christopher Raine had been her brother Paul, and Paul had died so long ago. She'd never, of course, breathed a word to James. Her older brother was not a man to whom one bared one's soul.

Honoria made her mouth move, striving to keep up her end of the conversation. "James simply wants you to himself, Diana. He'll be pleased that Mr. Templeton will take me off his hands."

Diana gave her a look that was all too shrewd. "Yes, but will you be pleased?"

Honoria stopped herself plucking her skirt or swallowing or in any way betraying her nervousness. She was practiced at it. "Why would I not be pleased? Mr. Templeton is a respectable Englishman with fine business prospects in America. And I've been on the shelf far too long. It's time I got out from underfoot."

"You are mixing your metaphors."

"I am sorry," Honoria snapped. "It's been a trying day."

Diana's features softened into a smile. "It has at that. I will be happy when we return to my father's island."

Honoria felt suddenly contrite. She'd looked forward to residing alone here in London with Diana in Diana's father's house. Diana had gallantly taken Honoria to the best of the London sites, helped her buy a new wardrobe, and introduced her to prominent people, like Lady Stoke and Lady Featherstone, who had in turn introduced Honoria to Mr. Templeton. Honoria ought to have known that Diana's heart was not in it. Scandals in Diana's past made London uncomfortable for her, not to mention the fact that she was married to the notorious pirate hunter James Ardmore. Only the influence of Lord Stoke and Diana's father with the Admiralty let the two ladies live in relative peace.

"I know you miss James," Honoria said, reaching out to touch Diana's hand. Honoria's own relationship with her brother was problematic at best, and she always breathed a sigh of relief when he ran off to chase pirates. But Diana needed James the same way a body needed air.

"The inconvenience of being married to a villain," Diana said, smiling a little.

"You like him being a villain," Honoria said.

"I do, that." Her smile turned playful. "Who knows? Perhaps Mr. Templeton will prove to be one, too."

"Nonsense," Honoria said, though her heart was not in the banter. "Mr. Templeton is far too respectable to be a villain."

Diana's eyes sparkled. "But you wish he would be. You have the same craving for excitement that I have, Honoria, and you know this."

"Don't be silly, Diana. Excitement only leads to trouble." *And I should know.*

Diana gave Honoria a long look, assessing and shrewd, as only Diana Ardmore could. Her sister-in-law was far too perceptive and often saw through Honoria's shell, especially on the occasions when Honoria did not want her to.

"I beg your pardon," Diana said. "I know I go on too much about James. I am certain it becomes cloying."

"Not at all." Honoria made her voice brisk under Diana's too-knowing gaze. "I think it mighty fine that you won James's heart. I was never aware that he had one."

Honoria's pen hovered over the blank page of her journal. A droplet of ink trembled on the nib, waiting for her to change it into words.

Her fingers were cold, despite the fire that had been built high. She and Diana had calmed themselves with hot tea and a late supper in the sitting room, chatting of the pleasant island of Haven on which they would spend much of the summer.

Or at least Diana had chatted. Honoria's mind had only whirled with thoughts of Christopher Raine, despite her attempts to tamp down the memories.

His name had never been recorded in the book that lay flat on her bedroom table, waiting for her to write in it, nor in any journal she'd kept since she'd met him the first time.

James had brought him to the Charleston house long, long ago, along with the irritating Grayson Fin-

ley, who was now lording it over London as Viscount
Stoke. The three rogues had been young, arrogant,
and breathtakingly handsome. Grayson and Christopher were both blond, Grayson with mischief-filled
blue eyes, Christopher with eyes of cool gray. Her
brother James was black-haired and green-eyed and
the most arrogant of the three.

Honoria had been a giddy girl of eighteen and
madly in love with Christopher Raine. She'd saved
every penny pamphlet, every newspaper story, every
exaggerated picture book about the notorious pirate
Captain Raine. Christopher had a French father and
an English mother, captained a crew of mixed nationality, and was loyal to no one.

At the time, Christopher had been twenty-two,
strong, tall, and well-muscled. He'd worn his wheatblond hair in a plait down his back and dressed in a
dark blue coat and breeches and ivory linen shirt.
She'd met him in the garden room, a chamber of
lovely coolness, colorful tile, and a whispering fountain. He'd regarded her with eyes as clear as ice and a
smile that sent her thoughts rocketing to unimaginable places.

Not that James had introduced them. In fact, James
had forbidden Honoria to leave her rooms while
Grayson and Christopher lurked in the house. Why
they'd been there at all, she'd never learned—probably to discuss some nefarious scheme that James was
hatching. It had been Paul, Honoria's young brother
and her other self, who had noted Honoria's excitement and promised to distract James so that Honoria

could slip downstairs and at least have a look at the famous Christopher Raine.

And there Christopher had stood, alone in the garden room at the far end of the house, the quiet broken only by the trickle of the fountain into its basin. Honoria had crept forward and asked in her timid, well-bred voice if he'd autograph the pamphlet she held crumpled in her damp hand.

He'd taken the pamphlet, his blunt fingers brushing her small ones, opened it, and read it. The pamphlet had amused him. The corners of his gray eyes had crinkled as he leafed through it. He stopped and read out some of the more amazing bits in his faintly accented English, and made her laugh.

He agreed to sign the book with the ink and pen she'd brought for the purpose, then he'd softly requested a kiss for its return.

No, that was wrong. That memory was Honoria trying to place a romantic glow on what had really happened.

What he'd done was to hold the pamphlet over his head, grin impudently, and tell her he'd give it back only if she kissed him. She'd grown annoyed at his presumption, and told him so, but his smile had outdone her. So she'd risen on tiptoe, trembling all over, and pursed her lips. He'd bent to her, eyes closing, and kissed her.

In an instant, every bit of playfulness between them had vanished. He'd kissed her again, and again, drawing her closer. The pamphlet had fallen, unheeded, to the floor.

9

Her heart pumping hard, she'd twined her hands around his neck and frantically kissed him back.

She'd let him lower her to the cool tiles, let him twist his hand through her hair, let him do so many things.

She'd thought he'd want her virtue, but he had not asked for it. He'd touched her in every other way, but they'd not joined. Not then.

Afterward, he'd returned her pamphlet, said goodbye, and walked away as if he'd not cared. He'd glanced back at her once, though, and his gray eyes had held something unreadable. He studied her as if trying to understand something, then he turned and was gone.

She'd not seen him again for nine years.

In 1809, Christopher Raine captured a fabulous prize, a ship called the *Rosa Bonita,* which was filled to the brim with gold from Mexico and bound for Napoleon. Newspapers printed story after lurid story about the ship's capture and the devastating loss for the French, who were struggling to fund their ongoing war. The legend of Christopher Raine grew.

By then James Ardmore had turned pirate hunter. He'd gone after his old friend Captain Raine and caught him.

Christopher was brought in, tried, and condemned to death. Of the Mexican gold there had been no sign. Christopher refused to tell what had become of it, and typically, James had not cared. Let the world speculate on the missing gold; James wanted only one fewer pirate on the seas.

During the week Christopher was imprisoned, Charleston went mad for pirates. The newspapers printed stories about legendary pirates of old, a pirate fair was held near the docks, ladies hosted masked balls with pirate themes. Books on pirates became the rage, children begged for cutlasses so they could board and sink the neighbors.

Women of dubious repute flocked to the fortress where Christopher was being held. They begged to see him, begged for a lock of his hair or a scrap of his clothing. Ladies in fine carriages pretended they needed to pass the fort on their way somewhere else, and sent footmen to beg for an audience with the notorious pirate. A few footmen even asked on their own account.

But the only lady admitted, shrouded and veiled from curious eyes, was Honoria Ardmore. To her surprise, the turnkey had let her in, taken her to the filthy cell in which he received visitors, and locked her in with him. She'd unshrouded herself and faced him with nothing to say.

Christopher was no longer an arrogant youth. Sandpaper bristles covered his jaw, his eyes and mouth bore lines at the corners. He wore an old shirt and breeches and scarred boots that had seen better days. But his hair was just as wheat-blond, his eyes as clear gray, his smile as sinful.

They'd studied each other for a long time in silence. Then he'd said he was glad she'd come. She'd touched his cheek and asked him to kiss her.

No, no, that memory was another glossing over of the past. In truth, Honoria had wordlessly clasped his forearms, sinking her fingers into his flesh, and he'd gathered her to him and kissed her. She remembered

11

the rasp of his unshaved whiskers on her lips, the strength of his arms around her back.

They were on the floor before they'd spoken more than two sentences. She'd let him. Proper, sweet, genteel Honoria Ardmore had let Christopher Raine take her to the floor of the cell and make love to her. The memory brought heat to her face, a flush to her body. He'd asked her permission—

No, again, her treacherous memories were trying to make the encounter sweetly romantic. It had not been romantic at all, but hot and panicky and rough and aching. He'd said in a low voice, "I'm going to die, Honoria. I want something to think about when they take me to the scaffold."

She'd touched his face, so rough and hard and unlike those of the proper Charleston gentlemen who courted her. She thought of the throng of women outside, each of whom would gladly throw at him what he wanted. "Why?" she grated. "Why do you want me?"

"Because you came to me," he'd answered. "And I love you."

He lied about the last part, she knew that. It was what a gentleman said to a lady to seduce her. Women longed to be cherished, not just wanted, and gentlemen used that fact to their advantage.

She'd said quietly that he could have her if he liked. *No.* If she made herself face the truth, she'd remember that she'd begged, "Please, yes, Christopher," and clung to him like a wanton. He'd laughed, kissed her and brought her to heated readiness, then thrust himself straight into her.

12

When they were finished, he'd kissed her gently, then helped her to dress. He'd made a last request of his jailors and, to her amazement, they'd granted it.

The next day, they'd dragged him to the gallows. The newspapers printed a flamboyant account of the hanging, which most of Charleston flocked to see. Honoria stayed firmly at home, shut herself in her room, and told everyone she was ill. She'd tied a black ribbon around her box of keepsakes and pushed it to the back of her drawer.

That day had been the worst of her life. Today was becoming a fast contender.

The droplet of ink fell from her pen and became an ugly blob on the paper. One transparent tear followed it.

Honoria quickly tore the paper from the book, crumpled it, and pushed it aside. Firming her lips, she touched the pen to the paper again and scribbled, "Attended a performance of *Love's Labor's Lost,* which I've always thought was a silly play. The actors, I don't believe, had ever been in love before. The *Labor* part of the title was the only truth."

She paused. Her fingers shook, and she quieted them. "I believed the actors fools. Or am I the fool? I thought I saw—"

She broke off. She could not write the name, even now. "I believe I am becoming senile. According to London's very low opinion of spinsters, I should be off my head by now. Thank heaven for Mr. Templeton's proposal or I should, as the quaint saying goes, lead apes into hell."

She lowered the pen, her fingers aching. Her head

hurt, and she could no longer think of bright, amusing things to say.

She heard Diana's muffled footsteps on the stairs as her sister-in-law ascended to the third floor. Just above Honoria's room lay the nursery, where Isabeau and Diana's baby son slept. They'd called the baby Paul. Honoria thought this a little unfair to the child, because anyone called Paul Ardmore would have very big shoes to fill.

She lifted the pen, wrote in the book, "My entire life is a lie."

She underlined "lie." Above her and far away, she heard Diana crooning, "Who's mama's ickle lad, then?"

Honoria carefully wiped her pen and placed it in the pen tray. Then she rose from her writing desk and turned toward the bed.

Christopher Raine was standing beside it.

Honoria stepped back abruptly. She upset the chair, which fell against the desk, dislodging her journal and pen tray. The pen tray crashed to the floor.

After three agonizing heartbeats, Diana's footsteps creaked to the stairs. "Honoria? Are you all right?"

Honoria dashed to the door, flung it open. "Yes, indeed," she called up breathlessly. "I dropped my pens, that is all."

Diana peered down the half-dark staircase. She had little Paul hoisted on one arm. After a long moment, she said, "All right, then. Good night," and retreated up the stairs.

Honoria shut the door firmly. She resisted turning

the key. If Diana heard the click of the lock, she might be down again, demanding to know what was wrong.

She whirled around again. Christopher Raine was gone.

"Oh, no you don't," she snapped. "I saw you this time."

He stepped out from behind the bed. He had moved so that the hangings would hide him from the door, in case Diana tread all the way downstairs.

He came to her as she stood, motionless, by the writing table. He certainly looked alive. His quiet footfalls, the brush of his sleeve against his shirt made him sound alive.

He'd been well-muscled and fine of body four years ago; he was even more so now. His shirt clung to broad shoulders; black breeches, shiny with wear, stretched over taut thighs. His boots, worn and black, tracked mud and tar onto Diana's lovely carpet. Candlelight burnished golden bristles on his chin and the finer curls at the opening of his shirt.

"*Why* are you alive?" she demanded.

"That happy to see me, are you?"

Something had happened to his voice. It had always been deep, with a faintly French accent, but now it had an edge to it, like it had been broken and imperfectly repaired. Gravel on a dry road had a sound like that.

She took several gulps of air. "Happy to see you? Why should I be happy to see you?"

He placed his hands on her shoulders. Heat burned through her silk dressing gown.

15

"The last time we met, you threw yourself into my arms."

"The last time," she repeated, barely able to breathe. "Why is there a this time?"

"Because there is. Stop asking questions and let me kiss you."

As demanding as ever. He bent to her, his breath on her lips, his eyes cool and clear and gray. Honoria silenced every screaming question in her mind and twined her arms about his neck.

She'd never kissed any man but him. She'd done it so many times in her dreams, but far too few times in life. Maybe he was a ghost in truth, and he'd thought it humorous to haunt her. She somehow did not care.

For a ghost, he certainly was solid. And hot. She'd never felt anything like it short of sticking her hand into a fire. But then, they said he'd gone straight to hell and been turned away. Even Beelzebub had not wanted Christopher Raine.

She ran her hands across his shoulders, down his long back, under his warm hair. No man could be more alive than this. His pulse beat strong in his throat, and his hardness pressed her thin dressing gown.

He nudged his bent knee between hers, pulling her full-length against his body. She found her dressing gown parting, his thigh resting between her legs, right against her opening. She wanted more than anything to slide along his thigh, to savor the sweet friction.

"That's the Honoria I remember," he murmured.

Each time they met had been like this. They'd spoken a few opening phrases, then had been unable to keep their hands off each other. He cradled her backside, dragging her still closer while his tongue flicked into her mouth.

She tried to push him away. It was like pushing a brick wall. She turned her head. The bristles on his jaw burned her skin.

"Christopher," she gasped. "We must talk."

His eyes were like smoke in the sunshine. "I didn't come here to talk."

"That is obvious. But you're supposed to be dead."

He brushed his thumbs over her collarbone, spreading heat beneath the dressing gown. "You keep saying that. Inconvenient for you, is it?"

The ties on his shirt were frayed. He smelled of soap and tar and the faint musk she'd remember until the day she died. "No. I want you to be alive." She traced the hard muscles of his arms. "But I don't understand—Christopher, we have so many things to talk about."

He framed her face in his hands, his thumbs warm on her cheekbones. "For once we have a convenient bed. But I think I prefer the floor, with you."

They had carpet this time, at least. But if she allowed him to take her there, she would surrender to him again, and that would be the end of Honoria Ardmore.

The years of absence had not diminished his strength. He rocked her back, threaded his hands through her loosened hair. He was right; questions could come later. She parted her lips, let him explore her in slow, familiar, intimate, breathtaking strokes.

The door clicked open and a cold draft poured into the room. From the doorway, Diana Ardmore said clearly, "Take your hands off her, or I will shoot you."

17

Christopher stopped. After one tense moment, he eased his lips from Honoria's. Looking neither puzzled nor angry, he steadied Honoria on her feet and turned to face the intruder.

Diana stood on the threshold in a green silk dressing gown, her glorious red hair hanging over her shoulders. She held a pistol in one firm hand, pointed it straight at Christopher.

In shock and sudden, shaking anger, Honoria stepped in front of him. "It is all right, Diana," she said in her clear, well-bred voice. "He is my husband."

Chapter Two

"I still do not understand," the red-haired woman called Diana Ardmore said.

She touched the creased piece of the paper that said Christopher Raine and Honoria Ardmore had been married in Charleston on the eighth of November 1809.

Christopher drained his glass of whiskey and carefully set it on the dining room table. He'd always heard that when ladies had something to discuss, they brought out the tea. The woman who had married James Ardmore had gone straight for the whiskey. She'd made Honoria drink a slosh as well.

Honoria had taken one sip and made a face. She'd put the glass primly on the table and held on to the arms of the chair like she was on a ship about to go down.

She refused to look at Christopher or Diana or the

19

license. But here was a fact. She'd kept the license. She even carried it about with her.

Her black hair tumbled loose, a curl snagging on the clasp of her dressing gown. Half-dressed and mussed, she looked good enough to eat.

Christopher had been following her all evening. When he'd seen her emerge from the theatre, he'd wanted nothing more than to sprint across the cobbles, snatch her up, and drag her off. She was his wife; they could find some cozy inn in which to settle down and become reacquainted.

He'd already discovered the whereabouts of the house in which she stayed on Mount Street in Mayfair. The house belonged to one Admiral Lockwood, whose daughter, Diana, had married James Ardmore. Unbelievable.

It had been simple to slip into the house and quietly climb the stairs to Honoria's bedchamber while the ladies consumed tea in the drawing room. He'd easily deduced which bedchamber was Honoria's, the painfully neat one with every book on the table lined up and her pens in an exact row in the pen tray.

He truly had meant only to speak to her, to discover what she still felt for him, but watching her enter the room and undress with the help of a sharp-faced maid had sent his blood into high temperatures. He was surprised the curtains behind which he'd stood hadn't suddenly bulged forward.

He'd waited until he was certain the maid would not return. Honoria had sat at the desk, posture correct, primly writing in the book before lifting her head and staring off into the distance. Her lips had parted, her cheeks had colored, and he'd hoped to God she'd not been thinking of this Mr. Templeton, or whatever his name was, that she planned to marry.

Talking had been suddenly out of the question. He'd stepped out of hiding, determined to go to her, yank her head back, and kiss her until all thoughts of Mr. Toodlewink had vanished from her mind.

She'd faced him, chin out, and demanded in her imperious voice just what he was doing alive. But her kisses were as sweet as he remembered.

He wondered if Mrs. Ardmore would have shot him if he hadn't let Honoria go. The look in her gray-blue eyes now said very probably.

He answered her. "It was a condemned man's wish. The chaplain who visited the prisoners was a romantic. He pulled strings to get the license, and then he married us. The next day, I was taken out to be hung."

Honoria's lips whitened. "Which, presumably, you weren't."

She sounded very put out about it. "I was let off," he said. "But the magistrates feared they'd cause a riot if they announced they'd let me go, so they put a hood on the next man in line for the noose, and told the crowd and the newspaper he was me. He went out in a blaze of glory," he finished dryly.

Diana Ardmore shifted the baby on her arm. The lad had a brush of black fuzz on top of his head. He was asleep, as limp as only a baby safe in his mother's arms could be. Men slept like that after making love. There was something about cradling oneself on the bosom of a beautiful woman that gave a man over to peaceful slumber.

21

"What happened to you?" she asked.

Christopher turned his glass on the table, throwing spangles of light over the dark wood. "They tied my hands and slipped me out the back to a cart. I still thought I was on my way to the gibbet. But things got quieter and I realized that we weren't anywhere near the gallows. When the cart finally stopped, I was made to get into a longboat. The jailor with me told me that my sentence had been commuted, but to keep it quiet. The boat took me to a ship, and the ship sailed out to sea."

"Where did the ship go?" Diana continued. The baby moved his fist, and she absently rocked him.

"China." Christopher pulled the decanter of whiskey to him, poured more amber liquid into his glass. "The ship was a merchantman, and I worked on it. I have no idea whether the captain knew who I was. I climbed yardarms and stood watches like one of the crew."

Honoria slanted him a frosty look. "I am surprised you didn't try to take over the ship. All that cargo must have tempted you."

He let himself smile. "I didn't have my trusted crew, my wife. Besides, the merchantman was paltry. I didn't mind being a common sailor for a while."

Honoria raised a brow. "After the *Rosa Bonita*, I am certain no mere merchant ship could live up to your standards."

He laughed. "Ah, yes, the *Rosa Bonita*. The take of a lifetime."

"Strange that the gold was never recovered."

He'd suspected that it had not been, but he liked

that Honoria confirmed the fact. "Your brother never found it?" he said lightly. "He's going soft."

"He didn't look for it, so far as I know," she said. "He didn't care about it."

"Is that why you've returned?" Diana Ardmore broke in. "For the gold?"

She was a woman who kept to the point. Christopher took a moment to sip his whiskey and place the glass back on the table before responding. "I returned for my wife."

He let his gaze rest on Honoria. He wagered that Mrs. Ardmore had never heard of the *Rosa Bonita* or the Mexican gold before this, but the woman was shrewd.

Mrs. Ardmore studied the license again. "Why were you let off after they'd condemned you? Did the governor decide to be lenient?"

Christopher raised his brows, surprised. "It was James Ardmore's doing. He got me released. He never told you?"

Diana looked quietly astonished.

Honoria said in a hard voice, "I feel certain I would have remembered if he'd mentioned it."

"Did you never tell him you'd married me?"

The placket of her dressing gown was parted slightly. She hadn't refastened it quite right, and the silk gaped to show a curve of her bosom.

"That is not exactly the sort of information I could impart to James," she informed him.

"He is your brother."

"We are not close."

No, but Honoria now lived with James's wife in

23

London. Christopher did not know the lay of the land here, and he did not like that. He had to tread carefully, and that was not easy with Honoria glowering at him while her pretty bosom went up and down.

If he could have finished making love to her upstairs, he could have sated himself and turned his mind quietly to other matters. Instead, he sat here randy as a sailor who hadn't had shore leave in six months. Two beautiful women perfuming the air, one of whom was his wife, and he had to sit behind the table and keep his thoughts at bay. He took a long drink of whiskey.

"Why would James save your life?" Diana continued, ever practical. "I thought he'd arrested you in the first place."

"He owed me a debt."

In truth, Christopher had been surprised at the man's generosity. Christopher had information that Ardmore had very much wanted to know, but he hadn't realized he could bargain for his life with it.

"So you have been in China all this time?" Diana continued.

"I worked my way from port to port," he said, glossing over disease and hardship and the times he believed he'd never find home again. "I also searched for my crew. I'd had a small fleet before my flagship was destroyed and my crew scattered. I want to find out what happened to them." He shrugged. "They're my family."

That was true in the deepest sense, but he had no wish to become sentimental before Honoria and Diana.

"What brought you to London?" Diana asked,

rocking her son again. She might be making small talk at a dinner party. He took on an ingenuous look. She would report anything he said to her husband, and Christopher knew it. She knew he knew it. He knew she knew he—oh, never mind.

"Still looking for my crew," he said. "My second in command is rumored to be in England. My ultimate destination was Charleston, but fate shortened my journey."

Honoria raised her brows. "Why on earth would you want to return to Charleston?"

He thought of the way her breasts had grown taut under his touch not a half hour ago. If he saw well enough, her kissable nipples were tightening even now. "To find my wife, of course. Lucky for me, I opened a London newspaper and saw her name in it." He let his voice cool. "Announcing her engagement to another man."

She did not even flinch, or hide her head in shame, or tumble from her chair in a swoon. "I thought we would come to that."

"Why else would I be here?"

Her lips whitened. "I thought you were dead. Long ago."

"I hope so. Else you could be arrested for committing bigamy."

"You were officially dead and hanged in Charleston," she said in rising anger.

"No. I was officially transported. There was never a record of my hanging and death. Did it never occur to you to check before you rushed into another marriage?"

25

"You gave me no reason to believe you were alive. You disappeared."

"But I have turned up again. And I claim the marriage."

She turned in her chair, one arm resting on its back. "Why should you?"

Her loose hair hung down her back in a black wave, a riot of curls haloing her face. Her limbs were long and shapely. She had the beauty of a deer, quick, lovely, graceful. He reflected that he'd love to see her run. Along one of the white sun-drenched beaches of a Caribbean island, perhaps, and she'd have left her dress behind. He would be pursuing her, of course, and she would not be trying very hard to get away.

"I didn't marry you in jest," he said. "I married you because I wanted you. So tell Mr. Tuppeny that you have a previous contract and are no longer able to marry him."

She reddened. "Mr. *Templeton* is a good and respectable gentleman."

"Then why marry him under false pretenses?"

Honoria glared, not one ounce of love in her eyes. "I will ask that you set me free so that I can marry him rightfully."

Christopher's famous temper stirred. He did not release it very often, but when he did, lesser fleets sailed for their lives.

He had not expected Honoria to welcome him with open arms. He had been, in fact, surprised to find her still unmarried. But in that cell in Charleston, when she'd promised to be his, he'd read in her eyes true grief for him, not just pity. She had loved him.

When he'd read the announcement of her engagement, his strong reaction had surprised him. Before that he'd thought he would speak to her, catch up on old times, let her go. But when he'd seen that she'd promised herself to another, he knew he could not sit back and tamely let her walk away. He would find her, remind her what she'd felt for him years ago. If this Tuzzlewitz truly loved her, he would be magnanimous and not stand in her way.

"What is right is a woman obeying her husband," he told her steadily.

Her eyes sparkled like a lightning storm on a vicious night. "You were my husband for all of a day."

"I have been your husband for four years."

"In name only!"

He smiled. She made his blood hot. "In all ways, Honoria. You gave me your maidenhead, remember?"

Her face went brick red. "I was distraught. I did not understand what I was doing."

"Really? I believe your words were *Please take me, Christopher.*"

"If you'd been a gentleman, you'd have sent me home."

He got to his feet. The whiskey burned through his veins, and he wanted to laugh very hard. "I was a *pirate.* I was about to be hanged, and you had half your clothes off. When a beautiful woman wants a pirate, the pirate obliges."

"Why are you trying to make this my fault?"

"You were made for me, Honoria. You know it, and your body knows it."

At the head of the table, James Ardmore's son

made a small mewl of protest as their voices penetrated his sleep.

Christopher threw Diana a look. "Will you excuse us, Mrs. Ardmore? My wife and I want to argue."

"I think I had better stay," Diana said quickly.

"Why?" He wanted to laugh and rage at the same time. "Are you afraid she'll try to make herself a widow?"

"I am not certain what I fear," Diana answered. "But I will stay."

Honoria shoved back her chair, jumped to her feet. The chair fell over backward. Baby Ardmore squeezed his eyes closed and let out an irritated wail.

"I beg your pardon, Diana," she said, her voice ringing majestically. "I certainly will not stay here and embarrass you further. Please have a servant show Mr. Raine the door. Good night."

She fled the room, banging a few more chairs in her haste. The dressing gown slid down her shoulders. It was a most enticing picture.

Diana crooned to her son and bounced him in her arms. After the bedroom door slammed—the draft rocketed down the stairs—and the key turned in the lock, the lad settled down again and sought his peaceful slumber.

Christopher let her go. There would be time, plenty of time. He had to search for Manda, and he could not leave England until he found her. Before he departed, he would scoop up Honoria. It was inevitable. She simply needed to become used to the idea.

Her body had fit to his again so easily. She belonged to him, he'd known it in his bones since the day he'd first met her. Circumstance had had other ideas, but circumstance had led him back to her once more.

It would be a fight. She would not come easily. But he would have her. Even if he had to drag her off kicking and screaming.

He took leave of Mrs. Ardmore and let himself out of the house. Outside, London was still misty, but a certain warmth had penetrated his blood, which began to burn hotter than the sun in the Pacific islands.

"Do you want to talk about it?" Diana asked, sitting on Honoria's bed.

Her sister-in-law had returned baby Paul to the nursery, looked in on Isabeau, seen the house locked for the night, then returned to Honoria's bedchamber. Honoria supposed Diana was tactfully giving her time to compose herself, but Honoria thought she'd never be composed again.

She felt limp and sick and worried, and at the same time very angry. How *dare* he come back to life just as she'd gotten everything sorted out and in order?

He'd done it on purpose. She was certain of it. She'd finally been ready to begin a normal life, to have a family of her own. So, of course, he'd choose just that moment to come back from the dead and turn her heart inside out.

"What is there to say?" she told Diana, her words muffled. She lay facedown on the bed, her head at its foot. She hadn't cried. Honoria Ardmore rarely cried. "You heard Christopher's story. It is true."

Diana leaned down and hugged her. "Oh, Honoria, why did you never tell anyone?"

"Who was I to tell?" She shrugged, as though it had not hurt to keep the secret. "James disappeared the day of the hanging, and I did not see him for months. And then it seemed pointless. The marriage had only lasted the day. I thought Christopher dead and gone, everything over." She sat up, pushed her hair from her face. "Are you going to tell James?"

"Well, I do not see how I can keep it from him."

Honoria took Diana's hands in hers. "Please say nothing for now. I do not want Mr. Templeton to hear of this in a roundabout fashion, nor do I want to face the gossipmongers."

"I would never say anything outside the family, Honoria," Diana said stiffly.

Honoria felt too much turmoil to apologize. Her body still quivered where Christopher had touched her, and she'd wanted to taste his mouth far into the night. If Diana had not interrupted them, Honoria would gladly have succumbed to him on the floor. Or on the bed. Or on the windowsill, for that matter, while passersby in Mount Street looked up in astonishment.

"Please let me think on it. Perhaps he will see reason and release me."

"An annulment is not as easy to obtain as you might think, especially when one party is unwilling," Diana said. "There must be very special circumstances or an embarrassing affliction on the man's part."

Honoria very much doubted Christopher would willingly say that he wanted an annulment because he was impotent. Which he wasn't. Honoria had felt that quite plainly. Even now she grew warm as her treacherous mind remembered the exact shape, length, and feel of his hardness against her abdomen.

"There is some precedent for a marriage ending when one of the parties goes missing," she said, her throat dry.

In these times of risky traveling and war and uncertainty, husbands or wives could be missing for years with no word. In that case, the remaining person could assume the other dead and marry again.

"Yes," Diana said slowly. "The trouble is, he's turned up. And you have the license, and he seems determined to keep the marriage."

"Why are you taking his side?" Honoria cried. "I would think you'd be distressed for me."

"I am, dearest." Diana put her arm around Honoria's shoulders. "I am simply pointing out the difficulties. If you like, I can ask my father's man of business, in pure speculation, of course, what legal steps might be taken."

"Please, not yet. I want to think."

Diana patted her shoulder, fell silent. Honoria hated to impede Diana like this, but she so wished no one to know her folly until she could decide what to do.

She needed to talk to Christopher, to explain, but that might do little good. Whenever they were together, she melted in a puddle of lust. Perhaps if they could meet somewhere neutral, on two sides of a very wide table, perhaps, with witnesses, they might see a way out of this mess.

The trouble was, she could not prevent Christopher from striding up and down London, proclaiming their nuptials far and wide. Christopher knew Grayson Finley, who was now Viscount Stoke. Wouldn't Grayson laugh to hear that the oh-so-proper Honoria had let herself be talked into marriage with Christopher Raine?

Grayson would tell his wife, the beautiful and lady-like Alexandra, and Alexandra would be shocked. Others would hear the news and delightedly spread it throughout the *ton*. Honoria could not run about London scolding everyone to silence. And when the news reached Charleston—and it would—she would be completely ruined.

All this was nothing, of course, to what James would say.

She needed to speak to Christopher and explain that it would be best if he went away again. James had set him free to begin a new life, he must begin it.

Surely, he would see reason. She closed her eyes, feeling again his hands on her hair, his warm lips parting hers.

Christopher would understand and go away. He had to. Because if he didn't, Honoria Ardmore would burn up to a crisp.

Christopher slid into the shadows of the Mayfair streets as he made his way south to Piccadilly. He probably did not need stealth, but it came as a habit. He liked to observe the world around him without being too closely observed himself.

Well, usually. Tonight, he was preoccupied with Honoria. With her scent, the feel of her, the taste of her, the glorious fact that she was still his wife.

His eyes and ears automatically registered the carriages and horses and people, the thieves who also tried to keep to the dark as his feet moved him toward Piccadilly and St. James's and his meeting there.

His mind and his heart, however, remained with Honoria. He wanted her with every breath. Their usual course of action was to see one another, stare for a few moments, then grab each other and start kissing. Laces tore, buttons popped, linen ripped while their hands and mouths sought each other's in desperation.

And then they'd be on the floor, her skirts raked high, his breeches open, his hands on her thighs, parting them for the inevitable and final phase of their greeting.

They simply could not keep their hands off each other. And, he reflected with a grin, why should we? She was a beautiful and sensual woman, and he was a man who needed her.

He realized he'd never be sated with her. After years apart, he still wanted her with an intensity that had become still more powerful, if that was possible.

St. James's Square, elegant by day, was a far more interesting place by night. The entire area of St. James's—the square itself, Jermyn Street, St. James's Street, Piccadilly—was riddled with clubs for the highest gentlemen in the land. Aristocrats, military leaders, and well-born gentlemen all gathered here to enjoy an atmosphere that reeked of old friends, old money, and old ties. A gentleman's club was more his home than his own house.

Or so Christopher Raine had heard. He'd never

had the pleasure of entering a gentleman's club and had no interest in doing so now.

The aristocratic St. James's had another side to it. Tucked between the respectable clubs lay the hells, gambling dens in which gentlemen rubbed shoulders with blacklegs and the less respectable. Aristocrats came to slum, to play games both legal and illegal, to talk with ladies who dressed well and enticed gentlemen to wager.

Christopher Raine came to meet a man who could help him. He entered The Nines, a tall, narrow establishment in St. James's Square, paid his fee, and went up to the first floor.

They call this vice, he thought as he looked about the gaming rooms. Compared with the vice he'd seen in the ports of Siam and China and Brazil, The Nines was a child's tea party. The cardsharps with smooth faces and watchful eyes kept to their places at tables. They busily fleeced young men who were confident that their names, their father's names, and their inheritance would allow them to lose whatever they liked.

Christopher easily found the man he was to meet. Grayson Finley stood at the foot of a hazard table, a tall man, broad of shoulder, his hair fair, his face tanned and weathered like Christopher's. He watched the dice and the thrower with a cynical expression, but Christopher noted that the man won nearly every wager he made.

Finley had once been one of the most ruthless pirates on the seas. Now he wore a frock coat and a cravat and sported a title and several estates. He'd once been a partner of James Ardmore, before Ardmore had turned pirate hunter. Finley had since married, had four children, and become a respectable aristocrat called Viscount Stoke.

Christopher did not join the dice game. Instead he took a turn at faro, a game in which the optimistic gambler wagered on what value a card would have when it was turned up. He won a few guineas and lost a few.

He found himself coming under scrutiny of a smallish man, about forty, with a pleasant face but a long, beaky nose.

"Not got the taste for it?" the man said, his voice friendly. "I notice you do not throw your family fortune down on the turn of a card."

Christopher's fortune could probably purchase the estates of a few of the aristocrats present. He shrugged. "I am a careful man, by habit." This, at least, was true.

"I am surprised you came to The Nines, then." The man smiled. "Not a place for a careful man."

"It is a way to spend an evening."

He chuckled. "A good answer, my friend. I, too, sought a way to spend the evening, although," he lowered his voice a fraction, "I do not know if I care for the company here. But a man must come to a gaming hell at least once in his life, mustn't he? I am sowing my wild oats, you see."

Christopher looked him up and down, brows rising. "You've left it a bit late," he remarked. Christopher's oats had certainly been wild, so much so that he could not remember a few years of his younger life.

The man laughed. "Too true, my friend. But I am to

be married in a few months' time, and so I decided better late than never. I have always been a careful man, myself. This is all new to me."

Marriage seemed to be catching. "Best of luck to you."

He brightened. "Thank you. I say, would you like to adjourn to a tavern? I much prefer conversation with a careful man over a comfortable pint to sowing wild oats."

Christopher glanced at the hazard table. Grayson Finley was still there watching the dice.

Christopher opened his mouth to form an excuse, but the gentleman thrust out his hand. "Ah, but we have not been introduced. The name's Templeton. Rupert Templeton."

Christopher froze for half a second before he forced a cold smile and took the other man's hand in a very firm shake. "Raine," he said. "Christopher Raine."

Templeton winced a bit at Christopher's grip, but his face showed no recognition. He'd never heard of Christopher Raine.

Christopher told Templeton to name the tavern, and then the two of them departed. Christopher felt Finley's puzzled gaze on his back, but nothing short of a volcano erupting in the heart of St. James's would keep him from walking to a nearby tavern with Honoria Ardmore's intended.

Chapter Three

The tavern in Pall Mall poured excellent ale and was full. Christopher and his new friend Rupert Templeton squeezed onto a corner of a bench and Christopher stood two pints, which Templeton said was very decent of him.

They could not have much conversation in the uproar of the regulars and those who'd dropped in on their way to or from somewhere. Near them, a few Scotsmen debated national issues with their English counterparts, and both proved that neither nation had yet bested the other in drinking ability.

Rupert Templeton was friendly, open-minded, and had not much wrong with him, to Christopher's annoyance.

The man turned to the subject of his upcoming nuptials easily enough. "Thought I'd be a bachelor into my old age, Mr. Raine, that's a fact. But when I met Miss Ardmore, I said to myself, Rupert, old man, why not give it a try? She's an American, of course, but I never held that against anyone." He chuckled.

"England is at war with America," Christopher pointed out.

"Yes, that nonsense. I have many business interests in America, and we'll settle in Charleston. She comes from a fine family, but she feels at a loose end, poor thing, since her brother married."

"Her brother," Christopher prompted, wondering what a respectable Londoner would make of James Ardmore.

Templeton took a long pull of his ale, then wiped his mouth. "I gather he is rather a legend. His wife, now, comes from a most distinguished naval family. I imagine much of his reputation is a mix-up."

Templeton was thoroughly wrong. James Ardmore was a law unto himself and damn all those who got in his way.

"I do admit," Templeton went on, "that perhaps her brother's reputation is the reason she settled for me. Perhaps better gentlemen than I did not want such a connection. I am not much of a catch, but I was pleased to be caught in her net." He chortled at his joke.

"Honoria Ardmore is a fine young woman," Christopher could not stop himself saying.

Templeton raised his brows. "Indeed she is. Do you know her?"

"I am a—friend—of the family."

"*Reee*-ly?" Templeton showed happy interest. "I had no idea. They've never mentioned a Mr. Raine, but then, I have not known them long."

"I've been away," Christopher said evasively.

"Quite a surprise when she accepted me, I can assure you. I never dreamed a lady like Miss Ardmore would favor me so. My mother was tickled something fierce. She has become very fond of Miss Ardmore. A stickler for propriety, is Mother, and Miss Ardmore is all that is proper, of course."

"Of course." Christopher traced the raised pattern around the bottom of his glass.

Poor Honoria. Christopher knew damned well she wasn't proper, and he'd just breezed back into her life to prove it. He supposed he could breeze out again and let her keep living the lie.

No, she was not getting off that easily. Honoria belonged to Christopher, even if Templeton was a likable rube.

He opened his mouth to continue the conversation, but Templeton was peering through the crowd with a look of delight. "Is that not Viscount Stoke?"

Christopher turned to see that, sure enough, Grayson Finley had entered the tavern. Templeton burbled happily, "I thought I saw him at The Nines. I had the great honor of being introduced to him once. He, too, is a friend of Miss Ardmore's family. Do you know him?"

"Yes," Christopher answered. He'd once had the great honor of moving Finley's nose to another part of his face in a fight long ago about who knew what.

Finley began making his way across the room as though he'd just noticed Templeton and was coming to greet him. Men moved aside for Finley. They generally did. Finley towered over lesser beings, and the hard cast to his face generally sent gentlemen scrambling for cover.

Women found him handsome, though, so Christopher had been told. They liked his light blue eyes and his crooked grin, and melted at his feet. Except Honoria. She'd never had anything polite to say about Grayson Finley. Another thing Christopher liked about her.

Finley's blond hair was a light smudge in the smoky darkness of the tavern. He stopped at the end of their table, and Templeton leapt to his feet. "My Lord, how excellent to see you. Would you join us? Unless, that is, you came to meet someone else?" He was a friendly dog, begging for a pat.

"I would be glad to," Finley rumbled. He glanced at Christopher, his expression neutral.

Christopher gave him a nod. "Your Lordship," he drawled.

Finley's expression did not change. A stool vacated itself magically, and Finley drew it to the table and sat. The barmaid, responding to the blue eyes and the grin, slid a tankard before him and blushed when he smiled at her.

"Mr. Raine was just telling me that he was acquainted with my betrothed's family," Templeton prattled as Finley took a long draft of his ale. "Funny how one encounters people by chance and they prove to have a connection after all."

Finley stopped drinking for a split second, then swallowed and set down the tankard. "I am always encountering Mr. Raine by chance."

"How odd," Templeton chirped.

Christopher said nothing.

It must have been Templeton's happiest evening ever. The man was ecstatic to have the attention of a viscount, though he seemed equally pleased to have met Christopher, a mere sea merchant—the tale Christopher had told him as they'd walked to the tavern.

Christopher watched Templeton and Finley talk like old friends, while Christopher contributed little. This allowed him to assess Finley, whom he had not seen in many years.

Finley's marriage and the children that followed seemed to have lent strength to him rather than diminish him. There was also a new stillness about him. Grayson Finley the pirate had always been recklessly brave, as though he'd not needed to stay alive. He seemed to have found a reason.

Christopher also noted that while Finley seemed to drink quite a lot, he did not, in truth.

At long last, Templeton professed that he must return home, although Mother would be *tickled* to know that he had spent his evening with a viscount. Finley gallantly offered to return Templeton in his carriage. Templeton tried to refuse, but Finley insisted, and finally, Templeton slurred an acceptance. The two wove their way out of the tavern, and Christopher quietly followed.

The carriage deposited Templeton in front of a plain house near Cavendish Square, then rolled south again toward Grosvenor Street.

Finley suddenly became much less drunk. "Where are you staying?" he asked Christopher.

"Lodgings near the docks."

"Alexandra will insist you take a room with us. We have many."

Christopher shook his head. "Colby and St. Cyr are there. I'll go back."

The carriage moved slowly through the dark, the light of the single lantern inside throwing huge shadows on the satin padded walls. "Fine coach, this," Christopher said.

"Alexandra's idea. A lordship isn't allowed to walk in the city, it seems. On the other hand, in the country I'm supposed to be terribly hearty. Eight-hour walks, three-day hunts, shooting in the freezing cold. The soft life of the aristocrat."

"Surprised you came back to claim the title at all."

Finley smiled, his face in shadow. "It had its compensations. You find another ship?"

"A brigantine. I'm refitting her in Greenwich. I've rounded up most of my crew—except my first officer."

"Manda," Finley said softly.

"I traced her to England. But my information is old. I have evidence that she came here, but that's as far as I got."

The news that Manda had gone to England had come from a Frenchman and it was not reliable, but Christopher had heard of her taking a ship across the Channel. France was knee-deep in war with England; that ship could have been commandeered, sunk, captured.

"I'll tell you truthfully that I have not seen her," Finley said. "I've departed the country several times since my marriage, but I've never noticed Manda." He chortled. "And she's noticeable."

"I know." The first thing men noticed about Manda was how shapely she was. The second thing they noticed was her boots kicking their teeth in. Christopher never intervened when a man tried to take Manda. It was more fun to watch what happened. But for all her willingness to fight like a man and sail a ship like a man, she was shy with men emotionally. He doubted she'd fallen in love and run off with one.

"I heard a name," Christopher said. "An offhand remark in a tavern near Dover. The name was Switton. Mean anything to you?"

It was a long shot. The man in question had said, "Wasn't she one of Switton's?" and the seaman with him had shrugged.

"Never heard of him," Finley said. "But I will ask my wife. Alexandra is a walking Debrett's Peerage. She knows every person in Mayfair, who their parents were, who they married, where they went to school, and the names of their butlers."

Christopher hid a grin. "You have a butler, Finley?"

Finley grimaced. "Not yet. Alexandra has her eye on one who works for a duchess. She's trying to entice him to give notice and come live with us. It's a hobby of aristocratic women to go after each other's butlers."

Christopher shook his head. "I still can't believe you turned into a viscount. The world has changed since I died."

Finley gave him a long look. "I knew you wouldn't stay dead. You never do."

The carriage halted before a tall, many-windowed house in Grosvenor Street. Finley asked Christopher to come in, but Christopher declined and departed to find a hackney to take him back down to the docklands.

Before parting, Finley invited Christopher to a fancy dress ball Alexandra was hosting the next evening. Their new friend Templeton would be there, Finley said with a grin, as well as Templeton's charming fiancée, Honoria Ardmore.

Christopher replied that he wouldn't miss it for the world.

The house in Grosvenor Street overflowed with guests for Lady Stoke's masked ball. Honoria and Diana arrived early and closeted themselves in Alexandra's dressing room with maids to ready their costumes.

They dressed as Greek ladies, in simple gowns that fastened at the shoulders and hung to the floor. After all, Diana said, it was little different from fashions nowadays, and the costumes would be easy to manage. Honoria tried to enjoy putting together the gowns with Diana, but she'd only been jumpy and irritable.

When at last they went downstairs, the house was thronged with guests. Alexandra's parties were always popular. At one of her soirees several years earlier, a horde of pirates, many of them naked, had swept the house, fighting the men and ravishing the women. That was the official story, the one reported by newspapers.

Honoria knew the real story, told to her by Alexandra herself. The truth had involved only one murderous pirate plus Grayson Finley. Only one man had been naked, poor Mr. Jacobs, Grayson's second in command, who'd dashed from a bedroom, sword in hand, ready to defend Grayson and the ladies of the house.

The sight of Mr. Jacobs, a very handsome and muscular young man wearing nothing but a cutlass, had sent most of the ladies into happy swoons. From that day forward, invitations to Alexandra's parties were much sought after, every lady inwardly hoping that such an occurrence would happen again.

Tonight Honoria wanted nothing more exciting than spilled lemonade. But when she saw the cluster of gentlemen waiting at the head of the stairs near the ballroom, she wanted to sink through the floor. Only Diana's hand on her elbow kept her upright.

Grayson Finley smiled down at the ladies as they approached. Next to him stood Mr. Henderson, a tall, fair-haired man who dressed impeccably and wore gold-rimmed spectacles. Mr. Henderson served as an officer aboard James Ardmore's ship, though he'd taken leave to travel to London with Honoria and Diana. He'd been looking for an opportunity to stay in a sumptuous hotel and buy new suits.

Next to them stood Mr. Templeton. He was dressed, of all things, like a pirate. Or at least like a fictional pirate. He wore striped trousers, a red shirt, a black sash, a papier-mâché saber that was too long for him, and an eye patch. He looked absolutely ridiculous. Grayson's eyes twinkled with mischief, and Honoria had a feeling she knew who'd engineered the costume.

But none of this made Honoria's blood freeze more than did the sight of Christopher Raine standing easily next to Mr. Templeton.

Grayson and Henderson wore evening suits rather than costumes, and so did Christopher. He looked perfectly calm, gray eyes dark in the lamplight, his tanned skin golden above his white cravat. The black coat only emphasized the gray of his eyes, the pale shade of his hair. He wore it in a plait, as usual, the hair that swirled back from his temples a darker blond than the rest.

A very large lump worked its way into Honoria's throat. She'd not slept at all the night before, and things had gone fuzzy about the edges. Seeing Christopher Raine hard and handsome before her was not helping matters. She wanted to do the little things a wife did for a husband, brush a nonexistent piece of lint from his lapel, smooth the coat on his shoulders, touch the strand of hair that was just going gray.

It annoyed her that she wanted to do this with Christopher but she had never, ever pictured herself doing such things for Mr. Templeton.

After glaring at Christopher for her own defects, she lifted her Grecian draperies in her hand and prepared to sweep past them all and into the ballroom.

"No," Diana said in her ear. Her sister-in-law's fingers on her arm were like vines that wrapped a trellis, light and thin, but strong enough to crush.

"Ladies," Grayson said. He had a half-grin on his face and that blasted twinkle in his blue eyes.

Diana smiled at him, held out her hand. Grayson bowed over it, sending Diana a warm smile. He bent over Honoria's hand as well, giving her a wink and an impudent grin. Honoria scarcely noticed. Christopher's presence filled up her vision, and all her senses tingled at the nearness of him.

Mr. Henderson only bowed and nodded, leaving their hands alone. Mr. Templeton greeted Diana with delight, and dared to press a light kiss to the backs of Honoria's fingers. He made some jesting reference to his costume, but Honoria did not hear a word.

Christopher's gaze was fixed on her, his eyes holding a mixture of amusement and impatience.

Her heart faltered at the thought of what might have been the four gentlemen's conversation before she'd come down. The very idea that Christopher and Mr. Templeton had met at all gave her palpitations. What on earth had they discussed? Had Christopher said, "Good evening, I'm Honoria's husband, I believe you are engaged to her?"

No, from the look of things, Christopher had kept silent, at least to Mr. Templeton. What Grayson and Mr. Henderson knew, she could not tell. They didn't behave any differently, but both were men who knew how to hide their thoughts.

"Mrs. Ardmore," Grayson was saying. "May I present Christopher Raine? Raine, Diana Ardmore. She married my good friend, James."

Good friend, my foot, Honoria thought distract-edly. The enmity between Grayson and James was legendary.

Christopher took Diana's hand and lifted it to his lips. Neither his look nor Diana's steady gaze betrayed that they'd already met.

"And Honoria Ardmore, James's sister."

Christopher turned to her. His hand, ungloved, closed over Honoria's. Their eyes met. The look he gave her was possessive. He was obviously not going to step aside and let her engagement to Mr. Templeton stand. The fireworks would begin soon, it was just a matter of when.

"We've met," Christopher said.

"Ah, yes," said Mr. Templeton. "So you told me last night."

Last night? Honoria glared at Christopher and snatched her hand from his grasp. "Mr. Raine and I are acquainted, yes."

"More than acquainted," Christopher said.

Honoria's heart beat swiftly and lights spun before her eyes. He could not announce it here, could he? Not now. She was not ready. She gave him a hard look, wondering if she could send her screaming thoughts straight into his brain.

Christopher continued, "I am an old friend of her brother's."

Her panic shifted to rage. Was this what he would do all night—begin the startling announcement and then back off at the last moment? Light the fuse, then stamp it out before it reached the bomb?

She wished Mr. Templeton's papier-mâché cutlass were real. She'd ask to borrow it, then she'd back

Christopher into a corner and demand to know what he thought he was doing.

Christopher was calm, that was one thing. But it was the calm of the eye of a hurricane; the winds could shift at any moment and bear down on her with devastating force.

Grayson was speaking. "My wife bade me to send you to her, Mrs. Ardmore. She's in the ballroom. The dancing is about to commence."

Diana made some polite answer that Honoria missed, removed her fingers from Honoria's arm, and glided away. Honoria felt suddenly bereft. Diana's grip had propped her up; she would fall any second now.

"Excellent," said Mr. Templeton. He offered his arm to Honoria. "I claim the honor of the first dance, Miss Ardmore. But I am generous. I will give each of you fellows a turn."

Christopher's gray eyes flickered, and he said nothing. Mr. Henderson, who could write etiquette books if he chose, bowed and said, "I would be most honored to join Miss Ardmore in the cotillion."

"I'll fetch you for a country dance," Grayson promised. Honoria tried not to flinch. Grayson was a good dancer, but a most exuberant partner.

Attention turned to Christopher. It would be impolite in the extreme for him not to offer a dance as well, but she had the feeling he didn't care two pins for what was polite. Just as well. She would not be able to plead him to silence on the dance floor, and if he touched her—

Well, she knew what happened when he touched her. Even that brief touch through her glove had

49

stirred her troublesome lust, the same lust that had kept her awake all night.

Had she been lying in bed trying to rationally think of a way out of the situation? No, she'd been reliving his kisses. Every kiss, every touch, the feel of his body against hers, the knowledge that he only had to part her dressing gown and slide his hand between her thighs to find her ready for him. Over all this lay the glorious, exciting fact that he was still alive and had come for her.

If he took her hand on the dance floor, she'd melt. He'd have to scoop her up in his arms and carry her off, cradling her against him. She would love it.

She looked at him with the others and struggled to keep from biting her lip while the silence stretched too long.

"I don't dance," Christopher said at last.

Disappointment wove dark fingers around her heart. *Relief,* she scolded herself. *That's what I should feel, relief.*

"Pity," Mr. Templeton said. He looked slightly pleased that he possessed a skill that such a handsome, well-fitted man lacked. "My mother, now, she always likes a caper. Ask her, and she will teach you a few steps."

Christopher's eyes flickered. Honoria glared at him, forcing her thoughts into his head. *Don't you dare.*

He almost smiled, as though he'd heard her. He gave Mr. Templeton an unreadable look. "I'll think on it."

His gaze returned to Honoria, and she wanted to scream.

Then Mr. Templeton was pulling her away, leading her to the ballroom as the musicians began. Honoria felt Christopher's gaze on her back all the way. Mr. Templeton babbled to her about his costume, how the viscount had suggested it, and wasn't it a good joke? The viscount had also invited Mr. Raine, wasn't it interesting how they all knew each other?

Honoria ground her teeth as Mr. Templeton swept her into the square for the minuet and thought of all the things she would later say to Grayson Finley and Christopher Raine.

Christopher Raine knew he had a reputation for patience. He'd been known to lie in wait for weeks for a prize if it was worth it. He'd planned for months before taking the *Rosa Bonita,* and he and his crew had executed every piece of that plan as though it had been a stately dance like the cotillion Honoria had promised to Henderson.

Christopher was notoriously slow to anger, but those who did manage to anger him never forgot, and never did it again. A slow match, Manda called him. He burned long, but when the gunpowder was reached, nothing equaled the explosion.

He was rapidly approaching the end of his slow match. The delay in finding Manda troubled him and now his dear sweet Honoria expected him to tamely release her so another man could claim her. He found Templeton amusing, but that did not mean he'd step aside and give him his wife.

Christopher would give her this night to enjoy herself with her friends, and then he would force the issue. He had plenty to do without waiting for Honoria to make a choice.

He wanted to ask Finley if he'd discovered anything more about the name Switton, but Finley was busy playing host, and guests thronged the hall. Finley seemed to like the role of viscount, and, as usual, had plenty of women simpering at him.

Christopher idly wandered into the ballroom. Most of the guests were costumed, dressed like gypsies, kings and queens of old, jesters, shepherdesses, or clowns. He liked Honoria's costume, plain white muslin hanging to the floor in a straight line from her shoulders. Her body moved enticingly under the draperies as she danced the minuet with Templeton, letting Christopher know she was unfettered beneath it. Clasps at her shoulders held the costume in place, and he enjoyed thinking about what would happen if he loosened one of those clasps.

He watched her, this lovely picture in mind. Templeton knew the steps of the dance, but he moved in jerks while she glided gracefully to and fro, her costume flowing.

Christopher needed to claim her quickly. If she delayed too long, he'd simply sweep her into his arms and carry her somewhere to rip her clothes off. Preferably his ship, which was nearing completion. And then off to find Manda and his legacy.

"Mr. Raine?" A slender woman with thick red-brown hair and fine brown eyes stopped at his elbow. Christopher had met Finley's wife, Alexandra, earlier tonight and at last understood why Finley had given up everything to become a viscount. Finley was besotted, and no small wonder. The woman was breathtakingly beautiful.

Alexandra went on. "A number of people have requested to be introduced to you." She dropped the stiff politeness and smiled, dimpling. "They begged me, actually. They have concluded you are a pirate, and pirates are quite popular at my gatherings."

Christopher had heard the tale of Alexandra's famous pirate-infested soiree. It had been, and still was, Finley said, the talk of the Town.

He conceded, amused, and Alexandra led him to the first group of guests. Most were ladies, although two gentlemen stood behind the women, eager expressions on their faces. The ladies gazed at him with wide eyes and wider smiles. Each time Christopher bowed over a hand, the lady stepped back and fluttered her fan rapidly, as though the temperature in the room had suddenly risen thirty degrees.

They moved on to the next group, who behaved identically. More giggles, more titters, more simpering. He glanced back at the first group and saw the ladies watching him intently, fans waving.

By the time Alexandra had circulated him to the end of the ballroom, he must have met every lady in London. He'd shaken hands with quite a few gentlemen, too. The married and widowed ladies, and a few of the unmarried misses, had fluttered lashes at him and given him promising smiles. He'd had more unspoken propositions than a gigolo in a ladies' bathing house.

53

As Alexandra at last excused herself to return to other hostess duties, Diana Ardmore stepped next to him and gave him a knowing smile.

"They are hoping you will take your clothes off," she said.

Chapter Four

Christopher looked down at her, nonplussed. "What the devil for?"

Diana laughed. Her hair burned gloriously red against her white skin. "It is why Alexandra's parties are so popular. The chance of glimpsing a naked pirate."

He quirked a brow. "The people of London need more to do."

"You are a handsome specimen, Mr. Raine."

She was being matter-of-fact, not flirtatious. Still, the other ladies in the room watched enviously as Diana took his arm. The only lady who had missed the entire show was Honoria.

Honoria was dancing with Henderson now, doing much justice to the stately cotillion dance. They were well matched, the aristocratic-looking gentleman and the well-brought-up lady.

"Give her time," Diana said gently. "You startled her. She's frightened and confused."

"And angry," Christopher observed. "Very, very angry."

Diana sent him a severe look. "I do not blame her. You men simply sweep in and decide we should be yours. You barely give us time to grow used to you before you carry us away. James was just the same."

Christopher understood well why Ardmore had swept this woman away. She was not only stunningly attractive, but she had a core of steel inside her. She had to, to withstand Ardmore. Honoria possessed that same core of steel, as well as the Ardmore traits of coldness and stubbornness.

He watched his wife now parade through the steps of the cotillion. "It may have been abrupt for her," he said, "but not for me."

In the last four years, he'd many times thought he'd never see this side of the world again, let alone live through the night. Thoughts of Honoria had kept him from despair. Even in the direst of nights, he'd warmed himself thinking of her green eyes that could swiftly darken with passion, of her lips that parted so readily beneath his. He had worked and fought and lived with one thought foremost in his mind—seeing her again.

"I have no doubt that you care for her," Mrs. Ardmore was saying. "You do not bother to hide it. But you must give her time."

"Time is what I have short supply of, Mrs. Ardmore. I have things to do and no time to wait for Honoria to sort out her feelings."

"Perhaps you should run your errands, whatever they are, and then return for her later," she suggested.

Christopher studied Diana's guileless eyes and chose his words with care. He might admire this woman, but she was married to James Ardmore. "And give her a chance to marry Templeton?" he answered lightly. "I'm not here to fight a battle, I simply need her to choose."

Diana gave him a skeptical look. "You say *choose*, but there is only one choice you want her to make."

He let himself smile. "Of course. She's a beautiful woman, and I want her."

Diana rested her tapered-fingered hand on his arm. "I believe I know what you mean. But if you only seek a companion, there are several dozen women who would be happy to oblige you. You could leave Honoria alone."

"That isn't the point. I'll tell you bluntly, Mrs. Ardmore, that I've never needed to work very hard for female companionship. I'll also tell you that I've never known a woman like Honoria. She was worth coming back for."

"She won't run to you tamely when you call." Diana's eyes suddenly sparkled, teasing. "I think you simply like a challenge, Mr. Raine."

"It adds flavor," he admitted. "I'm going to win, Mrs. Ardmore. I'd be obliged if you didn't stand too much in the way."

"Honoria is my dear sister now. I want only her happiness."

"Then make certain she doesn't marry Templeton."

They both looked at Mr. Templeton, who was chatting animatedly with his mother and pretending to flourish his false sword. Their glances met again. "I believe you are right," Diana said. "I just wish I knew more about you."

"Ask your husband," Christopher said. "He'll give you an earful. But wait until Honoria and I are far away."

She gave him an assessing look, then nodded. Christopher felt a small taste of triumph. An ally was a useful thing to have.

Templeton approached them then and asked Christopher if he'd show him the proper way to use a pirate sword. Christopher's mood had lightened enough that he led the man out of the ballroom, fetched a real sword from Finley, and took him down to the garden.

Honoria watched them go with direst forebodings. When her dance with Mr. Henderson ended, he led her politely back to her chair, then brought her an ice, which she did not want. She was about to push the ice on Mrs. Templeton and rush after Christopher, but Grayson turned up to claim his country dance. When she started to beg off, he said, "Oh, no you don't," and dragged her to the middle of the floor.

The former pirate danced with enthusiasm. He whirled Honoria with such force, she feared she'd fly across the room if he let go. But he also danced with feral grace, and other ladies cast her looks of envy.

The part of her mind not worrying about what Christopher was saying to Mr. Templeton reflected that Alexandra's ballroom seemed to be neutral ground for them all. Grayson and her brother James had been enemies for years. They'd fallen out over a woman, and then Paul's death had complicated things. They'd subsided for the sake of Diana and Alexandra, but an undercurrent of tension still existed between them.

Then there was Mr. Henderson, who worked for James. Grayson disliked him, but Alexandra counted Mr. Henderson as a friend and so did Diana.

Tonight Christopher Raine, a pirate and not ashamed of it, strolled Alexandra's ballroom like he owned it, while conversing at length with the wife of the pirate hunter who'd arrested him.

They were all connected, and yet disconnected. On the open sea, James, Grayson, and Christopher would likely do their best to sink one another. But here in the ballroom, they'd called a truce, no matter how uneasy.

She wished she could call one with Christopher. She wished she did not want to turn her head whenever he walked by, did not want to let her gaze linger on his broad shoulders, on the golden highlights in his wheat-colored hair or the light gray flecks in his eyes. She should not care that other ladies had watched him as though they'd like to lap him up, suit and all. He was hers to lap, if anyone would do any lapping.

Good Lord, what was wrong with her?

She must make Christopher see that their hasty marriage no longer mattered. She must gather her courage and tell him that they should set each other free. Strings could be pulled, and Grayson, as a viscount, could pull them.

Grayson finished the dance and thanked her for it. Honoria, breathless, sought the terrace, needing air after dancing with Grayson.

The terrace was dark and relatively empty. She let out her breath, happy for the silence and the coolness on her aching brow. She would rest here a moment, and then scour the house for Christopher and Mr. Templeton. If Christopher had revealed their secret, she would—she would— Well, she would speak quite sharply to him.

She leaned on the balustrade, drawing in air scented with roses, coal smoke, and whatever happened to be in the River Thames tonight.

She suddenly wished that Christopher would enter the terrace behind her, come to her, and slide his broad hands around her waist. She closed her eyes, seeming to feel his warm breath on her neck, to hear his gravelly voice whisper into her ear that he wanted her.

She had no business dreaming that. Or thinking of how his gray eyes darkened behind his golden lashes as he leaned to kiss her. But she did think it. She drew her hand slowly across her abdomen as heat coiled there.

A noise below startled her out of her reverie. She opened her eyes, face hot, and looked down into the garden.

What she saw froze her blood. Several men stood about, their attention riveted on two others near the fountain. One man was Mr. Templeton. The other was Christopher.

Mr. Templeton held his makeshift sword clumsily, fearfully eyeing the real, steel sword in Christopher's hand. As Honoria watched in horror, Christopher came at Mr. Templeton with the sword, backing him across the garden stroke after stroke.

She wished she were a pirate. Then she could leap to the top of the balustrade, grab the ivy, and swing down. But she was a Charleston lady in a flimsy costume and would likely only break her neck.

She whirled and dashed from the terrace and through the ballroom, pushing through the crush of guests now lining up for another country dance. Never in her life had she shown such ill manners to anyone. Now she shoved people aside like she was a common woman on the streets. Her strange behavior would be all over London tomorrow, the talk of the town. Which would not matter as long as she stopped Christopher killing Mr. Templeton.

She flew down the stairs and through the dark back hall to the garden. The ring of steel, the sound of male voices cheering spurred her on. She burst through the back door and ran across the grass toward the fighting men.

Mr. Templeton had his back against the garden wall, his ridiculous costume bright against the dark ivy. His sword hung uselessly in his grasp, and Christopher's sword was at his throat.

"Yield," Christopher said in a ferocious voice. "Yield, or I'll not be merciful."

"Christopher, no!" Honoria shouted, then her dancing slipper slid across a wet stone, and she went down into grass and mud in a flurry of draperies and a sharp stab of pain.

* * *

Sometime later, she saw Christopher bending over her. His tanned face was drawn in concern, but also with annoyance.

Mr. Templeton peered over his left shoulder, safe and sound. No sword protruded from his throat, belly, or any other mortal place.

"What the devil were you doing, Honoria?" Christopher said.

She looked at him through a numb haze. "I had to stop you from killing him."

To her astonishment, and her fury, the men gathered around began to laugh. Including Mr. Templeton.

"Your kind heart becomes you well, Miss Ardmore," Mr. Templeton said. "But there is no need to swoon. Mr. Raine was simply teaching me the ins and outs of swordplay."

Honoria did not believe that for a minute. "He was, was he?"

"He was," Christopher answered. He held out his hand to help her up.

Honoria's draperies had loosened at one shoulder. She snatched at them, fearing they'd tumble down altogether, grasped Christopher's hand, and made to stand.

Wrenching pain made her gasp. Christopher caught her with his strong arm, more gently than she imagined he could. "What is it?" he asked.

"I believe I have sprained my ankle."

She writhed in embarrassment. She sounded like a heroine in a silly romantic novel. Heroines were always hurting themselves or swooning and having to be carried to safety by the melodramatic hero.

Christopher looked anything but melodramatic. He frowned, as though he thought her up to something.

"Sprained," she repeated. "I can't walk."

The circle of men closed. She looked up at a mass of black cashmere splashed with waistcoats of ivory white, banana yellow, violent purple, and cherry red, topped with white cravats tied every way imaginable. These were Corinthian gentlemen who disdained fancy dress but were mad for anything sport, such as an impromptu sword fight in the garden. They began offering various words of advice—"Bind it up," "No, walk it out," "I know a doctor chap who's the end on ankles," "Shall I carry you to a couch, Miss Ardmore?" "Stubble it, I'll carry her."

Christopher put an end to the debate by lifting Honoria in his arms himself and starting for the house. Mr. Templeton trotted beside him, looking relieved that *he* wouldn't be expected to carry her.

Christopher took Honoria all the way to the second floor and to Alexandra's bedchamber. The Corinthians dropped out one by one, the excitement over. Diana and Alexandra hastened to Honoria's aid. Mr. Templeton, once they reached the door of Alexandra's bedroom, suddenly announced that he'd better go down and tell Mother what had happened. He would not even look inside the obviously feminine room, but turned away, red-faced, and dashed off.

Christopher carried Honoria inside and laid her carefully on the bed. She'd registered their progress upstairs only dimly. The rest of her had felt nothing but his strong arms, his hard chest, the beating of his heart. She'd known she'd melt when he touched her. It was nothing to what she felt when he held her.

Diana slid off Honoria's slipper. Christopher reached down and took the ankle between his large hands, probing it gently. "It's not broken."

"Thank heavens," Alexandra said, a hand on her heart.

"I'll wrap it for you, dearest," Diana said. "Then we'll go home."

Honoria lay back, feeling wretched. "No, do not spoil your evening. I'd rather lie here and rest than ride in a rocking carriage."

Diana frowned, but acquiesced. Alexandra brought a clean bandage while Diana untied Honoria's garter and stripped off her stocking. Christopher, who'd remained, took the bandage and wrapped the foot himself. Diana, her treacherous sister-in-law, let him.

His lashes shadowed his cheeks as he watched his work. His touch was warm through the pain, which began to recede. She probably hadn't even sprained the wretched thing, just twisted it.

Alexandra, once she realized that everything was all right, returned to her hostess duties. Diana lingered and bathed Honoria's face with a cloth dipped in scented water.

"I'm fine," Honoria said. "Thank you."

Christopher lowered her foot to the bed. His hand rested on it, his thumb stroking the sensitive skin of her instep. "Why did you think I was trying to kill Mr. Templeton?" he asked.

"Weren't you?"

Diana looked at Honoria sideways but continued to bathe her face.

"No," Christopher said. "He wanted a real pirate sword fight. So I gave him one. At least, a stage one."

"I saw you with your sword at his throat."

He eased his thumb over the top of her foot, most distracting. "If I had wanted to kill him, Honoria, I would have done it much more quietly. Someplace private, with no witnesses."

Her heart chilled. "Why does that not make me feel any better?"

"I don't plan to kill him. I don't need to. You and I are already married."

"So you keep reminding me."

He did not answer. He lifted his hands from her foot. Why did she want to cry out in disappointment?

"I tore the license in half last night," she said, giving him a weak glare.

The corners of his eyes crinkled. "If that were all it took for divorce, everyone would be doing it." He turned to Diana, who watched, chewing on her full lower lip. "Mrs. Ardmore, will you excuse us?"

Honoria's pulse sped in alarm. "No need to go, Diana."

Diana looked from Honoria to Christopher, frowning. Honoria felt her panic rise. She'd seen Diana and Christopher speaking together in the ballroom, Diana nodding at what Christopher said. Surely Diana, her own brother's wife, would not turn against her.

"Do not tire her," Diana said. Honoria stared at her in dismay. "Please send for me when she is ready to go home."

"Diana!"

Diana turned to her, blue eyes troubled. "You need to speak to him, Honoria. He deserves that, at least."

Honoria glared at her. Diana did not even look ashamed. She eased a coverlet over Honoria's legs, then quietly left the room, her back straight.

Leaving her alone with Christopher Raine. When she could not run away.

Christopher did not give her time to begin her opening argument or to order him to depart this instant. He leaned over the bed and kissed her.

Cool and smooth, his lips caressed hers. His lashes swept down to hide his eyes, and his warm hair brushed her face. She tried to murmur, *no,* but she was too caught up in kissing him back.

She loved the feel of his skin beneath her fingers, the strong muscles of his neck moving as he kissed her. She'd pretended to herself that she'd long forgotten him, but she had relived memories of him all too often.

When the house in Charleston had been at its emptiest, the servants below stairs, and the loneliness unbearable, Honoria would retreat to her room, shut the door, and remember. She lay on her bed, arms at her sides, and went over every moment of Christopher Raine making love to her—every kiss, every caress, every touch, every feeling. The way his sweat coated her as they'd slipped and slid together, how the smooth round of his backside felt to her fingers, how the unbearable heat of his lips on hers burned. She'd loved him and craved him, love and lust getting all mixed up, propriety forgotten.

In the darkness, she'd hug her arms about her chest and cry her climax. She would dissolve into tears at the false joy, which only made her remember the real joy she could never again have.

Honoria's ankle throbbed, bringing her back to the present.

She placed her hands flat on his chest. She did not bother to push because she knew exactly how strong he was. She could feel the strength of his muscles beneath her palms. They were such lovely muscles.

"Christopher, we need to talk."

He retreated a mere inch. A loose strand of hair touched her face. "I'm busy right now, sweetheart."

"You know this is impossible."

He eased himself down on the bed, his hip resting near her shoulder, giving her a nice view of his taut-muscled thigh. He lifted her hand, slowly peeled off her glove, traced a circle on the inside of her wrist. "Seems possible to me."

"You know what I mean. Being married."

His gray gaze rested on her. "You and I are married, Honoria; we have the marriage license. There will be surprise, but it's done. Fait accompli."

"Why didn't you tell me?" She thought about her years of loneliness. "Why didn't you send word? I would have waited for you."

"I didn't have the chance, love. By the time I was able to send word, it would have reached you the same time I did."

That was probably true, but she did not feel one bit reasonable. "I thought you out of my life forever."

"Then why didn't you marry again?"

"I did. I mean, I will. To Mr. Templeton."

"I meant that you waited a long time."

He kissed her palm, then her wrist. Hot sensations crawled up and down her spine.

"I was content being unmarried. There are so many advantages to being single, such as a man not driving you mad."

His lips twitched. He kissed her wrist again. "What changed?"

She hesitated. "James brought home Diana. They have a family now, and I don't belong in it."

"Diana is fond of you."

"She is dear to me. But she wants to be with James. Alone." She looked at him limply. "So I took Mr. Templeton's offer."

She knew he didn't understand. But he could have no idea what it felt like to have Diana always making certain Honoria was included in everything, when Diana and James were so obviously wrapped up in each other. That and Diana was now mistress of the Charleston house. Honoria had run it for years, and Diana tried to make her feel she still did run it, but Honoria knew everything had changed.

He traced a line along the inside of her arm, blunt fingers rough. "If you simply need a husband, you have one."

"A *pirate* husband. On a pirate ship."

His face registered no sympathy, but he continued the light, maddening patterns on her skin. "Honoria, I need to leave England as soon as I can. I don't have time to wait until you sort out your feelings or talk

68

things over. As soon as I put my hands on my second in command, I am setting sail, and I want you on that ship. You will have to break the news to Mr. Templeton, say your good-byes, write your brother a note."

She started to sit up, but her ankle twinged, and she sank back to the pillows. "It is much more complicated than that, Christopher Raine."

He drew a lazy circle in her palm with his thumb. "Why?"

"Because I don't love you any longer."

He stilled for a heartbeat, then said, "Is that important?"

"It ought to be if I am married to you."

He laid her hand at her side. "Do you still want me?"

Her tongue felt thick, and she said nothing.

He drew his finger along her cheekbone, traced it to her lips. "I want you," he said in a low voice. "I'm about insane with it."

She struggled to breathe. "You seem very calm."

"I have to be. And I tell myself that I'll have time. It's a long voyage across the Atlantic."

"Are we going to Charleston?"

He smiled a little, and she realized she'd said *we*. "Is that where you want to go?" he asked.

"I belong there."

"You belong with your husband."

She half-rose on her elbows. Her ankle throbbed again, but less so. "Do not begin again about wifely obedience. We married in haste, and now we are repenting."

Christopher lowered her to the pillows with his

hands on her shoulders, and bent over her so that she could not rise without pushing him aside. "I don't feel repentant. In fact, I feel more alive than I have in years."

Her heart beat hard. "Perhaps that's because you have been able to take regular meals and have baths and a bed to sleep in."

He leaned closer. "Perhaps it's because I found you again after so long. Speaking of beds, I'm happy to finally have you in one."

His shirt smelled clean, of washing soap, overlaid with the male scent of him. Not fair. She loved him so near, she'd always loved that. Perhaps that is why every time they met, she flew into his arms.

"We were speaking of Charleston," she reminded him.

He kissed the line of her hair. "We can have beds there, too."

"We'd live there? You're a pirate. Besides, everyone in Charleston thinks you were hanged."

"People can be amazingly obtuse, my wife. But we can live anywhere you like. I'll buy you a house, two houses, three even, in case you get tired of the first one."

She touched his jaw, enjoying the feel of the sandpaper bristles there. He'd shaved since the night before, but his whiskers grew fast. "Where I'd live while you went out pirating? Until my brother caught you again?"

His face hung close to hers, his body heavy and warm. His breath smelled of brandy. "I have more imagination than that. You can have anything you want, your own tropical island if that's what you like. And I'd be there with you. Every day. Finley retired from pirating, so can I."

"Only because he became a viscount. And had a daughter. And fell in love."

His lips curved. "I'll never inherit a title, I promise you that. But I fell in love. As for a daughter, well, that's up to you."

"Is that what you want? Children?"

"I want you. If children come, so much the better."

"And you do not care if I can't love you?"

He traced the pad of her lower lip. "Not at the moment. Because I know you want me."

She swallowed, her throat dry. "How can you know that?"

Christopher twisted his hand and the remaining clasp holding her gown came away. He'd distracted her by touching her lips, now he tossed away the clasp with a satisfied look. He lowered the muslin to bare her shoulder and one breast, which was already lifting and tightening to fit his hand.

"I can feel you wanting me." He slid his fingers under the loosened gown to her abdomen, his palm warm. Without meaning to, she arched her hips to him.

Giving a soft laugh, he moved his hand obligingly over the heat between her legs. "As brazen as I remember."

Her face warmed, but she could not bring herself to squirm from his touch. It felt so right. She loved it.

71

"Wanting isn't love," she gasped.

"No, but it is enough for me. I've learned not to expect too much."

"And you'd stay with me, just because I want you?"

He smiled a dark smile. "For now. But I get to try to change that lust to love, my wife."

She barely heard him. His fingers began teasing the sensitive folds between her legs. A dark tingling wove its way inside her.

He went on, "As I said, it's a long voyage." He slid one finger firmly inside her. She gasped.

"Every night," he went on, and his finger did too. "I will persuade you to fall in love with me. I will try every method I know, and if that means I seduce you every night, so be it. By the time we're across, if you still do not want to be my wife, then I will take you to Charleston and let you go. But you will give me this voyage."

He pressed a second finger into her, his touch strong. Her mind whirled with sudden excitement. "All right," she whispered hoarsely.

His eyes were dark, pupils swallowing the cold gray irises. "Excellent. Shall we seal the bargain?"

"With a handshake?"

"No." He snaked his other hand to the nape of her neck, pulled her to him, kissed her. A slow, hot kiss filled with promise of a very exciting voyage indeed.

As he finished the kiss, he eased his fingers out of her. The disappointment was unbearable. "No, Christopher, please don't stop."

"You'll hurt your ankle."

"I feel much better. I think I only wrenched it."

He brushed his palm over the join of her thighs one last time. "I love your fire, my wife. You bury it behind your proper lady's mask, but it's there."

"No one but you has ever seen it."

"Good." He touched his fingers to his lips, tasted one with his tongue. "Mmm. Sweet as ever."

He gave her a warm smile, and her heart turned over. He stretched out on his side, draped his arm over her.

"Tomorrow I will take you to my ship," he said. "You'll need to send for or buy what you need. I'll give you the money for it. Shop to your heart's content."

"Tomorrow?" she exclaimed. "No, that's too soon. I need—"

He stopped her lips with his. "It's not too soon. We've waited four years."

Her ankle still hurt, the throb cutting through the fierce longing he'd stirred, then deserted. "You rush me into things every time, Christopher Raine," she argued. "I never have a chance to think about what I want, or how I feel. We never talk about what we feel."

He lifted a loose curl from her cheek. "No, we act on what we feel."

"But what if it's the wrong thing to feel?"

The warm glint left his eyes, and he made an exasperated noise. "You like to talk things to death, my wife. We feel instinct. We can't keep our hands off each other. Nothing more to be said."

He was already driving her mad. Instinct, he said.

73

Jennifer Ashley

Instinct was killing her. "But we really should discuss—"

He growled and kissed her, effectively silencing her. He slid his hand beneath her costume again, across her bare flesh.

"Now rest," he ordered. "I want you well enough to board my ship on your own two feet."

He pulled the blanket over her, started to rise. Honoria caught his arm. Words welled up in her throat and she could not say them.

He waited, his eyes watchful, though his face was calm. She traced the muscle of his arm. "Stay," she finally managed. It came out a croak.

He hesitated. She thought he'd shake his head and leave her cold and forlorn, but he lay down beside her again. The bed sagged with his weight, rolling her against him.

She could not explain that she needed time to savor him, to become used to the idea that he was alive and whole. "I'm not ready yet," she whispered.

He obviously did not understand, but he did not argue. He drew her back against him, his chest to her back, draped his arm over her side. She snuggled into him, feeling oddly contented.

Her sleepless night, her dreadful day, and the shock of seeing him again dissolved against his warmth. Her body relished the feeling of his hardness pressing into her hip. He wanted her, he'd whispered, but he'd hold it at bay for now.

Her limbs loosened, and she slept.

When she awoke again, she was in a room full of people. Christopher still lay behind her, his hand

74

heavy on the curve of her waist. She started up, clutching her costume to her, and met the gazes of a shocked Alexandra, a dismayed Diana, a surprised Grayson, and a furious Mr. Henderson.

Chapter Five

It was over. Honoria was alone again, sitting deject-
edly on the bed in Alexandra's chamber. The cheval
mirror sitting opposite her revealed that she'd stood
before her friends and family confessing her sins with
one layer of her costume loose. The dark aureole of
her right breast pressed against the flimsy material.
No wonder Christopher had looked amused.

The others had not. The news that Honoria was
married to Christopher had come as a great surprise
to all except, of course, Diana.

Mr. Templeton had behaved very well. He had accepted Honoria's apology with dignity and promised
that the engagement would end quietly. He declared
he would not ask for compensation for breach of contract. After all, he'd wanted to marry for companionship, not gain.

He'd been so reasonable, Honoria had almost
grown angry at him. Grayson had watched her, look-

ing torn between laughter and curiosity. His wife, Alexandra, had seemed puzzled and worried. Mr. Henderson had been enraged, but then, Mr. Henderson had once tried to court Honoria, and behaved as though some sort of bond still existed between them.

Now Christopher and Grayson were off talking about other matters, as though relieved all the nonsense was over. Honoria balled her fists. *Men.*

Diana entered the room, followed by Alexandra. Diana's sweet perfume engulfed Honoria as she enfolded her sister-in-law in her arms. "That was brave of you, dearest."

"Indeed," Alexandra echoed. She sank onto the bed and gave Honoria her winsome smile. "I much admired you. I, too, know what it is like to win the love of a pirate. It is most difficult to explain to your friends."

Honoria leaned into the comfort of Diana's embrace. She said to Alexandra, "At least yours is a viscount."

"In name." Alexandra smiled a small, pleased smile. "Not in spirit."

"And mine is an out-and-out villain," Diana said. "Not easy to explain to your great aunt in Coombe St. Mary." She smoothed Honoria's hair. "Would you like me to break the news to James?"

"No, I will do it. I am not afraid of him."

Alexandra bit her lip. "He will have much to say."

"Then let him say it," Honoria said frostily. "I am no longer interested in James Ardmore's opinions."

The other two exchanged a glance. Diana was madly in love with James, and Alexandra had always had a soft spot for him. Why, Honoria could not fathom. James could make you grind your teeth to nubs. He was so *arrogant*. But ladies had always been attracted to James Ardmore. Heaven knew why, the man had never learned a modicum of politeness.

"I am happy you both are pleased for me," Honoria said, then she, who seldom cried, burst into tears.

The home Christopher took her to was a brigantine, a two-masted ship, moored off the docks in Greenwich. He'd christened it the *Starcross*.

The *Starcross* lay small under a graying sky, her bare masts black, her sides rich wood. The ship had been stripped and her hull refinished, the quarter deck removed to render the top deck one long surface. The captain's quarters had been rebuilt below and fitted with many-paned windows called lights. The beams and walls and ceiling had been painted white, giving the cabin an airy look, but the quarters were cramped.

Honoria's ankle had mended enough that she could climb down to the captain's cabins without much pain. The main cabin held a desk and cabinets and the captain's logbook. A small room opening to the port side contained more cabinets and a bed built large enough for two.

Honoria studied the bed in some irritation. She knew that ship's carpenters built the bunk to fit the man, so that the sleeper had a better chance of staying abed in high seas. She glared at the obvious double bed and then at Christopher.

"You assumed I would come away with you, or you'd not have had a bunk made so wide."

Christopher leaned against the door frame. He'd said little between Mayfair and Greenwich, sitting in the shadows of the carriage, not offering conversation.

"The carpenter finished it this morning, before I came to fetch you," he said.

It was a box, bare of mattress and coverlets. Honoria had brought a few quilts with her, courtesy of Diana, but she saw that she'd have few comforts here.

Christopher entered the tiny room behind her, slid his arms about her waist. "It's a fine ship. Good bones. Do you like it?"

She leaned back into him without meaning to, liking the feel of his arms across her abdomen. She knew something of ships, enough to know that this one was sleek and solid and well built. "It's a bit small," she said.

"Small and fast. Built for speed." He reached up, fondly touched a beam. "She'll take us where we need to go."

Honoria also knew enough about men with ships to know they could go on about them for hours. "And where are we going? Charleston?"

He gave her an unreadable look. He hadn't answered her about Charleston the night before, either, and it seemed he had no intention of doing so now.

There was just enough room in the bedchamber for them to stand together. The rest was taken up by the bed and the cabinets. That meant he'd have to stand very close to her at all times. He filled the cabin with his body and his presence, warming her to her toes.

"We'll leave soon," he said, his breath stirring the fine hairs at her temple. "Take the time to get settled. I have unfinished business in London."

"If we are not leaving immediately, you might have let me stay with Diana a little longer."

He stepped away from her, and she felt suddenly cold. "We must be ready to leave on an instant, Honoria. I won't have time for your tearful fare-wells."

She glared at him. "So like a man. I am surprised you let me bring any luggage."

He looked surprised. "Why wouldn't I?"

He'd abandoned the gentleman's suit and returned to breeches, boots, and a shirt. The shirt was open enough to reveal the end strokes of the tattoo on his collarbone, a Chinese dragon with overlapping scales. He had another tattoo on his hip, that of a lion, a Chinese creature with claws held ready to attack. The last time she'd seen it, she'd traced it with her tongue.

He caught her gaze on him, and his look turned knowing.

She flushed. "I was in such a hurry I didn't bring enough," she babbled. "I will need bedding."

He smiled a slow smile. "I know. I plan to bed you every night."

She scowled, flustered. "You know what I mean. A feather bed—for the bed. And a chair."

"Very well. I can bed you in a chair just as well."

"Christopher!" His eyes were sparkling, teasing, but behind the teasing lay a watchfulness, anger retreated but still present. "I meant that I cannot live in a bedroom without a chair. I need someplace to sit."

"Sit on that." He pointed to a small benchlike seat in the corner with a lid and a clasp.

Honoria knew what *that* was. When the lid was raised, a round hole opened to the water below. She'd be able to relieve herself here, in private, instead of making her way to the bows and the head, where she'd be visible to the entire crew.

She gave him her best proper-lady look. "I meant somewhere more elegant."

Christopher's hint of a smile told her that he knew good and well what she'd meant.

He led her back into the outer room and pulled a pouch from one of the cupboards. It jingled. "Take the money here, go to Greenwich, and go shopping. Buy what you like. Curtains, carpets, whatever fripperies you need to make yourself comfortable."

He was being much too accommodating. "Anything I want?" she queried, studying the money pouch. "What if you don't like what I buy?"

He took her hand, placed the pouch into it. It was heavy with coin. "Then I'll throw it overboard. Enjoy yourself."

Honoria took the pouch, toyed with the drawstrings. "Will you come with me?"

"To feather the marriage nest? No, love, that is your preserve. I have pirate things to do."

"What?" she asked, suddenly suspicious. "What did you need to speak with Grayson about last night? That is the true reason you came to Alexandra's ball, wasn't it? It had nothing to do with me."

81

"No," he said with painful bluntness. "I've been reduced to begging help from Grayson Finley."

"Help with what?"

"Help finding the last of my crew. Rescuing her if necessary."

Honoria stared at him. "Her?"

He nodded. "Manda Raine. My sister."

Christopher made his way back upriver and met Grayson and the ubiquitous Mr. Henderson in a tavern near Covent Garden. Smells of ale, cabbage, horses, humans, and warm river wafted through the open door and settled inside the close room.

Finley looked at home in the tavern in loose coat and shirt, worn breeches, and boots. Henderson, on the other hand, wore a fine cashmere suit, dandified cravat, and boots so shiny he must have to polish them every time he crossed a street. His hair was carefully combed, and his spectacles gleamed. Christopher wondered how the man worked on a ship where baths were scarce and dirt was a way of life.

Finley, Christopher knew, had given up his pirate life when he'd inherited his title. He'd fallen in love with his next-door neighbor, Alexandra, married her, and settled down to raise his children, though the Admiralty called on him from time to time for help. Alexandra was beautiful, Finley's home lavish, his wealth vast, his position in society assured. Yet he still looked more at home in a tavern.

"You miss it," Christopher observed.

Finley seemed to know exactly what he was talking about. "I do sometimes."

"You could leave."

He shook his head. "Alexandra has her social calendar. The ladies, as you'll come to know, like that."

Honoria could do all the socializing she liked during the day. At night, however . . . "What about you, Henderson?" Christopher asked. "Why aren't you out with your captain scouring the Barbary Coast?"

Henderson took a fastidious sip of port and wiped his fingers on his handkerchief. "I needed to visit my tailor."

"You'd brave interrogation by the Admiralty to visit your tailor?"

Henderson looked surprised. "His Bond Street shop has been making suits for the Hendersons for generations. There is no better in the world."

Finley shot Christopher a *don't ask* look and drank his ale.

Christopher shook his head. He wondered how such an obvious landsman had ever taken to sea. He knew Finley had run away to it as a boy and had taken to the life well. Christopher himself had been born and raised a pirate. He'd learned to tie lines and climb rigging as he learned to walk.

Christopher's father had been a small-time pirate of French birth who ran between Barbados and the Carolinas. His mother had been a captain's daughter on an English merchantman bound for the West Indies. Other pirates had raided the merchantman, murdered the captain and most of the crew, stolen the ship, and condemned Christopher's mother and the few remaining crew to a longboat.

Christopher's father had taken the survivors on

board. Mr. Raine had liked the look of the young Englishwoman, snatched her away to his cabin, and likely raped her. He'd fallen in love with her in his own fashion, and kept her with him. Christopher had no idea if they'd ever officially married, but his mother always behaved as though she were his father's legal wife.

His mother had tried to raise Christopher to be a good Anglican, with poor results. His father pretended to fear God, but in truth, he feared nothing. When Christopher was ten years old, their ship was attacked by other pirates, their hold stripped of its contents. Christopher's father had planned to sell that cargo to get them through the winter.

Mr. Raine, brave and stupid, had told the pirate captain where he could shove himself. The pirate captain shot him dead. The pirate captain then started to rape Christopher's mother. Christopher had grabbed one of the pirates' pistols and shot the pirate captain through the head.

The other pirates had said good riddance and elected a new captain. That captain divided the spoils and set the Raine ship alight because it was not worth saving. The new captain told Christopher's mother to come with him, and Christopher's mother had obeyed. A few months later, she had escaped ashore into the Carolinas, without taking Christopher. Christopher never saw her again.

He had found a home among those pirates who had burned his father's ship. His father and crew had been small-time criminals; these men were tough and fearless and smart. He'd admired them. They'd taught

Christopher how to track a ship, how to tell if it was loaded or running empty, how to assess cargo for the best yield, how to sell it safely for the best price. By the time Christopher reached the age of fourteen, he'd been as much a pirate as any of them, as ruthless and cruel as only the young can be.

Now that he was twenty years older, different things mattered.

He wrapped his hands about his ale glass. "Discover anything more?" he asked Finley.

Finley nodded, blue eyes quiet. "Alexandra had the right of it. I knew she would. A Lord Switton, an earl, lives in Surrey, near Epsom. I don't know him myself, but Henderson has heard of him."

That explained Henderson's presence. "Where do I find him?" Christopher asked him.

"A man does not pay an impromptu call on a lord," Henderson said, his tone disbelieving. "He makes an appointment, which might or might not be granted."

"Sorry, I forgot to bring my etiquette book," Christopher said dryly. "But I have a lord sitting right here. Finley can pay an impromptu call on him."

Finley gave him a look. "I haven't been introduced. He's an earl, I'm only a viscount. A hanging offense."

"You may laugh," Henderson broke in. "But you ignore the rules at your peril. If you cannot get Lord Switton to speak to you, you will never learn anything from him."

"True," Christopher said. "All right, we'll play your game. What do I do to garner an appointment with this great man?"

"You cannot. But I can. He and my father went to school together. I'll write to him tonight."

"That's kind of you," Christopher said. "But why should you? You looked ready to shoot me last night."

Henderson gave him a withering glance. Finley answered, "Because my wife asked him to help. And Henderson will do anything for my wife."

His tone was ironic. Christopher sensed an irritation between the two that went beyond the banter at this table.

He was not interested. He drained his ale. "Whatever his reason," he said, "we'll go to Surrey tomorrow."

By the time Christopher reached Greenwich again, the night was inky black and well advanced. Honoria would have done her shopping by now and finished making up the bed. She'd be tucked under the blankets, probably asleep, her flushed face pillowed on her arm. His heartbeat quickened in anticipation.

She'd come to see his way of things eventually. He had this voyage in which to teach her.

She'd nearly come to climax under his hand last night with very little petting. That pleased him. She could pretend to be coldly indifferent to him, but her body knew better. She wanted him, and even she knew it. She'd put her hand on his arm, said, "Stay," with a catch in her voice.

Forever and ever, my wife. The taste of her honey had almost undone him. For four long years that remembered taste had kept him alive. He looked forward to tasting her again tonight.

The ship, when he arrived, was in an uproar.

A dog barked incessantly in the bow. Christopher heard voices raised in argument; one was Colby, his man in charge of the crew. Christopher's third in command, a tall Frenchman called Jean St. Cyr, stood by, arms folded, silently observing the scene around him as usual. The rest of the crew aboard were on deck, obviously enjoying the show.

Colby was exchanging irritated shouts with men below him on a longboat. The boat was laden with—things. Boxes, crates, unidentifiable dark bulks under blankets.

Christopher climbed the steps into the ship. "All right, Colby, what is it?"

Colby, a huge bear of a man, swung around just as Honoria emerged from belowdecks. Instead of being snuggled up in bed, she was wide awake, looking composed and efficient in a plain lawn dress and a white cap. A matron's garb. She'd decided to embrace the married state all the way.

With her was Colby's wife, a former barmaid. Mrs. Colby wore a look of vast amusement on her face.

"Colby," he repeated.

Colby glowered. "This bloke here says he's putting all this junk on board. And he wants money for it."

The bloke in question turned an angry eye up to Christopher. "It's been ordered. I'm not leaving without my coin."

"Well, I didn't order it," Colby growled. "Neither did St. Cyr."

"*I* did," came a frosty reply.

As Christopher had expected, Honoria stepped forward. She gave Colby a cool look. "It is all right, Mr. Colby. I placed the order and instructed him to transport it here. Mr. Raine is paying for it."

"Honoria," Christopher said in a warning voice.

Honoria ignored him. "Bring it this way, please. Down to the main cabin. Do hurry, it's growing chilly."

Christopher's eyes sought Honoria's. She paused and returned his gaze. Colby looked hopeful. Christopher could imagine the phrases in the man's head—"He'll sort you out, missus. You don't know who you're dealing with."

Christopher turned to Colby and shrugged. "Let him board."

Colby stared, openmouthed. Christopher raised a brow. Colby scowled back at him for a moment, then muttered something foul and stomped away.

Honoria looked tranquilly at Christopher. A few black curls had escaped the cap to brush her forehead. "You did tell me to buy what I needed, Christopher. I did not have quite enough money, so you will need to pay him for delivering it all."

A defiant spark lit her eye. She expected Christopher to shout at her, to rail and tell her what a terrible wife she made. She wanted him to very much.

He arranged his face into bland lines and signaled for the man to begin unloading. Honoria looked the slightest bit disappointed. She glided away to watch the process.

An odd assortment of things began finding their way to the deck. There was a lady's armchair upholstered in petit point and a footstool to match. A pile of quilts and bedding and pillows followed.

She'd certainly been busy. She'd bought boxes of soap, towels, swaths of linen, pewter mugs, jars of tooth powder, and another basin for hand washing. She'd bought odd things, too, like a crystal candle holder, silk cushions, and an Egyptian-style statuette that would fall over during high seas and hurt someone.

Some of the purchases were practical, like the rattan cabinet for clothes and the square trunk designed to slide under a bunk. Others were—

"What is that?" Christopher demanded as a brass oval basin was hoisted over the side.

"A bath," Honoria answered.

"Honoria."

She held her head up. The tapes of her cap floated in the breeze. "Yes?"

"At sea, there's not enough clean water to spare for a full bath."

"No?"

She knew that. She'd lived in a seafaring family all her life. He clenched his jaw. "Very well. Put it below."

She kept her gaze deliberately neutral, but she was not pleased by his reaction—or rather, his lack of reaction. She was spoiling for a fight.

Challenge me all you want, my wife, he thought. *I'm always up for a challenge.*

He looked over everything without a word, stopping only when he spied a crate containing an entire set of cutlery and porcelain plates.

"Are you planning a dinner party?"

"Those are for you," Honoria said, her green eyes glittering.

"For me?"

"A ship's captain must be distinguished from his crew. These are for you and those officers you invite to dine with you."

"We're pirates," he said tersely.

A pirate crew trusted their captain to make decisions, guide the ship, and lead them in a fight. Any captain who started strutting about like a bloody English admiral got thrown overboard. But Honoria knew that.

He eyed her levelly. "Take it all below. I'll speak to you there."

Honoria merely nodded and turned away, but he caught her small smile of satisfaction. Mrs. Colby went with her, and the two murmured together.

He moved to St. Cyr. The Frenchman had a chiseled face and flyaway hair that was very light blond and matched his light blue eyes. He always reminded Christopher of a quiet iceberg. Defying the stereotypes of Frenchmen, St. Cyr rarely drank anything stronger than water and believed abstinence to be the key to good health.

"I'm beginning to see your way of thinking," Christopher told him now.

St. Cyr remained unsmiling. "A glass of port mixed with water once a week is all that is needed to keep the humors in balance." So he'd said many times before. Colby claimed that St. Cyr was insane.

Christopher went on. "When I'm not with Mrs. Raine, make certain she stays out of the way of the crew, but any disciplinary measures involving her or because of her will be handled by me, not Colby."

Colby usually kept order among the men, and he was good at it. He was evenhanded and fair and made sure everyone followed the rules. He meted out the specified punishment when the rules were broken, no more, no less.

"Yes, sir," St. Cyr said.

Christopher couldn't be sure, but he thought he saw a twinkle of amusement in the iceberg's eye.

"Make sure all this junk gets stowed, then shut down for the night."

"Aye, Captain."

Christopher turned away. He did not tell St. Cyr about the lead on Manda, not wanting to spread false hope. He had only a name and a county. This Lord Switton might have nothing to do with Manda, know nothing about her. Christopher might have misheard the name, or it might be a completely different man called Switton. No knowing until he and Henderson visited this earl.

He chuckled to himself. So Henderson had a soft spot for Finley's wife. Interesting man. A fop and a fool on the surface but Christopher would wager a good amount of money there was more to Henderson than met the eye.

Christopher made his way below. He found Honoria and Mrs. Colby in his sleeping cabin. Honoria was sorting linens, and Mrs. Colby was making up the bed. She beamed her barmaid smile at him as she plumped the pillows.

Mary Colby was forty years old, round of body, and

good-humored. Barmaids learned early how to turn men up sweet, whether in bed or during a rousing chorus of pub songs. Mrs. Colby had the knack for bringing that ease to the entire ship and for keeping the volatile Colby pacified. She had a refreshingly earthy view of the relationships between men and women, and spoke calmly of ribald matters in a way that made even pirates blush.

Now she gave Christopher a knowing wink and his pillow a pat. "Enjoy yourselves, my dears. You have much time to make up for. Now I need to get Colby into his bed before he tears down the ship."

"Thank you for your help, Mrs. Colby," Honoria said.

"Never you mind, my dear. This is going to be a real pleasure." She winked at Christopher again as she went past. She closed the door of the outer cabin with an audible click.

Christopher folded his arms and leaned on the door frame. He let his gaze rove over the bed piled high with a feather bed and quilts, the upholstered lady's chair strewn with cushions, and the bronze Egyptian statue in the corner. Honoria stood in the middle of the crowded cabin, her glorious eyes flashing.

One lantern hung from the low beam, the candle spreading a soft yellow glow. Through the open window at the stern came the faint swishing sound of river water. The ship was quiet, but it had an expectant feel to it, as though impatient to get under way.

Honoria was waiting, too, but she betrayed her impatience. The halo of curls about her face moved in the quiet breeze, and her green eyes sparkled in defiance, waiting for him to shout at her so she could play the dignified martyr.

Unfortunately for her, Christopher had more patience than she did. No, *patience* was not the right word. He'd learned how to wait, like a stalking leopard, for prey to come near enough before he pounced.

"I enjoyed my shopping," she said. "I could not find everything I need, however. I will have to make another trip to London before we go."

"Tomorrow, we are going to Surrey."

She frowned, surprised. "Why?"

"To speak to an earl who might know the whereabouts of my sister. I'll need a wife with me to make me look respectable."

Her black brows rose. "You will never look respectable, Christopher Raine. Especially not to an earl."

"Henderson will be there to guide me." He paused. "Tell me, what is the real reason Henderson is in London?"

Her brows rose higher at the abrupt question. "I haven't the faintest idea. He came to order more suits, I supposed. Why are we talking about Mr. Henderson?"

"Because you want me to talk about your shopping expedition. But I'm not interested. Buy whatever you like."

She had braced herself for a torrent of anger, had wanted it, for some reason. She frowned in frustration, but tried to rally. "Well, I am pleased with your approbation."

His gaze fell again on the faux Egyptian statue. It was the ugliest thing he'd ever seen. The bronze, poorly cast, had a greenish tint, and the face was lopsided. The man who'd made it had obviously never seen a real Egyptian statue, nor had this statue ever touched the sands of Egypt. It was hideous.

Christopher stepped past the chair, lifted the statue, moved to the open window.

"What are you doing?" Honoria cried.

"Throwing it overboard."

He rested the thing a moment on the sill, then toppled it out the window. A faint splash told him the river had swallowed it whole.

Honoria stared at him, openmouthed, but she did not seem distressed. She'd known the damn thing was hideous. She'd only bought it to see what he would do. A passing waterman would dig it out someday, probably sell it back to the same shop it had come from.

He lifted a pillow from the bed.

She cried out. "Not the pillows. I need the pillows."

He held it for a moment longer, just out of reach of her seeking fingers. Then he plumped it slowly and dropped it back on the bed. "Come here, Honoria."

She let her hand fall, her green eyes filled with deep suspicion. "Why?"

Christopher pulled the window closed on the cooling night air, latched it. "You've had your turn trying to convince me you are a terrible wife and to abandon you. Now it's my turn to convince you to stay."

Her gaze shifted. "I have more unpacking to do."

"You can unpack tomorrow. It's time for bed."

The bold defiance suddenly left her, and her eyes darkened. Her lips parted, the red, moist space between betraying her longing.

His loins tightened. His passion with her had been interrupted twice, once by Diana Ardmore and her pistol, once by Honoria's friends rushing into the bedchamber where they reposed. This time, he had St. Cyr to ensure that there were no interruptions.

"Turn around," he said.

Her pulse beat hard in her throat. "Why?"

"Are you going to question every order I give?"

"Very likely, yes."

He narrowed his eyes. "Some orders you do not question. When we're at sea, and I give an order or tell you to get out of the way, you do it. It might be your life or someone else's if you don't."

A momentary spark returned. "I know that. I have been at sea before."

"But you've never taken orders from your husband before. Some wives love to answer back, even at the worst of times."

"Some husbands ought to be questioned."

"Not when I give you a command as a captain."

She looked about the room with exaggerated care. "I see no immediate danger here. I certainly see no need to turn my back simply because you ask it."

"You don't?"

"No." Her eyes narrowed. "I don't."

He shifted his stance, gave her a level look. "The window behind me is plenty large enough for your lovely body."

The pulse in her throat quickened. "You would not throw me overboard."

"I will if you continue to disobey my orders. Now, turn around."

She hesitated for one moment, then she pivoted swiftly and dove for the door.

She made it two steps before he closed his arms about her waist and pulled her back. She struggled for a few seconds, then stilled as his hand moved up her bodice to the hook at the top.

She involuntarily leaned back against him, her round bottom nicely pressing his thighs. She'd put up her hair under the cap. Fine wisps of it floated at the nape of her neck. They were silken beneath his lips.

She made a faint noise that was neither defiant nor questioning. The clasp of her bodice yielded to his fingers, parting the garment. He dipped his finger inside to trace the warm hollow of her throat.

"I like fastenings," he murmured. "They give way, little by little, to reveal the woman inside."

As he spoke, he moved down the bodice, flicking open each catch. With the other hand, he parted the placket, slid his fingers inside.

Her breasts rose and fell against his touch. A chemise separated him from her, but her breasts molded the silk. The nubs rose for him, tightening, wanting.

His own arousal rose in response. He'd been hard since he'd closed the door of the cabin. He'd tried to distract himself with the argument and the damn statue. He wanted to take her slowly, not in a clumsy wash of passion. She'd only be angry and unhappy; he wanted her smiling and pliant.

Then again, he might not mind her angry. Let her pin him on the bed and pour enraged kisses all over his body, he wouldn't mind.

She smelled—well, a little bit like coal smoke and fish, the smells of Greenwich—but her own fragrance was there, too, like the subtle scent of rose petals. He teased the nape of her neck with his tongue. She made another surrendering sound.

Yes, there was something about unfastening a bodice, pushing it, loosened, to her waist. Something about catching the fabric as it fell, baring her skin to him.

Her shoulders were white, with a smattering of tiny dark dots that black-haired women often had. He kissed them, one at a time.

Her breath quickened. He rested his hands on her abdomen, stroking softly through the silk.

"Christopher," she whispered, "were you intending to take me to bed?"

He nibbled the shell of her ear. "Yes. Eventually."

"We can't."

He tamped down on annoyance. He wanted her. He *needed* her. He would not walk away this time. She was his wife, and she'd better get used to it.

He tugged free the ribbons that held her chemise in place, and slid his hand inside to her bared breast. "We can and we will."

"You don't understand."

He kissed the side of her neck. "Are you having your menses?"

"No."

"I didn't think so. You aren't more irritating than usual."

She threw him a glance. "Only a *man* would say that."

He pulled at the tightening nub under his fingers. "So I am a man. And your husband. The bed will be involved."

"But we cannot."

"Oh, I think we can."

"No, because—"

He bit the curve of her shoulder. "I'm not terribly interested in your explanations." In one firm motion, he stripped the chemise to her waist and cupped both breasts, while he nibbled his way to her ear. His arousal throbbed and hurt.

She tried to pull away, but succeeded only in pressing herself harder into his hands. Her backside rubbed his aching erection, not helping.

"Listen to me, you arrogant man."

He tightened his hold. "I'll listen to anything you say once we're in bed."

"Damn your hide, Christopher Raine."

"Damn yours, Honoria Raine." He wrapped his arms around her, pulled her back with him, and sat down hard on the bed.

He remained still for one stunned moment, then a sharp, searing pain penetrated his senses and his backside.

He leapt from the bed and shoved her away. "What the hell?"

Honoria spun and faced him, eyes wide. She hurriedly jerked the chemise over her bare torso. "That is why," she gasped.

Christopher glared at the bed. He reached down, grabbed the feather bed. It crackled. Sharp edges bit through the fabric.

"They're wood chips," Honoria said, voice agitated. "They didn't have any feathers."

Christopher Raine's famous coldness stood no chance against the fire of anger, annoyance, and need that swept him now. The bride he'd fought across years and distance to find was staring at him in fearful consternation, covering herself like a maiden from her ravisher. His bed was a pile of raw kindling, and he'd just had a piece of wood shoved into his backside.

He didn't bother to soften his roar. "Why the devil is my bed full of wood chips?"

"I told you, I could not find a feather bed. He told me that if you cover it with enough quilts and pillows it's soft, and warm, too. Dogs like to sleep on it."

He balled his fists. "Damn it all, Honoria, here is one fact you missed—I am not a dog!" He grabbed her wrists as she tried to back away. "Don't you dare play the feeble wit with me. I know exactly why you got it. The same reason you bought the bloody statue and all the other loads of junk. You want me to throw you off my ship and sail without you. I didn't cross half the world to be put off by your idiotic games. You belong to me, and to hell with your wood chips."

She stared at him, frozen, face white. She probably *was* afraid he'd send her overboard after that statue. And he was almost ready to.

Instead, he jerked open the window, seized the misnamed featherbed, and stuffed it through the opening. It stuck, and he pounded it, then he backed up and kicked it through.

When he turned around, Honoria had sunk to the floor, her bodice pulled up again, her face buried in her hands.

"Oh, damn, that's all I need." He dropped to one knee beside her. His breeches tightened over his backside, digging in the splinters. They hurt like hell.

"Stop crying, Honoria. It was stupid, but I'm not going to divorce you for it, so give up the idea."

She pressed her hands tighter over her face, her shoulders shaking. And then he realized she was not crying.

He snarled a few livid French curses and climbed to his feet. She peeked through her fingers at him, eyes streaming, mouth wreathed in smiles. She was beautiful when she smiled.

He growled. "Don't laugh at me, damn you. I've got a splinter in my backside."

She pressed her hands to her mouth, shaking all over.

"Stop looking so smug," he snapped. "You get to take it out."

Her eyes widened in sudden alarm, and she came to her feet. "I'll send for Mr. Colby."

"Oh, no, you will not." Christopher imagined Colby's great roar of laughter, his bearlike form shaking as he held himself up on the door frame. He'd insist on bringing down the rest of the crew to view their captain in distress. "On your feet, my beautiful wife. Tend to your husband."

He unbuttoned his breeches, shot them down to his knees, then turned around and leaned over the bed.

Chapter Six

Honoria studied the firm muscles of his buttocks, the tight thighs beneath them, and her laughter died. The Chinese lion on his hip stretched a little with his movement, as if restless itself.

She had difficulty breathing. Always he'd defeated her by having a body that stunned her senseless. God made the body, one of Honoria's governesses had once told her. He made it in his image, so there was nothing shameful about it. One should look upon it and rejoice.

She'd always wondered a bit about that governess, but she had to admit that God had certainly done well with Christopher Raine. His broad shoulders tapered to a slim waist and hips; his backside was smooth with muscle, pale in contrast to the rest of his tanned body. She had not seen him without his shirt since he'd returned, but she remembered the planes of his back, brown and flat and strong.

He looked over his shoulder at her now, his gray eyes narrow. His thick plait of hair had loosened in their struggles, blond wisps straggling over his shirted back. "Well?"

Droplets of blood surrounded the sliver that had worked through his breeches and into his flesh. She felt a twinge of remorse.

"It's quite large," she said.

"I'd be flattered if I didn't know you meant the splinter."

"There's more than one, I'm afraid." She came closer, gingerly put her hand on his back. His flesh was warm through the shirt. She did remember kissing the lion on his hip, quite wantonly, but she was suddenly shy. She was a different person now; so was he.

He watched her, not patiently. "You'll have to take them out. I can't reach."

"I know."

She smoothed the hollow of his hip, drew her fingers toward the first sliver. She closed her fingers around it and pulled.

"Ouch!"

"I can't see." She rose, unhooked the lantern from the ceiling beam, and set it down on the privy, training its beam on his back. She returned to the bed, sat down, gently took hold of the sliver.

"Take it out all at once," he said tersely. "Don't dig around."

"I will if you'll hold still."

He looked away, his muscles rigid. "All right, I'm rea—Ow!"

Honoria held up the longest sliver. She gave it a triumphant look, then took it to the window and dropped it out. "Only three more to go."

"Bloody hell."

Honoria returned to him. Braver now, she put her hand on the small of his back, a bared half-oval of skin beneath his shirt. "Christopher," she said as she worked the next free. "The pamphlets about you told stories of you being shot."

"What of it?"

"Well, that must have hurt more than a few splinters."

"It's not the same thing."

She stopped. "Why not?"

He shifted a little, whether trying to get comfortable or not wanting to answer, she could not tell. "Because when you get shot, you are in so much pain that either you pass out or someone pours opium down your throat. *This*—I feel everything."

"You are amusing, Christopher Raine." She resumed prying at the next-longest splinter.

"That sounded almost affectionate." His voice lost its edge. "Tell me why you fell in love with me, back all those years ago, when you read newspaper stories and wanted to meet me." He grimaced. "It will take my mind off the excruciating pain."

She fell silent, focusing her gaze on her work. "I suppose because you were nothing like what I knew. Most of the gentlemen in Charleston I'd known all my life. They went to university, started work in their fathers' businesses, looked for a wife to settle down with. They said the right things and knew the right people and married into the right families."

"And bored you senseless."

She thought about that. "I tried not to let them. I knew I would marry one of them, it was just a matter of which." She sighed. "Unfortunately, there is a streak of adventure in the Ardmore family. My brothers were able to fulfill it sailing the seas and fighting pirates, but I had to stay home. I found my adventure reading about you and imagining things."

"What did you imagine?" he asked, his voice dark.

"Nothing I will tell you," she said firmly.

She was glad his face was turned away and he could not see her blush. Good heavens, what she had imagined! She used to lie awake long into the night inventing adventure after adventure about herself and Christopher Raine until her body had grown rigid with excitement.

One of her favorites involved herself stowing away on Christopher's ship. He'd find her and, enraged, clap her in irons and prepare to execute her. Then he'd be struck by her beauty and innocence, and he'd fall in love with her. She'd prove herself clever, saving the day in some adventure or other, and he would promote her to be one of his officers. He would confide in her, and she'd help plan his missions. Then one day she'd save his life in a heroic battle, nearly losing her own in the process. He'd stay by her side until she recovered, and then he'd kiss her and profess his devotion to her, and they would marry, cheered by a grateful crew.

She'd had several versions of this tale, which she'd happily run through night after night, never tiring of them.

"And then I met you," she said softly.

The girlish fantasies had swiftly died that day, to be replaced by something deeper and more disturbing. She'd learned in the garden room what a man truly was, and what he truly wanted of a woman.

"I remember," he said. "You were so pretty with your ringlets and your blushes and your shy smile. You were a delectable little morsel, and I vowed to eat you up."

"Which you proceeded to do, as I recall," she said coolly.

"Yes, and you tasted fine—damnation!"

Honoria held up another splinter. "Almost finished. The others are quite small."

"Thank God for that."

The last two came free with very little resistance. Christopher was silent except for a single grunt and a very bad word as the last gave way.

Honoria disposed of the slivers and rummaged for a towel. Once found, she wet it in the basin in the outer room and returned. She cleaned the wound, touching him with more confidence, certain he'd be grateful that she had thought to purchase the towels.

She ran her fingers across Christopher's taut flesh, pleased she found little more than faint scrapes in his skin. She smiled to herself. Men carried on about the littlest things.

Unable to resist, she traced the lines of the springing lion on his hip, and then she leaned down and kissed it.

"Mmm," he murmured.

He smelled so good. His shirt tickled her nose, and

his skin tasted faintly salty. Her fingers rested firmly on his backside, right over his wounds, but he did not seem to mind.

He reached behind him, drew his hand through her hair, dislodging the matron's cap she'd put there.

It slid to the floor, and cool air touched her hair. A few curls trickled from their pins to brush her shoulders, their touch feeling like his light kisses there had. He gave her a slow smile, as though knowing what she thought.

Any moment now, he'd throw her to the floor and land on top of her, then their lovemaking would proceed in a frenzy of lust and ripped clothing, as usual. But he only said, gray eyes dark, "I missed you, Honoria."

She did not answer. She continued tracing the lion, watching her fingers. His skin was smooth, warm. The hem of his shirt moved across it as he breathed.

"Did you miss me?" he asked.

"No."

He stilled. "A minute ago, you were in love with me."

"I was. When I was a girl. I was quite infatuated with you."

More silence. She leaned down and traced the outline of the drawing with her tongue. He tasted heavenly, a tang that she'd never forget.

He asked, "Did you love me when you married me?"

"Yes."

"But not now?"

She flicked her tongue back and forth across the intricate ridges on the lion's tail. "No."

"You're acting very brazen for a woman not in love."

The edge had returned to his voice. She looked up. "It isn't brazen. You are my husband."

He rolled away suddenly, tugging his breeches over his backside, hiding the tattoo and everything else enticing. "One of us is confounded here."

He sat up, his back against the wall. She knelt next to him. He did not button his breeches, but they hid him. Most of him. Her eyes were drawn to a tantalizing line of flesh below his navel.

He sighed, reached out to thread his fingers through her hair. "I should be angry at you, Honoria. But I crave you too much right now. If you believe you are only doing your wifely duty, so be it."

"That's not what—"

He tightened his fingers, pulled her to him. His breath was hot on her lips, smelling of ale and his own spice.

She forgot what she wanted to say. Excitement began to push aside any other thought in her head. Regret would come later. For now her heart beat hard, every limb tingled, and desire snaked through her with an intensity that almost hurt.

She leaned forward and kissed his lips.

He made a noise in his throat, pulled her closer. She tasted his lips, ran her tongue over the sandpaper bristles of his chin.

He caught her face in his hands, kissed her hard. His tongue tangled with hers; he tasted of spice and heat.

Still kissing her, he pushed her loosened chemise and bodice back down to her hips. He slowly raised her to her knees, traced his lips from the hollow of her throat to her breasts that hung before him, tight with excitement.

She let her head drop back, closed her eyes, cradled his head in her hands. He caught her breast in his mouth, suckled her, his mouth fierce. It hurt her, and was glorious.

It was like a thunderstorm every time they came together, a tense buildup, then a sudden explosion of wind and lightning. The buildup was over, their tension wound high. The release was going to sink the ship.

He shoved her clothes downward. Kisses fell on every inch of her bare flesh. His muscles worked as he lifted her to her feet, set her on the floor. "Take off the dress."

Her hands shook as she obeyed him. She pushed it down her hips, stepped out of the circle of fabric. At the same time, he slid off his boots and breeches, kicking them both away. Still in his shirt, he lay down again and dragged her on top of him.

She straddled him while his warm hands roved her torso. She felt a bit shy being bare for him; the other times, they'd never taken the trouble to unclothe themselves completely.

But the shyness dissolved as she lost herself in the absolute beauty of him. His erection, long and hard, rested against his abdomen, crisp curls of dark blond hair at its base. She shifted until the hardness lay right between her legs. She rubbed herself on it a little, the friction promising more joy to come.

"You're always wet for me, Honoria," he said, voice

husky. "I never have to wonder if you want me. Are you open for me, too?"

She nodded. She was swelling and parting, already feeling him inside her. He lifted her, his fingers sinking into her flesh. His hardness stood up between them, and he slid her onto it.

He stretched her wider than she'd ever been stretched. In the cell in Charleston, everything had been quick, wicked, burning. Now he moved her slowly down onto him, inch by slow inch, getting her used to him. His hands were slick with sweat, just as she was slick from wanting him.

He pulled her down, farther, farther, while he rose inside her, hard and engorged. His eyes darkened as he watched her, candlelight touching his lashes, the bristles on his face.

"God, Honoria, I missed you so much," he whispered.

He pulled her the rest of the way down, closing the last bit of space between them. Her head rocked back of its own accord, her loosened hair softly brushing her shoulders. Her flesh rose and tingled, the points of her breasts hardened, becoming dark red against the white of her skin.

He lay almost quietly beneath her, muscles playing under the shirt he still wore. She wished he'd take it off so that she could run her hands over his body, but he did not. His bronzed throat showed in the V of his collar, shiny with perspiration.

And inside her was the blunt, rigid length of him. It loosened what had been tight for so long. She welcomed the burning at her cleft, wanting it and wanting him.

This was *right*. The only time she felt complete, whole, was when she and Christopher Raine came together.

She did not understand why this should be; she only knew that she wanted to pull him deeper into herself, as deep as he could go.

"Harder, please, Christopher."

He drove his hips upward, complying. Perspiration beaded on his upper lip. His gray eyes were heavy, like a drunken man's, and his warm hands engulfed her thighs.

She let her head drop back again, closed her eyes. He thrust his thumb between their bodies, where they joined, and squeezed her mound. Her eyes flew open, and she screamed.

Her climax came, the apex of the storm. She cried his name, tried to pull him ever deeper inside her. He thrust and thrust, and then suddenly he was gone

Her opening burned for him, and she cried out in disappointment.

He pushed her down into the quilts, his breathing hard, his body a heavy weight on hers. She sank into the pillows she'd insisted on buying, then he moved her legs apart and entered her in one long stroke.

Her climax went on, her voice rising to echo from the beams. He pinned her with hard hands, his sweat dropped to her chest. He sought her mouth, closed his eyes as he kissed her hard.

He rode her silently, his arousal hotter than anything she'd ever felt. It wanted her, widened her, possessed her. She felt aching and tight around him, a heavenly pain she'd never forget, had never forgotten.

He dragged in a breath, his eyelids fluttering. He groaned her name, then he rode out his climax, breathing hoarse, eyes closed.

After a very long time, he slowed, stilled. He raked her hair back from her forehead and kissed her.

Their storm finished, quieted. He kissed her swollen mouth, and she returned the kiss in gentle tiredness.

For a long time they lay quietly, he kissing her, she in limp tranquillity. The ship moved slightly as the river ran beneath them; a church tower on shore chimed eleven.

"Christopher," she whispered.

He nipped her neck. "You taste so sweet," he said, as though she had not spoken.

"When I said I did not love you—"

He raised his head. Strands of blond hair stuck to his throat, and his eyes were heavy. "I really don't want to talk about it right now."

"I want you to understand."

He put his fingers over her lips. "Honoria, we'll have plenty of time to talk about our feelings. For now, let's just pretend we're lovers."

"We are husband and wife, not lovers," she said.

His eyes held a glint of self-deprecation. "Thank you for correcting me. In that case, I order you to kiss me, wife."

She wanted to laugh. "I have been."

He seized her wrists, pinned them together above

her head. "This is another kind of order I expect you to obey without question."

The candlelight made wild shadows of the planes of his face. He looked frightening, but she felt heavy and happy. She lifted her head, kissed his mouth.

His lips brushed hers, then he kissed his way down her throat, skimming her breasts, dropping kisses to her warm stomach. His shoulders bunched as he drew his tongue across her abdomen. He kissed her navel, then laid his head down on her breasts and was silent.

His warmth soothed her, and her limbs felt loose. She drifted to sleep listening to the faint whisper of river, men speaking in low voices above them, a dog barking on shore.

She opened her eyes again to a bright moon. Christopher's head lay on her shoulder, his warm hair across her breast.

His whisper broke the silence. "God, I can't do this."

"Hmm?" Honoria murmured.

He waited one moment, traced her sensitive skin with his finger. "Go back to sleep, my wife."

"You cannot do what?"

"I wasn't talking to you."

She smoothed a pale lock from his face. "I never thought of you as a churchgoing man. Or of talking to God."

"Oh, I can pray, Honoria."

"What things does a pirate pray about?" She felt playful, despite the stern note in his voice. "Ships heavy with treasure, run by a crew that gives up without much fight?"

He grunted, his muscles tightening. "When they took me out of the prison that morning, I prayed. I prayed I'd die fast. Without lingering, without doing any of the horrible things a man can do when he knows he's dying."

Honoria touched his face, her heart throbbing with hurt. "I don't like to think about that. I couldn't come out of my room for three days." She traced the plane of his cheekbone. "I am grateful that God answered your prayer."

His lashes shadowed his cheek. "Yes, he spared me the noose and sent me straight to hell."

His eyes had lost every bit of mischievousness, every bit of warmth.

"But you were saved," she reminded him. "You were taken to the ship."

"Have you ever been on an English merchantman?"

"No."

He simply gave her a look, his gray eyes resuming their usual coolness. "A pirate's life is better."

"Pirates are cutthroats."

"We steal cargo," he corrected. "Believe me, Honoria, the East India Company is far more worried about the cargo pirates carry off than the crew who die. If we simply murdered everyone and left the goods and the ship, there would be no pirate hunters."

Honoria remained silent. She had heard often enough from James how grateful a merchant captain would be to him for saving his cargo. They seemed to think that losing a half-dozen sailors and two officers a good price for hanging on to their crates of crockery and sweet wine.

"My brother Paul was killed by pirates," she said softly. "As were his wife and daughters."

"So I heard."

She studied the lines of his face, hoping to find some sorrow there for her, some indication that he'd felt compassion when he'd heard the news of Paul's death. But his expression held only cool neutrality.

"Tell me about your sister," she said. She'd been surprised to learn that Christopher Raine had something as human as a sister.

"Half sister."

"What is she like?"

His smile returned, crinkles deepening the corners of his eyes. "Mean. There's not a better person I'd want at my back. She is absolutely loyal to me, and I trust her completely." He traced a pattern on her shoulder. "She disappeared the same time your brother arrested me. I haven't seen her since."

"I am sorry," she said softly. "I really do hate James Ardmore."

He gave her an odd look. "Strong words."

"It is the truth. He decides what everyone's life should be, and God help you if you do not agree. He never once asked me, his own sister, what would make me happy. I wonder you do not hate him yourself."

Christopher shrugged with infuriating patience. "He was doing his job." He traced a second pattern. "You seemed pleased enough that he made you a widow."

She rose up on her elbows, and his hand slid away. "How can you say that? I told you, I was ill for days when I thought you dead."

"You recovered."

"You think I did not care?"

"I think you did, in your own way."

"In my own way?" She sat up. "I told you I loved you, Christopher, that I grieved for you. You can have no idea how I felt. You know nothing about me."

"Now, that is a true observation."

She glared at him. His eyes were clear gray, the same color as diamonds. "Then why did you come back?" she asked. "If you don't believe I cared for you and were not surprised I was engaged to another, why did you bother?"

He stilled. His body just fit between her and the bulwark, a solid wall of flesh covered by his shirt and tangled in quilts. "Because every man is allowed to be stupid about a woman once in his life."

She sensed that his anger went beyond anything she comprehended. "And you were stupid about me?" she asked, her throat tight.

He tossed the covers aside, climbed over her, and rose to his feet. He took up his breeches, casually leaned over, and put them on. Candlelight gleamed on his hip, making the Chinese lion dance.

He fastened the breeches, then bent over the bed again, his hands on either side of her head. He smelled of lovemaking, and his seed, and maleness.

"Oh, yes, Honoria. Very, very stupid."

A small pain filled her heart. "Do you not want the marriage, then?"

He kissed her, no longer playful. The kiss was meant to bruise her and possess her, to put her in her place. "We are keeping this marriage, Mrs. Raine," he said, his words stern. "I want some compensation out of this."

He rose and abruptly stripped the quilts from her body.

Cold air touched her, raising her flesh in sudden chill. He took his time looking at her, raking his gray gaze over her bared breasts, her soft abdomen, her thighs that had parted so readily for him.

The gaze was possessive, one of a man looking over what belonged to him.

My wife, he called her, but he was treating her more like a courtesan than a wife. She, a properly brought up young woman, ought to be very upset about that.

Instead, the crawling excitement of all her dreams and fantasies rocketed back to her. He liked looking at her, and she liked that he liked looking at her. Without consciously realizing she did it, she opened her legs a little and touched the tuft of dark hair that grew between them.

His face darkened. "Damn you."

He shoved her back down into the quilts at the same time he popped open the buttons of his breeches. Another thunderstorm, but this one a whirlwind of cold rage that frightened her at the same time it exhilarated her.

He pressed her legs apart with hands that did not care, and thrust himself into her without preliminary. Hard and fast he pumped into her until she was screaming with need.

He made a raw noise as he spilled his seed, and then he pushed himself abruptly away from her, refastened his clothes, and slammed out of the cabin.

She fell back to the bedding, cold, spent, and alone. But she would not cry. She was Honoria Ardmore, and she'd endured hardships far more frightening than the rage of Christopher Raine. A lady of one of the first families of Charleston did not bow her head because her husband was angry at her.

Confusion wrapped her. The excitement he gave her twisted her all around until she did not know what she felt. She ached from lovemaking, and her body wanted more. She'd promised herself she'd acknowledge the marriage and do her duty, but she had no idea what duty was anymore.

She rolled over into the quilts that still smelled of him, wrapped them around her, and stared, dry-eyed, at the wall.

Chapter Seven

The saddle on the horse Christopher rode to Surrey did nothing for his backside. He'd not felt his torn skin while he'd made love to Honoria, but now the irritation was almost unbearable.

To his left rode Finley, looking as uncomfortable on horseback as Christopher did. Christopher liked the sea—land transportation was a necessary evil to him. Horses were fine beasts in theory, and he didn't mind handing them carrots or patting their warm flanks.

But once a man was aboard the beast, horses became demons with minds of their own. He'd once ridden down a mountain road in China in the freezing cold on a stubborn mount who enjoyed hugging the edge of the cliff. The beast would just miss its step, sending rocks into the chasm below, and dance backward as though surprised. When they'd reached the bottom, Christopher had dismounted, turned the horse to face him, and cursed it thoroughly, much to the amusement of the Chinese man he'd hired it from.

The road to Epsom lacked treacherous cliffs and the summer weather was warm, but this horse entertained itself by spooking at every fly, bee, dragonfly, mosquito, and butterfly that flew past its nose. Christopher growled at it, but the horse danced on, oblivious to Christopher's temper.

Mr. Henderson, a gentleman who'd had English countryside born and bred into him, sat his mount with easy grace. He was one of those irritating Englishmen who could ride anything, who probably owned stallions called Beelzebub or Mephistopheles and could make them docilely do his bidding. Henderson knew it, and rubbed it in by easily avoiding the muddy holes in the road that Christopher's horse seemed determine to stumble straight through.

A landau rolled behind the three horsemen, its top raised against the sun. Owned by Grayson Finley, the landau contained Honoria and Alexandra.

Grayson explained to Christopher as they rode that the two women would take the opportunity of this journey to dissect their characters thoroughly and at great length. He'd said this fondly.

Christopher imagined Honoria describing to Alexandra the horrors of their night together. The two would either exclaim that Christopher was an unfeeling brute, or, worse, they'd laugh. He glowered back at the landau, and his horse tripped over another hole.

Ostensibly, the five were simply friends enjoying a day out in the country. Switton's Surrey house lay near Epsom Downs, and the man had replied to Henderson's letter that he would be happy to give Henderson an appointment.

After much discussion of etiquette—mainly by Henderson and the ladies—it was decided that Henderson would keep the appointment alone. Finley and Christopher and their wives would take rooms at a public house in the next village and pretend to enjoy rustic picnicking on the downs.

At least Christopher pretended. The others seemed to be having the time of their lives.

Once the picnic was set up, with much girlish laughter on the part of the two ladies, Christopher paced restlessly to the top of a hill. From here he could look out to the road that Henderson had taken. Switton's estate lay out of sight over a few low hills that were surrounded by tree-lined streams. Hedges enclosed patchwork fields where faraway farmers bent in labor or led oxen or horses across them. Sheep grazed on open greens, including the very hill Christopher stood upon. One sheep, not five feet away, pulled up a mouthful of grass and watched him with mild interest.

Down the hill, Finley's baritone guffaws intertwined with the lighter laughter of Alexandra and Honoria. The two ladies had planned this outing down to the last detail, from selecting the correct foods to obtaining a large enough basket to worrying about what to wear. As they'd set up at the bottom of the hill, Honoria and Alexandra had chattered, even giggled, heads together, each wearing a filmy, lacy cap with fluttery tapes.

121

Jennifer Ashley

Christopher wondered if other men rushed into marriage with lovely, green-eyed wenches they'd give anything to wake up beside, only to discover they'd brought home a punctilious woman who grew horrified if you suggested the napkins did not have to match the picnic cloth.

A good many, he imagined. From the way Finley looked at his wife, the man had been happy to drown in the pool of female follies.

Honoria had looked radiant deciding whether lobster sauce went with jellied shrimp. But whenever Honoria caught Christopher's gaze on her, her laughter would die and her expression would cool. Another reason he'd walked away and up the hill.

She was so different from anything in his life, fragile like the tiny yellow blossoms that poked through the tough grass he stood on, yet strong enough to grow there. Thinking of her for four years had been the only thing that had brought him home.

And, once he'd found her again, she'd stared at him like he'd gone mad. He could tell she wondered why he hadn't left well enough alone. He wondered why himself.

"It's a lovely view."

Her soft Southern tones drifted over his senses, and he started to remember why again.

Honoria stopped beside him. She wore a yellow gown, thin muslin for summer, and not much beneath it. To entice him? She'd made clear last night she wanted him, whatever else she might feel for him. He'd be a fool not to take full advantage.

When she'd made that little gesture as he prepared

122

to leave, silently asking, *Do you want me?*, only a hurricane could have stopped him.

"Alexandra says," she went on, as if they were mere acquaintances at a picnic, "that from here you can watch the Derby race and see everything without all the dust and noise."

The woman who had screamed for him never to stop was worried about dust and noise.

"Perhaps," she continued, "when you find your sister we can all come and watch the races. It would be another fine picnic."

"I don't give a damn about horse racing," he snapped. "Or picnics."

She studied him a moment. The sheep looked at them both, took another mouthful of grass, chewed while listening.

"You are out of sorts today," Honoria observed. Her expression softened. "I suppose you are worried about your sister."

"You could say that." He turned his gaze back to the road, furious at the trees that hid his view. If Henderson didn't return within another hour, Christopher was going to storm the place, and damn Henderson and the earl if they were shocked.

Christopher's idea of negotiation was to put a sword to the other person's throat and tell them to do what he said. He'd always found it effective.

Honoria smiled—a polite, neutral smile, nothing warm for Christopher Raine. "Well, do not let Alexandra or Mr. Henderson hear you say you don't care about horse racing. It's very un-English, apparently. You'll be ostracized."

"I'm only half English, and by accident." He kicked at a hank of dead grass. The wind took it and shards of dried grass floated toward the sheep. The animal regarded it in faint disdain, then went back to cropping fresh grass. "I don't belong here. Neither do you."

"I know." She gazed across the everlasting green fields. "I say it's lovely, but I don't really like it. I've seen the ocean from my bedroom window all my life, felt the breeze from it. I always pretend I can see all the way to the other side of the world, if I look hard enough. Here I feel—landlocked."

Christopher nodded. "So do I. Having to trust devious horses to get from place to place. They plot, you know."

She smiled in truth this time, her white teeth charming him. "They do not, Christopher."

"Don't tell me you have a way with horses, too."

Her dimples deepened. "No. I'm just more used to them."

"You can't steer the bloody things. They go where they want, just to spite you."

"Don't be silly."

Her eyes, green as the grass beneath them, sparkled with good humor.

"That's dangerous, Honoria."

"What is?"

She looked so damn ingenuous. "Scolding me." His voice went quiet. "And smiling like that when you do it."

Said smile vanished. "I have no wish to scold you. I beg your pardon."

"I'd rather have you scolding like a fishwife than being so bloody polite."

Her fine brows arched. "Why should I not be polite to my own husband?"

"I don't want you being polite." He turned from the view, caught her shoulders. "I want you to spread yourself for me, like you did last night."

She flushed but held his gaze. "I'm afraid I was quite improper last night."

Maybe she was driving him insane on purpose, like the horses. He slid his arms around her, rubbed his thumbs in circles on her shoulder blades. "I don't want a proper wife."

"All men do."

"How do you know? You've only ever been married to me."

"I read books."

Now he wanted to laugh. He took her hand, pressed it to the hard lump in his leather breeches. "Does that feel like I want you to be proper?"

She looked at him coyly, dragged her palm downward. He grit his teeth at the harsh tingle that chased her touch.

"You want me to be brazen." She smiled. "I like being brazen."

"That pleases me, my wife."

"When you first touched me, I wanted you so much." She rose on tiptoe, put her lips to his ear, as though she wanted to tell him a secret, something the sheep could not hear. "I still want you, Christopher."

He felt her warmth through the cool country breeze. "Good."

"Everything is wrong and upside down from what it is supposed to be."

"I don't mind, as long as you keep doing that."

She hid her face in his shoulder and complied.

They stood for a long time, he holding her, she rubbing him softly and driving him mad.

"Christopher," she said. "When I told you I didn't love you—I meant it."

"I guessed that."

She looked up at him, her cheek resting on his shoulder. "I still like to touch you. I get so excited when you touch me."

He stroked the nub that rose through the silk of her bodice. "I see that."

"But that isn't the same thing, is it?"

Her hand continued its dance, and he was losing coherence. He pressed a kiss to the top of her head. "Right now, I don't care."

She traced the outline of his erection. It was getting difficult to breathe. "I love your body. I have always craved it, and because I'm your wife, now I am allowed to please it."

"I'm glad you've grasped your wifely duties."

"If we weren't out here, I'd want to bring you to climax with just my hand."

"You're very nearly there, love."

He tilted her chin up, leaned down, and kissed her. Her lips were practiced, but only with what he'd taught her.

Her hands ceased their delightful torture, wrapped about his neck, and held on, as she liked to. She squirmed a little, a delightful armful. He finished the kiss and held her close, stroking her back, burying his nose in the fine scent of her lacy cap.

Behind her, the sheep stared, bits of grass dribbling from its mouth.

"What are you looking at?" Christopher growled.

Honoria turned in his arms, saw the sheep, laughed. She shook wonderfully when she did that. The sheep gave them a bored look, lowered its head, and continued its luncheon.

Christopher moved to draw her back into his arms, but she stepped away and hastily straightened her cap. "Christopher, I want to explain why I say I can't love you."

He rolled his eyes. Why did she want heart-to-heart talks when they were both wound tight with desire? Save them for some boring day when they didn't have a chance to sate themselves.

"It doesn't matter," he said tersely. "This has been a shock for you. You'll get used to it."

She shook her head. Sable curls danced on her forehead. "No, please let me tell you. I want you to understand. When I say I do not love you, and I cannot, I mean just that—ever. You died, Christopher. I loved you, and you died."

He brushed her cheek with a light hand. "But I didn't, love."

Her voice hardened. "That doesn't matter. What do you think it was like for me to have had you and lost you in the space of a day? It hurt so much, I thought I would die myself."

He touched her hair again, but she pulled away, her eyes like hard emeralds. "So I let it hurt, and I

127

mourned you. And then I let you go. I had to, it was killing me. I put you behind me. I tied a black ribbon around my box of mementoes and pushed it to the back of the drawer."

She glared. "Do you understand, Christopher? I finished hurting for you. I had no choice. I lost the brother I loved more than my own life—he was my other self, and some pirate shot him when he was miles away. I lost him, and then I lost you. I cannot go through that again, and I never will." She paused, her breathing hard. "So I will be your wife because I made the vows and I signed the license. I will share your bed, but I will not let myself love you ever again."

Her eyes glittered as she waited for him to shout at her, to tell her how horrible she was.

"Are you finished?"

She gave him a nod. "For now. I just want you to understand—"

"Oh, you've made yourself perfectly clear." He caught her chin and twisted her face up to his. "If you want to service me and not engage your heart, you go right ahead. But you remember what you've said here, that you are my wife in name and body. I will hold you to that in every way. Do you understand *me?*"

"You want me to obey you."

"Every order I give," he said, voice hard. "So if I tell you to take off your clothes and service me right here, even with your friends waiting for us down the hill, you'd do it?"

She paled, but looked at him in defiance. "Yes."

Christopher yanked off the matron's cap, which he

already hated, and sent it dancing away on the breeze. "Play the martyr with me, Honoria, and you will live to regret it. I don't want a sacrifice."

He jerked her against him, forced his lips on hers in a bruising kiss.

He'd always known in the back of his mind that she would not have waited for him, but the illusion of that had kept him going when he otherwise would have died. To have her throw it in his face, in front of a sheep, how much she did not love him, stirred his slow, deadly anger to life. The explosion would soon follow.

But not now. He needed to get with Henderson and shake the Earl of Switton upside down until the man coughed up what he knew about Manda. If he knew anything at all.

Christopher broke the kiss, set Honoria down with a thump. She stared at him, her eyes wide, her loosened hair teasing her forehead. Disheveled, she looked . . . so delectable.

His mood foul, he seized her wrist, began dragging her back down the hill toward the waiting Finley and Alexandra.

She panted beside him. "But I thought you wanted—"

"You're lucky the sheep was here," he growled.

Mr. Henderson returned just as the picnic drew to a close. Honoria could eat nothing. She noticed that Christopher only pushed his food around his plate.

Grayson and Alexandra seemed oblivious to the atmosphere. They flirted and teased each other as usual until Honoria was ready to scream.

She should have known she could not make Christopher understand. He'd become angry, took it as a slight to himself.

Alexandra had warned her, in the carriage, that explaining one's feelings to a man was always a tricky task. Gentlemen, she said, so intelligent in other ways, often fell short when it came to their emotions. They simply did not understand that which came so naturally to women.

Honoria had not confessed to Alexandra the exact nature of her feelings, and she wasn't certain that Alexandra was right. She had confused Christopher, but she was completely confused herself.

She did thank Alexandra for her idea of very literally interpreting Christopher's order to buy whatever she wished. It had been quite useful. Alexandra had smiled, pleased. A similar thing, she said, had worked well on Grayson when he and Alexandra had been stumbling through their own courtship.

Mr. Henderson now adjusted his spectacles and gratefully accepted Alexandra's offer of wine and cake. He sipped wine, took a bite of cake, and dabbed his mouth with a napkin, the perfect English gentleman.

Christopher waited, surprisingly patient, for Henderson to set the plate down, clear his throat, and give his report.

The Earl of Switton was a congenial enough gentleman, Mr. Henderson said. Switton had been flattered to receive Henderson's letter, pleased to let him pay a call and catch up on old times. However, the man claimed to know nothing of a woman called Manda Raine.

Christopher's hands balled to fists, but his only change of expression was a whitening about his mouth.

Mr. Henderson continued that the earl had extended an invitation to them all to attend a garden party he and his wife were hosting the next day. If they attended, Christopher could question the man directly.

Christopher nodded once. Tension emanated from him, but he remained silent.

"But," Henderson concluded, "I do not believe the ladies should go."

The ladies, of course, at once clamored to know why not.

Henderson looked embarrassed. "The earl is a bit unsavory. He likes to talk about women, and I do not mean ladies."

"His wife will be there," Alexandra put in. "It will be perfectly proper."

"Yes, but he seems a bit odd. I haven't seen him since I was a boy; I don't remember him well." He sipped his claret. "I am not certain exactly what kind of garden party he has planned."

Alexandra's brows twitched together. "All the more reason we should attend. I will certainly not wait tamely while my husband is drawn into conversation about brazen women."

Grayson grinned, eyes crinkling, and slid his arm around Alexandra's waist. "No need to worry, love."

"We'll all go," Christopher said. He sat a little apart from them, his muscular arm circling his bent knee. He looked enticing like that. His coat hung open, and his loose shirt was parted at his throat. "Honoria and Alexandra can corner the earl's wife and question her while Finley and I tackle the earl."

"What does your sister look like?" Henderson asked. "I saw two ladies passing through one of the lower halls, but I could not see them clearly."

"Tall," Christopher said tersely. "Slim. Black hair. Looks like she could kick you from here to Jamaica, and probably could."

"Does she have black skin?"

Christopher's head snapped around. He rose to his feet in one smooth movement, like a lion that has scented prey. "You've seen her."

Chapter Eight

"Might have seen her," Henderson corrected. "There was not much light in the halls."

Honoria watched Christopher pull himself in, remind himself that any number of tall, slim women with black skin could be traipsing about the English countryside.

Mr. Henderson regarded him speculatively. "If you are contemplating rushing over there and beating information out of the earl, do not. He saw me watching the ladies and told me that they would attend the party. If we behave like civilized gentlemen—"

Grayson broke in. "We aren't civilized gentlemen. We're pirates. Think of the earl and his house as a pirate ship. We will board it and set Manda free."

Henderson gave him a deprecating look. "It's always best to get a feel for what the other captain will do. Or, in this case, the lay of the land. Charging in headfirst will do more harm than good."

"You probably learned that from James Ardmore, a man known for his prudence," Grayson said, an ironic glint in his eye.

"He is prudent," Henderson argued. "In his own way. Which is why he always wins."

Grayson's good-natured expression darkened, but he made a *I'll let this one go* gesture and subsided.

"We'll do this Henderson's way," Christopher interrupted. He'd gone cold as ice-covered granite, his eyes chill windows to the man inside. "We'll watch the house to see that nobody leaves it, then we'll attend this garden party. If the woman there is not Manda, we'll leave him alone." He let his gaze drift in the direction of the earl's house, as though he could see it straight through the trees and hills. "But if he has my sister, against her will, then God help him."

His words were quiet, but his hand curled so tight the skin over his knuckles whitened through his tan.

The silent gesture told her that Christopher must feel about this sister the way Honoria had felt about Paul. She would have died for Paul. If it had been Paul in the earl's house, Honoria would not have stopped herself flying there to rescue him by any means necessary.

She knew what he felt, although Christopher would likely not believe her if she told him. But the small measure of understanding brought her a tiny step closer to the man she had married. She said nothing and busied herself helping Alexandra clear up the picnic mess, but she felt just a little bit better.

* * *

The earl's wife looked a kindly sort of woman whose only vice was using too much rouge. The lady greeted her guests in the main hall of the crowded house the next afternoon with undisguised delight.

"Lord and Lady Stoke, I am honored."

Technically, Lady Switton was a step above Viscount and Viscountess Stoke in rank, but she appeared to be quite happy that Grayson and Alexandra condescended to appear at her party. Grayson, in turn, presented Honoria and Christopher.

The countess was just as delighted with them. Honoria put on her best manners as she curtsied, then took the lady's offered hand.

Lady Switton had met Mr. Henderson earlier in the day. "I am so pleased you returned, Mr. Henderson. You are alone now, but you will not be for long, I'd wager. I have some of the prettiest ladies in England in my garden." She tittered. Henderson's smile was strained.

They moved on. Alexandra and Honoria withdrew to an antechamber to freshen themselves while the gentlemen went on to the gardens.

The room was empty, to Honoria's relief. She sat morosely before a mirror, tucked a stray curl into her coif. Alexandra pinched her own cheeks and straightened a sleeve that had become twisted. "Well, Lady Switton does not look guilty of anything but being rather silly," she said. "I never see them in town. They keep themselves to themselves. Not really in anyone's circle."

"Perhaps they like the country," Honoria offered.

"You are being charitable, my dear. I think perhaps people simply do not like them."

135

Honoria withdrew a hairpin and reaffixed it. "I was trying to be polite." In truth, she cared very little about the Earl and Countess of Switton. Christopher had been closemouthed and chill the rest of the day and night, spending most of the time out with Henderson watching the Switton house.

She had wanted to explain that she understood his need to find his sister, and that she was prepared to help in any way she could but she'd not gotten the chance. He'd been tight-lipped, or simply not around.

He'd come to bed after she'd been asleep. In the gray light of dawn, he'd awakened her and made love to her swiftly and perfunctorily. Then he'd gone, leaving her hot and tired and bereft. She'd not seen him again until she'd descended from the landau at the Swittons' home.

"If Lord and Lady Switton are unpopular," she said now, trying to distract herself, "why are so many people here?"

Alexandra shrugged. "It is summer and garden parties are popular, and we are so near Epsom Downs. People will forgive anything for a few tips on the races."

"Oh, yes, the English are mad for horseflesh. They are in Charleston, too. Though Christopher seems to care little about horses and racing."

Alexandra smiled, flashing white teeth. "My dear, we married pirates, which makes us a little out of the ordinary."

Honoria studied her reflection. Her color was high, her eyes sparkling. She had to admit that she'd looked much better since she'd thrown her reputation to the wind and admitted she'd married Christopher Raine. No matter what the consequences.

Alexandra put her arm around Honoria's shoulders. "And you are at last with the man you love, my dear."

Honoria did not answer. Alexandra was giddily in love with Grayson Finley, poor woman, and simply assumed that Honoria and Christopher were living an idyllic dream. Diana had warned her that Alexandra existed in a world of honey-drenched optimism.

Alexandra's perfect white forehead wrinkled at Honoria's expression. "Everything is all right between you and Christopher, is it not?"

Honoria had also been taught to keep dirty linen hidden. "Yes, of course."

Alexandra did not look convinced, but to Honoria's relief, she did not pursue it. "Shall we join the gentlemen?" she asked.

Honoria nodded, glad to end the conversation, and they departed the antechamber.

The Earl of Switton's home was a Palladian house that had been redecorated in the austere style of about twenty years before. A black and white marble hall and a sweeping white staircase led upward amid portraits of Earls and Ladies of Switton.

The garden stretched out from the rear of the house and had been laid out by Capability Brown, or so the countess proudly informed them. Straight green or graveled paths led between pristine beds of flowers, pruned hedges, and topiary. Fountains trickled in corners, and the main path led to a series of fountains, each larger than the last, pouring water into huge granite basins. The spray gushed high, and a breeze showered everyone with droplets of water. Some guests laughed; others cursed and tried to dry their ruined clothes.

Alexandra and Honoria found the gentlemen on one of the lawns. They were speaking to another gentleman who must be the Earl of Switton himself.

The earl was much as Honoria had supposed he would be, a man in his fifties, plump from port and beefsteak, red-faced from the same. He was straight-backed and dressed impeccably, in short, an English country peer. She could see little to distinguish him from the English peers she'd met in London, or those who visited Charleston.

Christopher, Mr. Henderson, and Grayson stood arrayed before him. Alexandra paused and said behind her fan, "Are they not splendid?"

Honoria had to agree. Christopher's black coat stretched across broad shoulders, and his pantaloons were tight over well-muscled thighs and fine calves. More than one spindly gentleman who obviously had stuffed sawdust into his stockings, gazed upon Christopher's athletic body with envy.

Christopher's wheat-colored hair was plaited tightly into a single tail, held in place with a simple black ribbon. Tails were no longer in fashion for military or naval men, but Christopher's seemed to be accepted, and again, admired by ladies and gentlemen alike. Christopher, oblivious to this attention, kept his cold gaze on Switton while letting Switton prattle.

The other two gentlemen looked just as fine, although Christopher was the only one of the three who stirred Honoria's imagination. Grayson and Mr. Henderson were well turned out in black suits fitted over their tall, muscular bodies. Grayson's blond hair was pulled back in a simple tail, and Henderson's hair, the lightest shade of all, was cropped in the current fashion. Were she not nearly always irritated with Grayson and Mr. Henderson, Honoria might enjoy being in the company of such handsome men.

The Earl of Switton's conversation consisted mostly of joy that they had come. He liked new faces, he reiterated. When Mr. Henderson introduced Honoria and Alexandra, Honoria suddenly sensed why Henderson had not liked the Earl of Switton.

The earl's eyes were brown and wide and slightly soft. Those eyes focused narrowly upon her, as though he wanted to see into her entire being and turn it inside out. He betrayed no kindness or geniality, just pure prurient interest.

Grayson put a protective arm about his wife and drew her to him. His eyes held a cool watchfulness, blue like an icy lake.

Christopher was not as overtly protective, but under his stare, the earl withdrew the hand he'd offered to Honoria. She curtsied to him and held her fan demurely, incidentally covering her bare neck and bosom with the gesture.

"Charming," the earl said. His voice was a bit sticky. "I understand now why you did not want to leave your ladies behind."

Grayson's hand tightened on Alexandra's waist. Christopher did not touch Honoria, but Mr. Henderson edged a bit closer to her.

The earl turned to harmless topics like grouse shooting and the Derby that would occur in a few weeks, and what a devil of a mess the rains made of roads. Henderson and Grayson gave him noncommittal answers. Christopher spoke little but was tense as a violin string.

At last, the earl declared he would continue his duties as host and leave the gentlemen to the so-charming ladies. Only when he prepared to walk away did he make a statement that seemed the least bit odd.

"You will join me, won't you, for the pièce de résistance?" he said, lips quirking into a smile. Again, his gaze seemed to try to bore into Honoria's flesh. "At three o'clock. You will not be disappointed, I think."

Without waiting for a reply, he turned and strolled away.

"I do not like that man," Grayson growled.

"He's a boor," Mr. Henderson agreed. "I recall now that his grandfather obtained the title only because he knew some titillating gossip about Queen Anne. The peerage was apparently granted to shut his mouth. Trumped up—" He trailed off into mutter.

Grayson absently traced a curl that hung down Alexandra's white neck. "My love, I am torn between wanting to send you far from here and not wanting to let you out of my sight."

"I thought we were supposed to quiz the countess," Alexandra observed.

"I've changed my mind. You will stay next to me until this is finished."

Alexandra appeared in no way upset by this news.

Henderson growled, "We will have to find out things somehow. The sooner I can leave this place the better. The earl makes even conversing with Finley seem pleasant."

Grayson cast him a dark look. "Let us talk to people, ladies and gentlemen. And then meet for his pièce de résistance. I have a feeling it will be important."

He strolled away, Alexandra's hand firmly tucked under his arm. Henderson took out his quizzing glass and moved in the opposite direction.

Honoria was left with her grim-faced, silent husband.

"You know," she said softly, "society will look askance if you shoot the earl."

His eyes were hard. "Do you think I give a damn?"

"I did not say *I* would look askance."

He studied her with cool assessment. This was the first time they'd spoken alone since the hill, yesterday. "I've shot men who irritated me less. You'll see much if you choose life with me. I hope you are resilient."

"I do not swoon, if that is what you mean," she said crisply. "Nor am I a watering pot."

"Good." Abruptly he put his hand on her elbow and steered her toward the crowd.

She and Christopher spoke to no one. They moved through the garden, smiling politely, pretending to admire the flowers—or at least Honoria did. Christopher mostly bathed people in chill glances that made them draw back uncertainly.

Honoria saw no tall, slim black women circulating among the guests. A number of ladies, however, wore gowns cut scandalously low, painted their faces, doused themselves in perfume, and threw promising glances at Christopher.

Christopher ignored them as though they were boulders he had to avoid. Honoria ignored them as well, as a well-bred lady should. She wondered how long Christopher's patience would last before he tore the house apart to find out what he wanted to know.

They ended their stroll at the bottom of the summer garden. A fountain trickled quietly here, empty benches ringed around it. Behind a thin stand of trees, a green lawn led to a lake that stretched flat and gray to brown-green hills beyond. Few of the guests had trekked this far; most had stayed near the center of the garden and the food and drink there. Gentlemen here, she'd noted, had already indulged in much drink.

Christopher placed his hands behind his back and gazed at the silvered lake. His face was still, but a muscle moved in his jaw.

Honoria wanted to comfort him, to say *Don't worry, we'll find her*. But she knew finding Manda Raine was by no means certain. People disappeared all the time—they were lost at sea, or died of illness far from home, or became trapped in some remote place, penniless and unable to get home. If his sister had black skin, even though she might be a free woman, the chances of her being captured and sold as a slave were high.

The free black men and women of Charleston had to carry papers to constantly prove themselves free. The darker their skin, the more they were harassed. If

Christopher's sister had been raised aboard an English or French ship, if she had been free from birth with no papers to prove it, she might well have been captured to work the fields of some plantation in Jamaica or Antigua.

Honoria put her hand on his rigid arm, wishing she could offer comfort. But he'd know that anything she said would be false hope, and Christopher was not a man who embraced false hope.

His gaze swiveled to her, pale lashes hiding the gray. He made no indication whether her gesture soothed him or irritated him, nor did he shake her off.

She liked the feel of his arm. It was hard with muscle, rocklike, immovable. She knew the skin beneath his smooth coat was warm with life. She let her fingers drift, enjoying the solid feel of him.

Touching his bare flesh was so satisfying. No matter what her heart and her head told her, her body craved him, and she knew now that parting with him was out of the question. The wanting was too strong, the satisfaction too long denied.

I am in lust with him. Can one build a marriage on that?

And yet she knew that physical passion was very much a part of marriage. Diana and James did not touch each other much in public, but they could retreat into their bedchamber for hours and make muffled sounds that Honoria pretended not to hear. Grayson and Alexandra often gazed at each other as though the rest of the world had disappeared. Honoria's own parents had daily exchanged kisses and other gestures of affection, earning teasing remarks from their children. Her parents had never seemed very embarrassed about it.

Yes, she knew passion was part of marriage, but the intensity of Honoria's passion frightened her. She constantly wanted to look upon Christopher, to touch him, to bask in him. She remembered a girlfriend of hers in Charleston who'd found herself desiring her own husband. She'd told Honoria tearfully that when she confessed this longing to her husband, he'd grown disgusted, sent her to the seaside, and ordered her to take a course of remedies to cure herself of it.

Honoria doubted Christopher would be opposed to her desires, but then, this marriage was not normal. A hasty, secret ceremony, performed in a condemned man's cell, was not the same thing as a society wedding.

She stroked Christopher's arm, idiotically happy for even this small physical contact. She had no business wanting him in this overly ostentatious garden while he searched for his sister. But her loins ached, her body reacted to his nearness, his touch, his fragrance.

As though he sensed her longing, he slid his hand to the small of her back and pulled her to him for a kiss.

He tasted of champagne, and her desire built to a flood. She forgot where she stood and why she'd come. She was aware only of his tongue tracing hers, his warm hands on her back, his breath on her cheek. She wanted only to savor him. Perhaps they could sidle behind a hedgerow and continue what they'd started. Perhaps he would slide his hands over her body and never stop.

Thank heavens Christopher had self-control. He ended the kiss, eased his mouth from hers.

"It is three," he said. "On to our host's entertainment."

She took a step back, flustered. "Yes, of course."

Christopher tucked her trembling hand under his arm and guided her away.

As they moved back toward the main part of the garden, Honoria spied their host standing not far away. He was gazing right at them, a knowing smile on his face.

"Dear heavens," she said. "The earl was watching us. How embarrassing."

"He doesn't mind," Christopher said, his voice low. "He's a voyeur. He likes watching. He told us."

Honoria felt slightly sick. "How unsavory."

"For now, I want him to think me just as unsavory. That is, until I can get solid information out of him."

She stopped. Her skirts swished. "You think Manda is his pièce de résistance."

"If she is here, that is what she will be."

He propelled her onward, his stride slow but strong. Honoria glanced at the earl and bit her lip. If Manda did prove to be Switton's prize, his only worries would be which method Christopher would use when he killed him.

She spotted Grayson and Alexandra strolling toward the sweep of lawn to which most of the guests moved. Henderson followed not far behind.

"Does Alexandra know about the earl?" she whispered.

"No. Finley requested she not be told."

Honoria glanced sideways at him. "You told *me*."

"You are resilient," he said with no change of expression.

They joined the crowd. At the end of the lawn lay a small folly, the kind that wealthy gentlemen built on their grounds to pretend they enjoyed Greek architecture. The guests gathered around this as though it were a stage.

A large square structure muffled in silk curtains stood near the front of the folly. Footmen circulated the crowd with glasses of champagne and port, ratafia or lemonade for the ladies.

Christopher guided Honoria with his hand on the small of her back to where Grayson and Alexandra stood near the front of the crowd. Mr. Henderson positioned himself on Grayson's other side.

Henderson and Grayson told them about what they'd discovered, which was nothing about Manda. They'd found plenty of gossip, however.

"The Prince of Wales is here," Henderson said, sotto voce. "Somewhere. No one knows with who. He is supposed to be incognito. The newspaper accounts will be scathing." The corners of his eyes crinkled. "I cannot wait to read them."

"Oh, dear," Alexandra said, scanning the crowd. "I imagine we'll be in the newspaper, too."

Honoria turned her head and looked about as well. She recognized no august personages. In fact, she recognized no one but—

"Mr. Templeton!"

She said it aloud, so great was her surprise. Mr. Templeton stood alone, without his mother. "Hono—

er, Miss Ardmore—er, Mrs. Raine. Pleasant day for a garden party."

Honoria stared at him. Alexandra poked her arm, prompting her to remember her manners. "Er, quite."

Mr. Templeton, red-faced, bowed and edged out of sight.

Honoria glared at Christopher. "What is he doing here?"

Christopher's voice was low in her ear. "I have no idea, nor do I much care."

Alexandra fanned herself and watched Mr. Templeton try to lose himself in the crowd. "I am surprised he is here, if the earl is as unsavory as he seems."

"He's sowing his wild oats," Christopher told her.

Before Honoria could ask what he meant by that bizarre statement, the earl's footmen took up positions on the steps of the folly and the earl stood before the muffled structure.

"We must be cautious, my friends," he said, smiling a little. "We have a wild animal in our midst, and it must not be allowed to escape."

A murmur of excitement ran through the crowd. A few ladies fanned themselves. Gentlemen craned to look.

"Do not worry," the earl went on. "We will keep it caged. But in the event it escapes—" He paused, letting the words have their effect. One lady pretended to swoon. She fell artfully into the arms of the gentleman next to her.

Switton smiled. "But we have taken all steps to ensure your safety." He nodded. Two of the footmen approached the folly. "We are ready. Who here among you is willing to attempt to tame the savage beast?"

The footmen snatched the curtains away.

The object beneath it was a cage. Made of wood, it looked plenty sturdy, and was large enough for a man to walk about in.

Standing in the middle, head up, black eyes defiant, her form barely swathed in a leopard's skin, stood a woman. She was tall and slim with creamy black skin. She looked very, very angry, but her anger was nothing compared to what Honoria saw in Christopher's eyes.

Chapter Nine

Christopher's slow match burned out and the explosion began. He had no clear memory of handing Honoria off to Henderson, but he found himself moving toward the folly with the determination of a lava flow.

Manda turned her head and saw him. Her dark eyes flickered once in recognition and her breathing stopped. Then she deliberately turned away, her expression neutral, as though she had not just seen her brother alive again after four years of thinking him dead.

"Mr. Raine," the earl cried in delight. "Will you be the first to take on our Amazon?"

Christopher nodded tersely. He sprang up the steps to the cage's door. Laughter and applause sounded through the crowds and, this being England, men started calling out wagers. "Twenty guineas on the Amazon!"

"Let me in," Christopher said through his teeth to the footmen.

Switton beamed like a schoolmaster at a pupil who suddenly understands his lesson. "Mrs. Raine indulges you, does she? It is a fine thing to have an understanding wife." He nodded at the two footmen, and one produced a key. "If you take her down, you may have her," the earl said softly. "If not, we will try to remove you in one piece." His eyes twinkled.

Manda and Christopher exchanged glances, black eyes meeting gray. They'd learned to understand each other without speaking, and they did so now.

Christopher sensed Honoria watching intently. She had not offered argument or questioning, had not tried to stop him. She seemed to know what he felt and what he needed to do. His estimation of her rose.

Christopher removed his coat and cravat and rolled up the sleeves of his shirt. A few ladies in the front row sighed.

He nodded to the footman, who unlocked the cage with an unsteady hand. The footman quickly opened the gate and allowed Christopher to slip inside. The door shut, and a faint click told him that he'd been locked in. The crowd quieted a little, waiting for the entertainment to begin.

Manda paced the cage like an animal, nervous and restless. She had no weapon and wore nothing but the stupid leopard skin, which would no doubt drop from her body as soon as she began fighting. Manda would not care, but it was just another reason Switton would die.

He wondered if any man had bested her yet. From the fierce look in her eye, he doubted it.

He made a signal that would be visible only to her. She nodded imperceptibly, then came at him, launching her foot at his face. He easily blocked her kick, then they began sparring, falling into patterns that they'd learned years and years before.

By some chance, the leopard skin stayed in place, much to the gentlemen's disappointment. Wagers, however, came thick and fast, some on Christopher, most on Manda.

Manda's breath quickened and perspiration glittered on her dark skin. The gentlemen sang out lewd compliments to her. Manda ignored them. Her gaze was fixed on Christopher, watching for instructions.

They'd done this so many times, practicing to stay fit or staging fights in taverns to win wagers. She kicked again, he caught her foot and spun her away, he made to grab her, she easily evaded him. Four years since he'd seen her, and yet they had no problem communicating without words. His heart beat hard with relief and joy. She was alive, she was whole.

He'd had no clear plan when he'd sprung up here, only anger, burning and intense. He made himself calm, working out a strategy that would fit with what he and Finley and Henderson had already planned.

He signaled her again. She gave him another barely perceptible nod. When she next rushed him, she caught his shirt and pulled it from his body. The men laughed, the women squealed. He heard Honoria's audible gasp.

151

Manda quickly twisted the shirt into one long piece of cloth. When Christopher came at her again, she looped it about his neck and pulled it tight.

Manda was strong. Christopher tensed his neck muscles but still felt the burn of the lawn against his throat. He coughed. Her slim arms worked as she pulled him inexorably backward. He clawed at the cloth, not entirely pretending. The men cheered. Manda made a show of tightening the shirt about his neck.

"Please, someone help him!" Honoria's cry echoed over the noise.

Christopher heard Finley bellowing, quite close, "Get the cage open!"

The key rattled in the lock and the wooden gate swung open. Manda suddenly dropped the shirt, and as one, they sprinted for the opening. Finley had already pushed one of the footmen from the stage. Manda sent the other flying after him.

By now the crowd was in chaos. Ladies screamed. Gentlemen cursed. Men leapt forward, ready to stop Manda, ready to stop Christopher. He heard the sounds of fists hitting flesh as Grayson pummeled a path through them. Manda kicked and men ducked out of the way, but they were drunk and frenzied and most wanted to fight. The crowd of them was dense, closing around them.

He heard a sudden, high-pitched scream, the sound of a body falling. Alexandra cried, "Help, help! Oh, help! Mrs. Raine's collapsed."

Christopher grinned tightly. They were treasures,

both of them. He would show Honoria his gratitude for her help.

First they had to get away. At Alexandra's cry, about a third of the fighters turned back, pleased to find another activity less dangerous. The other two-thirds battled on gleefully, ready to pull the three of them down and pummel them senseless.

Then Henderson appeared. He had a pistol. At the sight of the pearl-handled gun held by a man who looked more than able to use it, more of the fighters changed their minds. They turned away with cries of "Steady on, man."

A clump of men barred their path. Half drunk on port and with fighting blood up, they prepared to take back the Amazon any way they could.

A small figure rocketed around Christopher and dove at the gentlemen in their path. The tails of his frock coat made him look more than ever like a small, determined comet. Rupert Templeton brandished something, someone's sword stick most likely, and shouted at the men in the way.

They stared at him as though a puppy had burst from the kennel and started growling like a wolf. The astonished amusement left their faces when he started jabbing them with the sword point. Men howled and reached for him, giving Christopher and Manda a clear path to the lake.

Manda ran. Her foot caught on a clump of grass, and Henderson caught her arm to steady her. She drew back, ready to hit him, but Christopher stopped her. "He's with us. Finley, get the ladies."

Grayson was already turning back. Christopher and Manda and Henderson ran on across through the elegant garden, down the green to the lake. As they passed Mr. Templeton, he stopped and saluted.

Christopher acknowledged this by dragging Mr. Templeton out of the way of the dandies he'd enraged and shoving the little man back toward the garden. "Take care of her, Mr. Raine," Templeton called through cupped hands before trotting off.

Manda, Henderson, and Christopher sprinted for the flat sheet of water stretching from the estate to empty hills beyond. One small boat lay at the end of the little pier. Once Christopher took the boat, any pursuers would have to swim for it, or hurry around by the road in hopes of catching them on the other side, but the road from the estate to the hills took an hour to traverse.

Much of the pursuit had dropped behind. Half the lords and gentlemen at the soiree looked as though they took little more exercise than a Sunday stroll. The other half, the fit ones, enjoyed the pursuit. They laughed, they made ribald commentary, they joked about what they would do to Manda when they caught her.

Christopher's boots sounded on the pier, and one by one he and Manda and Henderson dropped into the boat. Christopher found the two pistols he'd readied the night before and held them both up at the first gentleman to reach the dock. "Stop," he said clearly.

The gentleman threw up his hands and halted, his boots scraping the boards. The men behind piled into him.

Henderson unlocked the oars and rowed quietly away. The pier, not meant to hold ten drunken gentlemen pounding and shouting, gently crumpled and fell into the water. Christopher uncocked his pistols and sat down, ignoring the splashing chaos behind him.

Christopher was shirtless, Manda mostly naked. Henderson's clothes were still impeccable, his spectacles gleaming in the sunlight. Even his hair was unruffled.

Manda looked at Christopher and said, "What the hell are you doing alive?"

"Looking for you," Christopher said. "Here, Henderson, take the tiller. I'm too cold not to row."

They exchanged places. Henderson paused long enough to unbutton his coat and drape it over Manda's shoulders.

Christopher held his breath, waiting for her to grab Henderson's wrist and toss him overboard. Instead she stared at him, as though she'd never seen anything like him before.

She turned back to Christopher. "So you didn't get hung? I should have known."

"Raines are hard to kill," Christopher said, grunting a little against the pull of the oars. Now that his adrenaline was cooling, he wanted a strong drink and a good tumble with Honoria, and he wanted both right now.

Henderson cleared his throat. "I'd find this reunion more touching if I knew Honoria and Alexandra were safe."

"Finley will get them to the carriage as we planned." Christopher smiled to himself, thinking of drawing Honoria into his arms as soon as he saw her again. Of course, she'd seen the ruin of his torso when Manda had stripped off his shirt, and she'd have many questions. He saw Manda shooting him covert glances, wanting to ask, deciding to wait.

"I hope so." Henderson stopped, grimaced. "There's water all over the bottom of this damned boat. That is the end of my shoes. I hope you appreciate this, Miss Raine."

Manda stared at him again. Christopher didn't think anyone had referred to Manda as "Miss Raine" in her life.

"I don't call this much of a boat," she said deprecatingly.

"I call it the best we could find at the time," Henderson answered, voice clipped.

"I call you a strange rescuer," she went on. "Shouldn't you be having tea with the queen?"

Henderson growled. "I call you damned ungrateful. We barely got you away."

"From a crowd of dead-drunk dandies? I don't call that much of a challenge."

She was tense, her hands gripping the gunwale, her voice shaking. Christopher saw that, but Henderson looked peevish. "*I'd* call it your lucky day."

The boat pulled harder against the oars, and then a sudden wave of cold water engulfed Christopher's boots and pantaloons. "And this, my friends," he said, keeping his voice calm, "is called sinking."

"Good thing pirates can swim," Manda said. She threw off Henderson's coat and dove over the side in a graceful curve. Christopher shoved aside the oars and followed her.

He surfaced in time to hear Henderson say, *"Damn it all, this was a brand-new suit."*

The Earl of Switton sat on his chair before the fire, well-manicured feet in soft slippers pushed toward the hearth. His valet had left him alone to drink port and sulk. His deep velvet dressing gown hugged his limbs but could not compensate for the loss of his favorite exhibit.

Old Henderson's son had much to answer for. Switton should have seen that Raine was a ruffian despite having such a well-bred wife and being friend to a viscount. Switton had admired Raine's physique, but when the Amazon had pulled off Raine's shirt, Switton had experienced a moment of stunned horror.

Ruffian, that was the only name for him.

Henderson's boy, now, he was a real English gentleman, with fair skin tanned by sun and moon-blond hair. Henderson should have been paired with Raine's lovely black-haired wife instead. Raine was a common fighting man. A thug.

Depression trickled through him. Raine had stolen his black Amazon, the tall, strong-limbed, beautiful woman who could fight better than any man he'd ever known. He'd never find another like her.

A log fell in the fire. Flames shot upward, then subsided. The fire ought to have been better laid. Already it was waning, and it had to carry through until morning. Irritated, Switton reached for the poker.

Something cold pressed his cheek. Switton looked around in annoyance and found himself staring at the open end of a pistol.

Christopher Raine stood at the other end of the pistol. He wore nothing but pantaloons and boots, and Switton could see the whole horror of him. His gray eyes were ice-cold and his long braid was damp.

Switton's attention riveted to the ruin of the man's muscular side. It was as though someone had taken a statue of a perfect Hellenic athlete, hard marble and skillfully sculpted, and hacked a large, ragged piece from its left side. While Raine's shoulders were superb, his pectorals square and hard, the left side of his abdomen and torso degenerated into a concave mass of scars and white streaks, stark against his golden tan.

Someone had thoroughly ruined this man's body, and that defect, rather than the pistol, made Switton feel suddenly faint.

He tried to brave it out. "How dare you, sir? You came into my house under false pretenses and stole my property."

The pistol dug into his cheek. "She is not a slave. She was a free woman that you held in a cage."

"I paid her!"

"She says you neglected to and laced her food with opium so she'd be too exhausted to run away."

"She's a liar, then."

A blow caught him on the temple and sent him reeling. He fell to the hearth, his knees banging the stone. He gasped in pain and surreptitiously reached for the poker.

The poker clattered across the rug, kicked by Raine's muddy boot. "I am trying to decide whether or not to murder you," he said, his voice colder than anything Switton had ever heard. "My wife worries about the consequences of killing an earl, but I don't much care."

Switton felt his entire body shaking. "You will hang. You are a common criminal."

"I already have. And I'm still alive."

He gulped. "I'd have sold her to you if I'd known you'd wanted her so much."

"She is my sister."

Switton stared. Did the man have no civilized bone in his body? "That is nothing to boast about."

Switton found himself being pulled upright by the hair. Raine's cold face and horrible eyes came close. "I raised her from the time she could walk. I'm very fond of her. Do you know what I think of a man who put her in a cage?"

"You will not kill me. If you'd come to murder me, you already would have."

To his amazement, Raine smiled. It was not a nice smile. "Were this a pirate ship, yes, you'd be dead. The sharks would already be tearing apart your body. But I'm trying to be civilized."

Switton seized on the word. "Civilized. Yes, if you were civilized, you'd call me out, settle this like a gentleman." His mind worked feverishly. If he could get the ruffian to make an appointment for a duel, Switton could find some way out of it, or better still, find someone to stand in for him. Beg poor eyesight or something.

Raine's smile widened, making him look rather like the sharks he'd just mentioned. "All right, we'll make it more sporting." He leaned down, huge muscles working, and took up the poker. Then, still smiling, he passed Switton the gun.

Swiftly the earl turned the pistol around, cocked it, and fired. An explosion of sound rocketed through the room but could not drown out the deadly silence of the poker coming down.

Honoria let the delicate cup warm her hands and breathed the aroma of the hot coffee. She sat curled in a shawl in Alexandra's small drawing room and listened to the others tell their side of the tale. Diana had arrived, children in tow, when she'd heard of their return. Now she too listened avidly, her red hair bright in the candlelit room.

Honoria moved through her own story quickly. When she'd feared that Christopher and Manda would be set upon by too many, she'd decided that a dramatic swoon would be just the thing.

Alexandra and several helpful ladies had carried her back to the house, where Honoria had feigned recovery. Once left alone, she and Alexandra had hastened to the front drive, where Grayson had got them into their carriage. Because those chasing Manda and Christopher had gone through the gardens, the road before the house had been deserted.

They'd easily rendezvoused with the rather wet rescuers on the other side of the lake. Alexandra and Honoria had wrapped Manda in warm blankets, her leopard skin having fallen to the bottom of the lake.

Manda Raine had been absolutely astonished when Christopher had said casually, "The black-haired one is my wife," and had stared at Honoria all the way to London.

Grayson raised his glass of spirits to Honoria. "You are a fine actress, Honoria. I commend you."

Honoria thanked him politely, but she felt far from smug or clever. Christopher had not said a word to her. He'd been silent and withdrawn, and she had been able to think of little else but the horrific wound in his side.

He'd not removed his shirt in her presence, she realized, since he'd returned. Back in Charleston, on their wedding day, his body had been strong and whole, muscles pleasing and tight. Something had happened to him between then and now, and he had not wanted to tell her.

He sat casually on a straight-backed chair, arms on knees, glass of whiskey dangling from his fingers. He'd dressed in his own clothes, breeches and boots, loose shirt and coat hiding his ruined torso.

Manda told her own story briefly. She'd come to London looking for work and had met one of the Earl of Switton's lackeys. She was offered pay to pretend to be a wild woman of the Amazon for Switton's friends. She'd thought it a good lark and accepted.

Switton had decided the ruse went over so well that he wanted Manda to stay and perform again. When she declined and asked for her money, he'd refused to pay and would not let her go. When she tried to fight, he'd simply locked her in a room and starved her, then fed her food laced with opium.

She seemed none the worse for wear for this adventure. She sat with her legs folded under her, wearing a shirt and pantaloons, having refused Alexandra's offer of a gown. Her black hair hung down her back in wonderfully ropy curls. Her sable eyes, framed by long black lashes, swung to observe each of them with avid curiosity. Her wide mouth smiled or frowned openly, a young woman who did not bother to hide her feelings.

"He is disgusting," Mr. Henderson observed. "I'll see to it that the Hendersons cut him dead from now on."

Manda snorted. "I'm sure that will terrify him."

Alexandra offered, "Oh, yes, it will, Miss Raine. The worst thing that can happen to a gentleman is to be shunned by other gentlemen. He'll be cut by anyone who matters. When Grayson has a word with the Duke of St. Clair and others at White's, the Earl of Switton will have nowhere to turn."

Manda stared at them all in turn, then addressed Christopher. "Are they real?"

A faint smile touched his lips. "Finley's become an honest-to-God peer."

"Honest to God?" Manda asked him.

Grayson nodded somberly. "I'm afraid so."

"I meant to ask, *Miss Raine*," Henderson said, with unnecessary emphasis. "Why did you not try to get away?"

Manda's frown reappeared when she looked at him. The tension between the two seemed unnaturally high. "What do you mean, not try?"

"I saw you walking in the house yesterday with

Switton's wife. I will not believe that you could not escape from a lady armed with nothing more than a reticule."

The frown turned dangerous. "I was only allowed out when his wife pumped me full of opium. I was too disoriented to run anywhere."

The room stilled. Christopher said quietly, "I'm sorry I didn't kill him."

Grayson nodded, eyes grave. "Leave him to me. We'll get him, and I don't care if he is a peer. I'll make it my personal mission."

Honoria had not asked what Christopher had done to the earl. When Christopher had parted from them at the lake, his face had been so grim she'd not had the courage to ask what he meant to do. If Christopher had left the earl alive, the man was luckier than he deserved.

Manda shrugged. "I would have got out eventually. I never dreamed you'd come back to life and rescue me." She turned a smile on her brother that would have melted the hardest heart.

They looked much alike, Honoria observed. Manda's high forehead and firm jaw were womanly versions of Christopher's. Their eyes were a different color, but they were shaped the same, and both held the glint of people for whom the world did not hold much fear. Rather, the world needed to worry when it saw Christopher and Manda coming.

They sat across the room from each other, neither betraying joy or excitement at their reunion. Still, Honoria sensed the bond between them, one very much like the one she'd had with her brother, Paul.

Christopher and Manda had fallen into easy conversation, as though they'd been parted only days rather than years. Sometimes they finished each other's sentences without even noticing they'd done it.

Honoria's limbs were heavy with tiredness now the excitement was over. It had been a long and grueling day, but she did not want to sleep just yet. The conversation she'd had with Alexandra earlier that night danced through her head. Christopher had said they'd rest here for what little remained of the night and take ship the following morning. She hoped she'd have time to put her ideas into practice, and that she could stay awake for it.

It was already two. Christopher abruptly told Honoria she looked tired and should go upstairs and to bed. His look when he said it was far from amorous.

Honoria gave up. She made her good-nights and went up to the chamber Alexandra had given them. She lay in the heavy tester bed, having undressed, brushed her hair, and cleaned her teeth. She tried to stay awake, but her treacherous eyes kept closing.

He would not come to her, of course. He'd stay downstairs and talk with Manda and Grayson, probably all night. Despite Manda's apparent resilience, Christopher would want to ensure himself that she was well. That, and they had four years of conversation to catch up on.

Honoria's eyes had drifted firmly closed when she heard him enter the room. He shut the door and walked slowly to the bed. She smelled his spice as he leaned over and pressed a warm kiss to her hair.

Chapter Ten

Christopher had supposed Honoria would be asleep, but his wife opened her eyes and smiled up at him, her lashes long and seductive.

Downstairs, she had looked exhausted, her face flushed, her eyes drooping, but he was just as happy to find her still awake.

He kissed her softly parted lips, shifting the decanter of whiskey Grayson had pressed on him on the way upstairs. Grayson had said Christopher had the look of a man who needed to get drunk if ever he saw one.

"Mmm," she said sleepily. She flicked her eyes to the glass decanter, gave it a tiny frown.

He took his knee from the bed and crossed to the writing table where crystal glasses had been left for guests' convenience. Christopher sloshed liquid into a glass and held it up. "Want any?"

She sat up with a rustle of bedclothes, gave him a

ladylike look that was adorable when she was half asleep. "I do not drink spirits."

Christopher did. He silently drank the whiskey down and filled the glass again. He swallowed a deep draft of that, too, then took glass and decanter back to the bed with him.

She drew her knees to her chest. "Why are you trying to get drunk?"

He sat next to her, breathing the heady fragrance of her warmth under the bedclothes. The whiskey heated him, but it was surprisingly smooth. "I want to."

"How is Manda?"

He drained the glass, chasing the last droplets with his tongue. "Fine. Alexandra has her bedded down." He moved the glass vaguely. "Somewhere."

"You should talk to her."

He dribbled more whiskey into the glass. "What about?"

She gave him her most earnest, green-eyed stare. Her round cheeks were pink and pretty. "She went through an awful ordeal. She will need to talk about it."

He shook his head. The whiskey was at last loosening his limbs. "The last thing she'll want is to talk about it."

Honoria looked unconvinced. "Just what a man would say."

"Manda deals with things in her own way, usually alone." He pointed the glass at her. "So don't try to have a heart-to-heart with her. She won't like it."

Honoria said nothing, but a stubborn light entered her eye.

The throat of her nightdress was trimmed in lace, which moved up and down with her breathing. He thunked the whiskey decanter to the night table. "You should be asleep," he said thickly.

"I wanted to wait for you." A slow blush spread across her cheeks. "I wanted to show you something. It might soothe you to sleep, better than the whiskey."

He slid his hand over her nightdress, then withdrew before he touched her skin. The whiskey was beginning to cool his shaking rage, but he still did not trust himself. Not with her.

"Honoria," he said tightly. "If I take you tonight, it will not be the pleasant journey we had before." He was already stiffening with memory of that pleasant journey, but he ignored it. "I'll take you hard, and I might not be able to stop, even if you don't like it. And you are far too innocent for the ways I want to take you."

She watched him, eyes luminescent. "I am not innocent."

"You are," he corrected. "You let me have you, but that does not mean you are ready for all the things I can do."

"All what things?" Her voice was husky.

"I'll tell you when you're ready."

Her tongue touched her lower lip. She smelled of lavender, as though she'd scented her hair with it. His arousal grew tighter. She was his wife, after all. She had to do what he told her.

"Then you will not seduce me tonight?" she asked in a near whisper.

He deliberately put the glass to his lips, forced the whiskey into his mouth. "Not tonight, darling. I'm getting drunk."

"Good," she said decidedly. She pushed the covers aside, crawled out of bed.

Disappointment swirled through him. "What do you mean, good?"

She rummaged in the cupboard next to the bed. "If you are not busy seducing me, then I can do something for you."

He stopped the glass of whiskey halfway to his mouth. His head had been buzzing pleasantly, but now he came alert. "What?"

She came up with a glass-stoppered bottle. "I am going to rub oil on you. You will have to take off your clothes and lie down."

If he had been drinking the whiskey, he would have choked. He stared into the amber depths, looking for enlightenment, then he very carefully set the glass on the night table. "Why?"

She shrugged, but stood poised like a bird that waited to see whether he would stroke its neck or knock it aside.

Silently, he slid open the buttons of his coat and slid it off. He tossed it to the foot of the bed, then tugged off the boots. One irregular oval of dried mud, missed by Grayson's man's hasty cleaning, landed on the red and gold carpet. He popped the buttons of the breeches, one by one. Honoria watched with flattering scrutiny.

He rose to his feet while he pulled off the breeches

168

and tossed them to a nearby chair. His underbreeks followed, still a little damp from his swim.

He stood up, facing her, still in his shirt. The hem lifted with his arousal.

Honoria gestured to the shirt. "That, too." She held the bottle tightly. "I already saw what happened to you."

Christopher hesitated. The whiskey had warmed him, but he still felt a faint chill in his heart. Was he ashamed? He'd barely thought of the ruin that used to be his left side until he'd seen her. She was still so beautiful, whole, unchanged.

Quickly, before self-pity could establish its hold, he stripped off the shirt and stood naked before her.

She looked her fill. Her darkening gaze roved his shoulders, his abdomen, his legs, his erection. She looked at every part of him that was still tight and whole, before letting herself study his scarred side. Her mouth tightened.

He turned his back and walked away. He heard her draw a breath to call out, then she stopped as he locked the door and removed the key. The last thing he wanted while his wife soothed his body with oil was a helpful maid traipsing in with extra blankets or offering to stir the fire.

He placed the key on a marble-topped console table near the door. The tabletop was held in place by a bracket shaped like an Egyptian goddess. Her mahogany bosom swelled.

He preferred the living, satin bosom of Honoria. He returned to the bed.

169

Honoria stood beside it, cradling the bottle. Her fingers ran over the stopper in a scintillating pattern. "What happened to you, Christopher?"

He tossed himself onto the bed, landed on his back. He rested his hands behind his head and crossed his ankles. "Aren't you supposed to be oiling me?"

"Tell me," she said. "Please."

He drew a breath. "I was set upon and robbed. Somewhere in the East." He hadn't even been certain where he'd been at the time. China, Siam? It had been hot and wet and he'd stunk with fever. "They robbed me, and then they tried to butcher me."

Her eyes widened. Not in fascination, but in horror and anger. "How did you survive?"

"The kindness of strangers." An old farmer and his daughter, specifically. Neither he nor they had been able to speak the other's language, but the farmer had nursed him back to health and shared their meager food. Missionaries said that these races were heathen and damned, but the farmer and his daughter had been kinder to him than most Europeans he'd met.

Her fingers roved around and around the stopper, her gaze distressed.

"I lived, Honoria," he said, banishing memories of pain and humiliation. "It was just another adventure."

She continued to stare at him. She'd taken her hair down, gathered it in a thick tail at the back of her neck. Wild curls trickled across her shoulders, fine ones touched her forehead.

"You are so beautiful," he murmured. The whiskey must have been catching up to him, he thought.

She looked at the bottle as though just remembering it in her hands. Quickly she unfastened the stopper, poured a few drops of oil on her palm. The scent of jasmine and spice floated in the heated air.

She set the bottle on the dressing table, hiked up her nightgown, and knelt beside him on the bed. He removed one hand from behind his head and placed it on her warm knee. He edged the gown higher until he could see the curved line of her folded leg, a glimpse of her rounded thigh.

Honoria rubbed her palms together, then placed both of them on his chest. Her hands were cool, like springwater. She drew them apart across his collarbone, then down over his pectorals.

"Why did you not want me to see?" she asked.

He dipped his thumb into the warm fold behind her knee. "Vanity, I suppose. I didn't want to disappoint you."

No, what he really feared was that she'd take one look at him and flee in horror. She'd made no secret that the main reason she'd agreed to stay with him was attraction to his body. If she could not find him physically pleasing, then they'd have nothing.

Her fingers tangled in the curls on his chest. She circled his flat nipples, pale against his tan, then drew her palm to the twisted mess of his side. "I'm not disappointed," she said.

His heart warmed and her hands slid across his torso, slippery with oil. She explored him in hesitant, questing strokes.

He was already as hard as he could be, but she ignored this in favor of tracing the ridges of his abdomen. Her sleeves gently brushed his arousal, igniting fire in his belly.

"You are so prim outside the bedroom, my wife," he observed. "But inside—" He traced a circle on her thigh. "You're just right."

She gave him an oh-so-proper look. "What I do with my husband in private is no one's business." She swiped her palms up his arms, leaning forward to massage his knotted shoulders. "And I am not prim. Primness implies a want of feeling and rational thought. Propriety for the sake of it. I would rather think of myself as discreet."

He looked at her, amused. "Call it whatever you like."

She drew her fingers over the scars, letting them glide over the ridges. "You lived through this," she said, "and yet two nights ago a few slivers had you cursing and railing."

A smile tugged the corners of his mouth. "You enjoyed it."

"How can you think I enjoyed hurting you?"

Her green eyes were wide, glowing gems in the chamber's gloom.

He rested his hand on the length of her thigh, fingers indenting the softness. "You want me to be dead."

"I certainly do not."

"But things were easier for you when I was."

Her fingers moved in absent patterns on his skin, as though she sculpted him from the oil. "They were not easier. That is not what I meant at all."

He gently stroked her thigh, reveling in the softness of it, imagining himself pressing his lips there.

"I think we've already hashed this out as far as it can go," he said. "Get on with what you are doing."

Defiantly, her hands stilled. She opened her mouth, red lips wet, eyes indignant.

He closed his hand around her wrist. "You piously told me you'd agree to obey your husband and his demands on your body. So do it."

"Not if you are going to be rude."

He frowned. "I don't remember that in the wedding ceremony. I promise to obey my husband, except when he's rude."

"I'm pretty sure the authors of the Prayer Book meant that."

"All right, we'll find them and ask them."

She gave him an odd look. "They were dead hundreds of years ago, Christopher."

"Then what do they know about it? Now, get on with it. Your husband wants soothing."

"I can't if you don't let go of me."

He dragged her wrist to his lips, pressed a hard kiss to her fragrant skin. He released her. Her thick hair had fallen over her shoulder, curls snaking every which way.

"Do it," he said softly. "Or I'll take what I want."

Her glare could sting worse than a flogging. She turned to the bedside table, snatched up the bottle, jerked off the stopper, and poured a liquid dollop straight onto his chest. The oil landed with a sludge-like splash. The pool spread, oozing toward his sides and his belly.

Honoria slammed the bottle back to the table. She slapped her hands to his flesh, scooping the oil over his skin in quick, painful jerks. The slapping sound of palms hitting flesh rang across the room.

He seized her arms. "You little vixen."

"Don't move," she commanded. "You'll spill oil all over Alexandra's fine sheets."

"If you don't stop that, Alexandra is going to think something else is going on in here."

She stilled, puzzled. "What?"

God, how could she be so brazen and so hopelessly naive at the same time? "She'll think I'm teaching you a lesson. One you need to learn."

"Christopher, I have no idea what you're talking about."

"I'm talking about taking my hand to your backside. It's starting to seem a mighty fine idea."

Her mouth dropped open. "Alexandra would never suppose that."

"She might. Who knows what she and Finley get up to?"

Her eyes went dark, then light green again as she thought about this new concept. Her face was pale, sculpted marble in the darkness. Slowly the white marble flushed a very pretty and embarrassed pink.

"Well," she said finally. "I certainly will not allow you to do that to me."

He strengthened his grip on her arms. "Careful, Honoria. The husband decides what will be allowed."

She gave him an icy stare. He liked that. Other women of her upbringing would likely have been terrified of him by now, weeping and swooning and begging him to be kind. Honoria said do your worst and be damned.

She was like her brother, all right. James Ardmore had the reputation for ruthlessness. Ardmore would have shot Switton right away, without even speaking to him. Christopher had decided that drawing out the man's punishment would be much more satisfying. Every time the man looked into the mirror, he'd see the scar on his cheekbones and remember Christopher Raine.

Christopher wondered who was the crueler man, himself or Ardmore.

"Take off the nightgown," he said to Honoria.

Her eyes were green fire. "Are all husbands this barbaric?"

"I have no idea. Take if off."

Her glare returned, but the hands that moved to the hem of her nightgown shook. She slid it off over her head, further dislodging her hair, which tumbled down altogether.

He caught her hair in his hands, wrapped the warm strands around his palms. She was bare beneath her tangled curls, her breasts peeking out from between the ringlets, her firm buttocks resting on her heels.

"I wager the fine gentlemen of Charleston ate their hearts out over you," he said, his voice rough. "How many asked you to marry them?"

Her eyes had darkened again. She rested her hand, still slick with oil, on his thick biceps. "Fifteen."

He felt a dart of jealousy, which he covered with a sharp laugh. "Fifteen? Is that all?"

"Only two were worth serious consideration," the

proper Honoria said. "The others simply wanted connection with the Ardmore family and the Ardmore money."

He looked her up and down, so delicious and naked and smelling fine. "Oh, I'm sure they wanted more than that. Who were the two worth considering?"

"Gentlemen of good families whose wealth was enough that my brother need have no worries. A match with either would have been quite acceptable. In other circumstances."

"Such as not being married to me?"

She looked surprised. "Oh, no, these proposals were made long before I married you. I turned them down because the gentlemen had too many defects in their characters."

Christopher suddenly wanted to hold his sides and laugh until the tears came. "So you threw them over to marry a pirate who was condemned to death?"

Her breasts swelled with her breath. "Well, yes, I suppose I did."

"I'm glad you did." He slid his hand beneath her hair. "They were not good enough for you."

She inclined her head, still the proper lady, despite kneeling next to him mother-naked. "I suppose not."

"But a cutthroat pirate was."

Her brows drew together. "It was not the same thing."

"No," he said, "It's never the same after you've had a taste of it. Once a man has made you wet and dance with pleasure, you look differently at the men who haven't."

She balled her fists. The oil squeezed out. "My de-

176

cision not to marry had nothing to do with you. I never thought I'd see you again. The fact that I was not engaged when you returned to Charleston to be hanged is pure chance."

"The hell it wasn't."

"You are arrogant."

He uncurled her hands, pressed them flat to his chest. "You think it was chance that I didn't have a wife when I came back to Charleston? I tried to pretend that a little Charleston girl was not the only woman for me. I tried and tried to make you not matter. But when you came to me in that cell, I knew you did matter."

She stared down at him, eyes unmoving, like stars in black night. "I never should have come to you. I shouldn't have the first time, either, when I was a girl. Paul should have told me to stay in my room."

"Well, I'm glad he didn't." His blood heated at the memory. "You know, you were the kind of young woman I disliked most, dressed like a fashion plate, looking superior to every creature around you. I kissed you to teach you a lesson. And then you stuck your sweet tongue in my mouth." An intense heat had flared through his body, obscuring all reason.

He hadn't felt a gentle passion for the pretty young lady in her ringlets and muslin, her French perfume, and the tiny earrings that jingled when she moved. He'd felt carnal wanting like he'd never felt in his life. In two seconds, he'd had her on the hard tile floor, his arousal nearly bursting his breeches.

She'd clung to him and kissed him all the way down. He'd cradled her body from the cold marble, and she'd wrapped her arms around him and let him put his hands on her and drive her wild.

He'd kissed her hard to keep her from crying out, from alerting the household that he was ravishing the daughter of the family on the garden room floor. She'd nibbled his earlobe, tiny pinpricks of pain, and whispered, "Yes, please, Christopher."

If he'd fallen from atop a mainmast, smack onto the hard surface of the sea, he could not have hurt himself more. He'd hurt himself inside and out, and hadn't even known it.

He'd left that house feeling young and smug, never realizing that sweet Honoria Ardmore would haunt his dreams forever.

"Mine," he said now. He murmured the word with fierce intensity. "All mine."

"I suppose so."

The indifferent tone made his blood boil. For the second time in one day, Christopher found his temper flaring like gunpowder.

He rolled to his knees and jerked her up to face him. Oil ran like thick rain down his torso. He crushed her against him, the oil sliding her breasts across his rib cage like fine, soft velvet. He caught her hair in his hand, pulled her head back, and crushed a kiss to her mouth.

Lips and tongues met, and wildness began.

Chapter Eleven

Diana Ardmore napped in her chamber at her father's house on Mount Street, exhausted from her late night, from worry, and from saying good-bye to Honoria that morning.

The good-bye had given her the most wrench. She had wanted Honoria to remain in London until the time came for them to rendezvous with James, but Christopher Raine was adamant that his ship sail right away. Diana conceded the legality of Honoria's marriage to Raine and saw that he was in love with her, but that did not mean she trusted the man to be good to her. She didn't *know* him. On that point, neither did Honoria.

Diana had tried to talk Honoria into staying, perhaps making arrangements to join Christopher later, but Honoria had given her that stubborn Ardmore look and said that she'd accompany her husband.

Alexandra thought it all terribly romantic, but

Alexandra, though Diana loved her dearly, was a bit naive. Alexandra had found a generous-hearted man in Grayson Finley and tended to believe that her friends would perforce find the same happiness, no matter how odd the circumstances.

Christopher and his half-Jamaican half sister looked a wild pair whom no one would dare cross. Diana wondered, and worried about, how Honoria would fit in with Christopher and his sister, not to mention the rest of the pirate crew.

What James would do when he found out about Honoria, even Diana could not guess. He and Honoria had never got on. James might go on a rampage and drag Honoria back home, or he might give a cool shrug and say that Honoria had made her bed and must lie in it, literally.

Her worried speculation ran down as the June sun warmed the room. She tried to stay awake and keep fretting, but her limbs loosened as her body moved toward slumber. At last her eyes drifted closed, and she dreamed of her father's island, the cool air and savage ocean, and the sea-drenched caves where a green-eyed pirate hunter had dragged her into his arms for a kiss.

She was awakened by a callused hand stroking her hair from her face. The warm touch on her temple threaded its way through her body. She smiled sleepily, inhaling the familiar scent of ocean and spicy musk that meant her husband. Her dreams of him could be so real. She felt his warmth at her side. His strong hand moved across her belly to the curve of her breast.

She jumped fully awake. Her husband lay beside her, his black hair unbound, his green eyes as cool and assessing as they'd been the faraway day she'd met him—when he'd abducted her.

"James!" She flung her arms around his neck, buried her face in the curve of his shoulder.

He cradled her in strong arms, tilted her head back, and gave her a deep kiss that went on and on and on. He took his time exploring her mouth, and she savored every moment of it.

When she could speak again, she asked breathlessly, "What are you doing here? In London? In broad daylight?"

James Ardmore was a wanted man in England for his habit of boarding British ships and freeing press-ganged Americans. If someone from the Admiralty spied James Ardmore strolling about London, they'd arrest him on the spot, and she doubted even Grayson or Diana's father, with all their connections in the Admiralty, could save him from hanging.

"I finished my business," he said, as though he were an ordinary husband coming home after an ordinary day. "Gather the children and Honoria, and we'll sail tonight for Haven."

It was just like James to change the plans and the rendezvous place on an instant, without a word to anyone. He supposed a simple announcement of "We're leaving now" to be a sufficient plan.

He smoothed his hand across her belly, and his eyes went dark and full of promise. "But I guess we can delay a minute or two."

Diana kissed him again, losing herself for a few glorious moments in his warmth and his strength. "I missed you."

"I missed you too, wildcat. There was no one spitting fire at me. Or throwing food."

"I do not throw food at you all the time, James," she said, trying to sound reproachful.

"No. But I wouldn't mind if we could find some strawberries and a little bit of cream."

Her blood warmed. "I could speak to Cook."

"Later." He leaned against the headboard and pulled her up and onto his lap. "If you get up and go downstairs, you'll straighten your hair and button your dress. I like you a little disheveled. It's inviting."

He demonstrated by easing his hand inside her bodice, resting it on the curve of her breast. She closed her eyes.

Her conscience pricked her. He deserved to know and know at once, no matter how selfishly she wanted this moment to go on. She opened her eyes, sighed. "James," she said. "About Honoria."

"Mmm?" His lips brushed her hair. "What's she railing about now?"

Diana sat up. She brushed back her hair, put her hands in his, and drew a deep breath.

"Well," she said, "I am not quite certain how to tell you this . . ."

Far down the Thames a ship called *Starcross* rounded a headland and entered the Channel. The day was fair, the wind steady. The muted green of England slid along the starboard side. Sailors on the yardarms unfurled great sails that caught the wind and snapped taut.

Honoria sat on a bench against the stern gunwale, breathing the sweet fragrance of open sea. They'd left the stink of port happily behind them. No more fouled and muddy river, no more fish stacked on wharfs, no more towns of packed bodies. Just ocean and fresh wind.

Crew in breeches and open shirts worked the ship, tying off sails, scrubbing the deck, chopping vegetables for the night's stew, or whatever job they had been assigned.

The stiff breeze caught Honoria's tail of hair and flipped it every which way; she'd decided to leave it down because the wind would simply pull out any pins she pushed into it. The ship had started to heave in earnest now, but her heart soared with it. Voyages always reminded her of happy times sailing with James when Paul had been alive.

This voyage, however, was taking her to a new life. As a point of fact, she had no idea where they were going. Christopher had never definitively told her whether their destination was Charleston. Not even a pointed, direct question had brought Honoria an answer.

Her husband stood not far from her now, his back to her, his coat billowing like a flag. He steadied the ship's wheel and spoke with Manda and Mr. St. Cyr about shipboard things. Manda, dressed in breeches and shirt and coat similar to her brother's, folded her arms across her chest and nodded every so often at Christopher's words.

This morning, Honoria had said good-bye to her friends and Diana, severing the link to family and home, and had set off who-knew-where with a husband she barely knew. And strangely, she was not afraid. She had married a pirate and now sailed on his pirate ship. Still, she felt no panic as the shore receded and they headed to open sea.

She wondered very much where Christopher thought he was going, and what he'd do when he got there. England and America were at war, an added complication. Ports were blockaded and frigates prowled the seas. Blockades had never stopped her brother James, who viewed them as a challenge, and Honoria suspected that Christopher would behave the same. The American navy was pitifully small against the might of England, but the waters were thick with American privateers and merchants happy to harass English frigates. Christopher was French and English, but Honoria imagined that he would let neither frigates nor privateers of any nationality stand in his way.

Nor his wife, apparently. He'd simply given her an enigmatic look when she'd asked their destination this morning and said he didn't want to reveal it while they were still in port. They were well into the Channel now. She supposed it did not matter, the ship would carry her wherever Christopher wanted whether she knew the destination or not.

He glanced back at her now, his blond plait sliding over his shoulder. "Honoria," he called. "Take the wheel."

She blinked. "I beg your pardon?"

His brows shot together. He studied her not as a husband irritated at his slow-wit wife, but as a captain studying a disobedient sailor. He definitely had hanging in the rigging in the back of his mind.

There are some orders I expect you to obey without question, he'd told her. She'd understand an order to get out of the way to save her life, but to take the helm of the ship? In her blue lawn gown that lifted most perniciously in the wind? She had chosen to sit with her legs curled beneath her for that very reason.

She unfolded herself, letting the wind take her skirt, and padded across the small space of the deck. Christopher stood with one hand on the wheel, gray eyes impatient. "I'm shorthanded," he said. "You know how to pilot a ship?"

"Vaguely," she answered. She'd *watched* James and his pilot at work. James had never let her touch anything on his ship, at least not after she and Paul had pulled down the rigging on his bowsprit while attempting a few bravely stupid pranks. After that, James had restricted them to their cabins or sitting on deck where he could see them—at all times.

She'd been sixteen then. But even now when she rode on the *Argonaut,* James watched her as though his rigging lay in constant peril of her antics.

Christopher slid his arm around her, drew her to the wheel. "Hands here, and here." He took each one in turn, placed them on the spokes. "Sight down the bow, and keep her pointed that much to port of shore." He showed her a distance between his thumb and forefinger, which, when she sighted through it, she saw that it would give them a large slice of water between England's cliffs and open sea. "Just hold her steady."

She tried not to be distracted by his warm body at her back, his arms enclosing her, his breath in her ear.

She nodded, and he let go. Cold wind and disappointment took the place of his warmth. She toyed with the idea of asking him to show her again, but he'd already walked away.

Manda flashed her a grin, as if to say, *Good luck*, then followed Christopher and Mr. St. Cyr. Leaving her alone. To steer the entire ship. By herself.

"Christopher!"

He turned. Sun gleamed on his tawny hair and made his skin still more golden. "What?"

"What if we come to another ship?"

Plenty of craft sailed this sea, between England and France, England and Spain, England and the rest of the world.

"Don't hit it," Christopher said, then turned and strode away.

She ground her teeth at his retreating back. She started to call him names under her breath, but she soon found herself caught up in the task and, to her surprise, liking it.

The feel of the entire ship came to her through the tiller—every twitch of sail, every tightening of line, every gust of wind. It was exhilarating. The ship became a living, breathing being, communicating its every move from rudder up through the decks to the wheel and the muscles of her arms.

She moved the wheel the slightest bit, and the ship responded by swinging its bow to the left. She quickly straightened it again, before Christopher could notice and correct her.

She watched the coastline to make sure she stayed to Christopher's bearing. She felt new respect for James and his crew for keeping the *Argonaut* on course out at sea—it was easy to navigate when she could clearly see land on her right, but in the open ocean, especially when the sun was obscured by clouds, pointing the ship the proper direction must be a daunting task. The compass in front of her showed them sailing west-southwest, but the letters on the dial did not feel as real as the green-brown coastline beside her.

The sun made her remember another problem. Much as she loved staying on deck in the sun and wind, it would tan her skin until it looked like old leather. A lady had white, soft skin and did not look like a farmer's wife. Being from Charleston, Honoria was familiar with protecting skin from the sun, but she'd need something more than lace shawls and parasols here. She'd have to confer with Mrs. Colby about shielding themselves from the weather.

Manda appeared to care less about the sun or about being a lady. She dressed like a sailor, talked like a sailor, worked like a sailor. Christopher did not spare her anything, seeming to take for granted that his sister would climb to the crow's nest or tie off a sail same as any of the others.

Honoria studied the tall woman now, admiring her strong features and lithe body. Honoria had feared that Manda would view her with contempt or resentment, but Manda seemed, if anything, to be amused by Honoria. The ribald jokes the woman told indicated she thought Christopher's marriage the funniest thing she'd heard of in a long while. Christopher bore her teasing without comments or anger. Honoria, on the other hand, always blushed furiously, which made Manda laugh all the harder.

Honoria sincerely hoped that Christopher would not expect *her* to climb yardarms or furl sails. She looked up at the mainmast spreading its arms far, far above the deck. But, as on James's ship, everyone on the *Starcross* did everything. The officers were not like officers on a naval ship, with formal rank, but they had certain jobs—to navigate, to control the crew, to keep the charts, to command for the captain when he was asleep, to supervise the weapons and cannon.

These officers stripped down and bent their backs to the windlass with the other sailors when necessary or bailed or hauled lines without waiting for order. Even Mr. Henderson had helped raise sails this morning, because Christopher did not yet have a full complement of crew.

Honoria watched Mr. Henderson emerge from belowdecks now and begin conversation with Mr. St. Cyr. Mr. Henderson had exchanged his dandified London clothes for breeches, boots, and coat more suited to shipboard labors. Even so, he still managed to look like a gentleman out for nothing more strenuous than a walk in the country.

Why Mr. Henderson had chosen to join them at all still puzzled Honoria. He had turned up that morning asking that Christopher haul him along and drop him at Tangier, where he'd meet up with the *Argonaut*. When Christopher expressed derision at being used as a passenger service, Mr. Henderson snapped that he could be left anywhere, he didn't care. Christopher obviously needed more crew, and Henderson was a crack navigator.

It was Manda who'd said, "Oh, let him come, Chris. He probably got some society daughter in trouble and is running from her pa."

Mr. Henderson had bristled, but he'd boarded the ship.

Honoria had first thought that Mr. Henderson had come to keep an eye on her for James, but she abruptly revised her opinion as she watched him approach Christopher and Manda.

Mr. Henderson's gaze riveted to the tall black woman, a self-derisive look on his face. Manda did not notice him at first. When she turned toward him, Henderson's body stiffened, and his expression—no, his entire stance—became guarded.

Honoria narrowed her eyes, the ship almost forgotten.

Manda began bantering with him as usual. Honoria was too far away to hear what they said, but Mr. Henderson flushed, and his bearing went stiffer than ever.

Poor Mr. Henderson. Honoria found him far too correct and arrogant and *English* for her taste, but watching him now, she felt for the first time a touch of pity for him.

She also felt curiosity. She would certainly keep an interested eye on how things developed.

* * *

Christopher relieved Honoria of duty as the sky purpled in the west. The setting sun bathed the undersides of scattered clouds in golden light. Her arms ached, her face was chafed with wind and sun, her legs were weak from bracing against the roll of the ship. She felt glorious.

Did Christopher compliment her on her deft handling of the tiller? No, he simply told her, in captain's tones, that young Carew would be taking over and she should go below for the evening meal.

Carew was about twenty and had been sailing with Christopher since he'd been a boy. He gave Honoria a wink.

Honoria opened her hands. Or tried to. She parted her fingers halfway, and then agonizing cramps seized her and she cried out.

Christopher took hold of her hands, gently pried them open. They did not want to straighten. Red and white ridges plied her fingers and palms. "Damn it, Honoria." He rubbed her hands gently, his touch warming her.

"You needn't hold th' wheel so tightly, ma'am," Carew said in a kind voice. "Just rest your hands so." He demonstrated, laying his fingers on the spokes with a light touch.

Honoria tried to flex her fingers. "Yes, thank you," she said tersely. "I'll remember."

Christopher, looking displeased, led her away.

The captain and officers dined in the room reserved for the charts; the charts themselves were rolled up and stowed safely in mahogany cabinets. Light from candles in lanterns made the wood of the cabinets and table glow a rich red. The room had enough space for a table and six chairs; when the chairs were filled, they scraped the walls and cabinets. The cook, a short, spindle-legged black-haired man from Mexico, stood in the doorway, ready to hand around the dishes.

Christopher's chair was nearest the door. The rest of the table had filled by the time he and Honoria arrived, except for a chair at the far end, which Honoria would never reach except by climbing over the table.

At least Christopher did not make her do that. He jerked his thumb at Manda, who, grinning, unfolded herself and slid into the empty chair. Colby, the huge bearlike man, ungraciously moved to the next chair, vacating one for Honoria.

As soon as Christopher seated himself, the cook handed in a tureen. Christopher placed it on the table. "Sit down," he said to Honoria in a tone that did not invite argument.

Honoria's legs responded to the command and bent before she could stop them. She turned the movement into a graceful, rather condescending descent to the chair, which had been warmed by Colby's large body.

The board was covered with a cloth, dampened so that the dishes would not slide about. The cloth was yellow with age and frayed. On Christopher's other side sat the pale St. Cyr, with Mrs. Colby next to him. Mrs. Colby's red-dyed hair glowed with the same warmth as the cabinets.

Christopher scooped soup into her bowl, then his. Large pools of oil skimmed the soup's surface. Beneath it swam chunks of carrot and greens and pieces of meat. Despite its look, it smelled heavenly. Christopher shoved the tureen to his left and the sharp-faced St. Cyr dipped into it.

St. Cyr took soup, passed on the tureen, and made a perfunctory bow to Honoria. *"Bon appétit, Madame."*

Honoria's finishing school training took over. *"Merci, monsieur,"* she said, inclining her head as though they shared canapés at a garden party.

Colby snickered. Christopher raised a brow and said something rather rude in perfect, fluent French.

The phrase was one Honoria was not supposed to have learned in finishing school, but had anyway. She flushed. Amusement lit Christopher's eye.

For a moment, Honoria contemplated throwing the soup at him. Diana had told Honoria she'd once thrown an entire tureen of soup at James. Potato. Diana privately believed that was when James had fallen in love with her.

Honoria thought her own situation somewhat more complicated. At least James had given Diana time to get used to him before he'd married her.

She pretended to ignore Christopher as she spooned up the thin soup and brought it to her lips. Peppery, rich broth poured into her mouth. It was delectable.

"So, what's her share?" Colby asked suddenly.

Manda slurped from her spoon. "Why do you care?"

Colby tapped the handle of his spoon to the table. "We already know how we divided up the shares before. Stands to reason we all shouldn't take less just because the captain got married. She should get a cut of his."

Manda and Mrs. Colby watched Christopher. Mr. St. Cyr merely ate his soup in short, polite sips.

"She gets her own share," Christopher said.

"But that means we get less," Colby returned.

"We have fewer crew now, Colby," Manda said. "That means more all the way around."

"I say we put it to a vote. We voted when I got married."

"And Mrs. Colby gets her own share," Christopher said, his voice firm. "So will Mrs. Raine. There is no vote."

Colby opened his mouth to argue further, but he caught Christopher's gaze and shut it again with a snap.

The cook handed in a plate of bread. Christopher tore off a hunk and passed it to Honoria, just as the ship lurched. Everyone automatically steadied plates and jammed themselves against the wall. Other than that, they went on placidly eating. The ship ran up the swell and dropped through the next one. Dark wind whipped through the hall as the cook went out again.

Honoria carefully pried a bit of bread from the loaf and passed it on to Colby. He took it in a massive paw, tore off a large hunk, and shoved the rest at Manda. It was not very good bread. The loaf was dark with rye meal and molasses, and she felt definite grit beneath her fingers. She could put it back on her plate, or offer it to the Frenchman, but Christopher was watching her.

193

"My own share of what?" she asked.

"Huh," Colby growled. "Probably nothing."

All eyes turned to Christopher. "No," he said quietly. "I didn't survive all this time for nothing."

"I'll believe it when I see it."

"You'll see it," Christopher said.

Were they being deliberately cryptic to drive her insane? "See what?" she persisted.

Another glance went around the table. They all seemed to know what was going on without being told.

Christopher's gray eyes were light and smoke-colored. "Eat your bread, Honoria."

She scowled at him. The I-know-something-you-don't-know routine was very ill-mannered. If they had something to discuss, they should wait until she was gone, not drop hints about it in her presence.

She bit off a hunk of bread. Tiny pebbles rolled between her teeth. She stopped chewing. She couldn't exactly take it out of her mouth, but she couldn't eat it either.

Next to her, Colby said, "Damn stones," and spat a pebble across the table. St. Cyr ducked, and the pebble pinged into the wall behind him.

"Arthur!" his wife cried. "That ain't no way to behave. 'Specially not in front of a lady."

The ship lurched up another wave. Honoria's stomach lurched with it. She clapped her hand to her mouth.

"Oh, no," Colby said. "She's going to heave."

Honoria leapt to her feet. She nearly ran over the cook, who was returning with a jug that reeked of spirits. She staggered down the hall, holding the walls as the ship rocked. She dragged herself up the stairs and out onto the deck.

Cold wind hit her. The sunset had gone, swallowed by black night. A few clouds blotted the horizon with deeper darkness, but overhead, stars twisted across the sky like a smudge of diamond dust. Carew still stood at the wheel. A lantern at his feet threw golden light and shadow across his body.

Honoria reached the rail, leaned over, and spat the bad bread into the sea. The sharp wind blew her hair back from her face and brought with it the clean scent of brine.

She was a fool. She knew why she'd followed Christopher so eagerly, to this ship of people she did not understand. She'd told herself she did her duty, but duty and common sense had so little to do with her decisions these days.

No, she'd come for *him,* for the way his hands felt on her body, for the desire she'd come to crave. She could have stayed with Diana, found a legal way to slide out of the marriage—solicitors could do seemingly anything these days.

Honoria had followed Christopher because she'd wanted him, and now she paid for it.

She heard Christopher's step. She did not want to face her husband just now, but he gathered her against him, his warm body blocking the wind.

It was no use. Desire was her folly, and she enjoyed it. She turned in his arms and rested her head on the curve of his shoulder. He stroked her hair, pressing his lips to the crown of her head. He smelled rough and wild like the sea itself, his scent tangling with the fragrance of whiskey.

She raised her face to his. He bent to her, kissed her lips. The bite of whiskey lingered on his tongue.

"Share of what, Christopher?" she asked.

He smiled, a sinful, knowing smile, and breathed the answer into her ear. "Buried treasure, my angel."

Chapter Twelve

"You made a map to buried treasure on our *marriage license?*"

She clenched her hands, trying to ignore the pain of her still-cramped fingers as her voice rose and cracked. She'd returned to the chart room, and Christopher had closed the door. Colby was stationed at the stairs in order to announce anyone coming, particularly, Christopher emphasized, Henderson.

"Not a map," Christopher said calmly, candlelight chiseling his features into a hard cast. "The coordinates and heading."

The marriage license, in two pieces, lay on the damp table. Christopher's fingers rested on the faint numbers scribbled beneath his name. She'd always wondered what the numbers signified, had imagined the priest who'd married them had put them there for reasons of his own. Somehow they had never seemed important.

Now, of course, they took on vast significance. "I see," she said coldly.

Christopher offered no explanation, and the rest of his officers—and Mrs. Colby—seemed to not require one. Only Honoria stood stiff and indignant, her hands aching.

"This ship is built for speed," Christopher said. "If the weather holds fair, we should reach our destination in ten days." His gaze caught each of them in turn. "We tell the crew that we're making for Charleston until the last possible moment. We have an unwanted guest aboard, so I don't want the men talking about it until they need to know. That means this conversation goes no farther than this room, on pain of flogging." He turned his head and looked at Honoria. "That goes for you, too, my wife."

"I am not in the habit of discussing private matters with Mr. Henderson," she answered.

"With anyone," he corrected. "Not even one of us, without my consent. I don't want Henderson sabotaging my ship, or trying more dramatic means to stop us. He is a pirate hunter, after all."

St. Cyr interrupted. "Why not sail him to Tangier, as he requested?"

"Not with James Ardmore prowling that part of the world. I tangled with him once; I don't wish to do so again." His gaze darted around the room again, resting finally on Manda. "It was too hard a fight to find the lot of you. Ardmore might consider I've paid my dues, but he still might follow to see what we're getting up to."

"That, and you married his sister," Manda said. She

grinned. "Colby suggested we put both Henderson and Honoria in a boat and set them adrift. Let the pirate hunter have them."

"Colby is only miffed because she got the better of him," Colby's wife chortled.

Christopher's answering silence lay heavily in the room. "If anyone else suggests that we leave my wife behind, they can speak to me. I married her; she stays."

Manda raised her brows but offered no comment. Mrs. Colby still smiled. St. Cyr, a stoic man, said nothing.

"That is all," Christopher said. "Manda, relieve Henderson of his watch and send Colby to me."

The dark woman nodded. The others moved to leave the room. Honoria had to dodge aside so they could exit. Christopher folded the marriage license, slid it back into his pocket.

"Christopher," Honoria said when they'd gone. "We very much need to talk."

"Later." He softened the abrupt word by tilting her chin up and brushing a brief kiss to her lips. "At bedtime. We'll talk then."

"You never give me the chance then."

He flashed her a wicked grin, knowing very well what she meant, then pushed past her without another word. He beckoned to Colby, led the large man to his main cabin, and shut the door, polished wood and brass, in her face.

Fuming, Honoria made her way to the deck. It was darkly cold now, but Christopher had effectively blocked her way to the bedroom. No matter. He'd given her the opportunity to think. Plenty of time to come up with ways in which to tell him exactly what she thought of him.

A little way down the deck from Honoria, Manda said to Alden Henderson, "You're off watch. You can go below now."

Henderson did not move from where he leaned on the deck rail. "I like to look at the stars," he replied stiffly.

Manda shrugged, pretending she did not care. The wind ruffled his coat and his pale hair, but his body held the stillness of a waiting predator. His face was handsome in an English sort of way; even the spectacles didn't mar his features.

So why had he, a perfect hoity-toity gent, volunteered to come aboard a pirate ship, to raise sails and turn windlasses like a common sailor? If he planned to pirate-hunt here, he'd be quickly killed. He must know that. So why not wait in the comfort of his London hotel for his own captain to fetch him?

"You said you were a fine navigator," she said, her voice strained. "Does that mean you could find your way, by the stars alone, if you were stranded by yourself in a rowboat?"

He turned his head and looked at her. She could see only the lenses of his spectacles, made opaque by moonlight. "Only if you were stranded with me. I'd need you to row."

Why did the idea of being alone with him in a boat suddenly seem appealing? Ridiculous.

"Why did you rush to my rescue?" she asked sharply. "To a man like you, I should be nothing more than a servant or a slave—or a man's treat. It's all the same to you."

He looked out to sea again. "I am a gentleman."

"That's what I mean."

His calm finally shattered. "Can you never speak to me without deliberately provoking me?

She shrugged. "Can't seem to. And you didn't answer me."

His jaw tightened. "I told you, I am a gentleman. That bastard Switton had you in a cage. If it had been up to me, he'd have died on the spot."

An odd sensation coiled inside her. "Why should you care what happened to me?"

He made a noise of exasperation. "Are English gentlemen not allowed to have compassion? He had no right to take you, no right to lock you up, no right to defile you—"

"He never touched me."

"That's not what I meant. He defiled your dignity. He deserves worse than death for that."

They stood in a dark corner, between the pools of lantern light. She could not see his eyes clearly, just the glint of spectacles.

She reached up and touched them. "Take these off."

He pulled away. "Why?"

"I want to see your eyes."

"It's dark," he pointed out.

"Doesn't matter."

He heaved a sigh, unlocked the spectacles from

around his ears, pulled them off. He immediately shoved the spectacles into a pocket, as though he feared she'd snatch them and drop them overboard.

The moon was high and shining mightily through the clear sky. His eyes were starlight gray, somewhat like Christopher's, and just as intense.

As they faced each other, a mere foot of space between them, she found that she was nearly as tall as he was.

So she only had to rise a little on her tiptoes to kiss him.

For a moment he did nothing. His body went rigid, his lips unmoving. She expected him to wrench himself from her, make a noise of disgust, storm away.

Instead, he put his strong hands on her shoulders and pulled her toward him. Then he parted her lips and kissed her with a ferocity that she'd never felt in her life.

Honoria watched the kiss from where she stood in deeper shadow on the deck. Poor Mr. Henderson. Both he and Honoria were being quite taken in by the Raine family.

A treasure hoard, indeed. It sounded like the stories in the pamphlets about Christopher that Honoria had read long ago, the stories that had made her fall in love with him in the first place.

She'd been a giddy fool at eighteen, and she realized she was a giddy fool now. Why else had she sailed off so happily with Christopher? He had beguiled her with his wicked smiles and his warm caresses, and she'd mindlessly followed him—incidentally, bringing with her the piece of paper telling him where he'd left his treasure.

Now Christopher's sister was busily twisting Mr. Henderson around her fingers. It was too unfair.

Manda and Mr. Henderson broke apart. They stared at each other, each standing perfectly still. After a moment of tense silence, Mr. Henderson said something in a low voice. Manda's reply, which Honoria could not hear entirely, sounded mocking. Mr. Henderson snapped a retort, then turned his back and stalked away.

Manda watched him go. Her long hair stirred in the wind, and she stood straight and tall.

When she turned around again, she spotted Honoria standing in the shadows. Manda looked at Honoria for a moment, knowing she'd seen everything, then she turned and strolled away to the stern. Uncaring. Just like her brother.

The wind grew brisk, cold fingers racing across the sea to tease Honoria's dress and hair. Honoria knew she could not continue to stand up here and shiver, but she was not ready to approach the cabin she shared with Christopher. If she found him there alone, he would begin his game of seduction, of "persuading" her that marrying him had been a good idea.

Once he began kissing her, she would forget about her anger, forget about the hurt that carved out her heart, and let him bamboozle her yet again.

She made a decision, turned her steps to belowdecks, but to the galley, not the captain's cabin. The galley sat forward of the mainmast, aft of the forecastle, half submerged in the deck, and reached by a short ladder. The warm smells of soup and familiar corn bread met her as she entered. Mrs. Colby, who'd taken on the job of assistant cook, had returned there to help make supper for the sailors who'd next come off watch.

The galley was cramped, most of the space taken up by a table on which all meals were prepared. A fire roared on the brick hearth on the far wall. A black pot of soup hung over the fire on a crane, boiling away merrily. The dark-haired cook sitting before it tossed in the occasional vegetable or chunk of pork fat.

Honoria stood just inside the door and rubbed her arms. The room was stifling, but the warmth felt good to her cold limbs. Mrs. Colby looked up from industriously peeling potatoes. "You should be in bed, love. Dawn comes early at sea."

"I'm not very tired," Honoria replied, and then realized the lie. Her arms ached from her afternoon holding the wheel, and her eyes felt sandy.

Mrs. Colby chuckled. "Well now, your husband will be happy to hear you're wide awake."

Honoria blushed, which made Mrs. Colby chuckle again.

In Charleston, ladylike Honoria Ardmore would never have dreamed of conversing with a former barmaid, no matter how good-natured the lady might be. But they were both pirate wives now, she thought glumly, on a pirate ship. Class distinction and the proper order of things no longer seemed to matter.

At least, that's what the rational part of Honoria's mind prattled. The rest of her was just happy for someone to talk to.

THE CARE & FEEDING OF PIRATES

"You're good for him, dear," Mrs. Colby said, returning to her potatoes. "You've taken the edge off him."

Honoria blinked in surprised. "I have?"

"My goodness, yes. He's always been a hard man, albeit a fair one. He doesn't brook no disobedience, but he's good to his crew. Then again, he can be ruthless as a stray dog what takes over a pack. Now he's got something new to think about. Something nice."

Honoria eyed the woman in amazement. If Christopher had had his edges polished off, she was glad she hadn't known him with the edges on.

"He went through hardship in the Orient," Honoria offered. "Perhaps that has made him less formidable."

"Oh, aye. His adventures no doubt shook up his pride. But his toughness got him through those. It's you, dear, that's put that sparkle in his eyes."

"The one that makes him look like he wants to devour me?"

Mrs. Colby chortled again. "The very one. Let him enjoy himself, dear. He deserves a rest."

He deserved to be dumped overboard, Honoria thought privately. She glanced at the cook, but he had bent over his soup pot, seeming in no way interested in the chatter of women.

Mrs. Colby went on cutting potatoes. Honoria found herself sitting on one of the stools, arranging the uncut potatoes in order of size.

"He's had a hard time of it," Mrs. Colby went on. "Our captain got to watch his father be shot through the head and his mother walk away with the killers. That made him all hard inside, and him so young."

"Oh," Honoria said. Her treacherous heart began to ache for him. She wondered briefly if Mrs. Colby was telling her this because she'd seen Honoria's fury over the treasure map. Perhaps Christopher had instructed Mrs. Colby to turn Honoria's sympathies back to him.

"He'll be good to you, love," Mrs. Colby continued. "But in his own way."

"Does his own way include driving me insane?"

She smiled. "It's the way of love, my dear. When Colby courted me, I wanted nothing more than to slam a tankard right between his eyes. He'd swagger in and out of my life without so much as a by-your-leave and expect me to be waiting for him when he came back. And then one day, I wasn't waiting."

Honoria moved a large potato to the end of her row. "What did you do?" she asked, curiosity growing.

Mrs. Colby's smile widened in fond memory. "Oh, he did get that angry with me! He's mostly a gentle man, for all he's so big, but he has a temper. He tried to demand it from me, but I said if he cared so little for my feelings he could pay for the pleasure, same as he would a common woman." She shook with laughter. "He was that shocked. You wouldn't think old Colby was so prim. But he is. So he took me out and married me."

She reached for a potato in the middle of Honoria's careful line. "Then he wanted me, if you please, to wait in England for him. Not so, I said. Our vows said ''til death us do part,' not ''til your ship leaves port.' So I'm going. He needs a wife, bless him."

Honoria thought about the way she'd seen large Colby be grumblingly affectionate to his wife and the way she shooed him back and forth without embarrassment. They seemed to fit, the bearlike man and the plump little woman, she all smiles, he all growls. Honoria already sensed the strong bond between them.

She sighed. She'd always felt a bond between herself and Christopher, a tether that had wrapped itself around her even in the years she'd thought him dead. She'd told him she had let him go in her heart, but the truth was, she never could.

She could sense, for instance, that he'd entered the galley behind her. It was not only Mrs. Colby's sudden innocent expression or her abrupt interest in the potatoes that told Honoria who the footsteps belonged to. It was a change in the air, a tingling on her skin that told her he stood behind her before she even turned around.

His large body filled the doorway, and his gray eyes glinted knowingly. Honoria wondered how much he'd heard.

Mrs. Colby sent him a smile. "I was just keeping her warm for you."

"I'm grateful," Christopher said. The harsh light in the cavernlike room made his face harder than ever. He held out his hand. "Come along, my wife."

Mrs. Colby winked. If Christopher noticed, he pretended not to. When Honoria remained fixed to her stool, he took her by the elbow, pulled her up, and nearly dragged her out of the galley.

Jennifer Ashley

She went with him willingly enough. Not only did she have plenty to say to him, but he was also leading her to their warm and very interesting bed.

Christopher knew Honoria wanted to argue. She would begin by accusing him of returning for her only because he'd wanted the marriage license with its directions to the *Rosa Bonita*'s Mexican gold.

He'd tell her, "It was the other way around, sweetheart." She wouldn't believe him. But well-bred Honoria Ardmore would not sulk. She'd want to talk about it.

Honoria always wanted to talk about their feelings. Christopher only wanted to feel them.

He led her into their cabin, which the night wind through the open window had cooled. He shut the door. She opened her mouth to start the argument, so he abruptly pressed her back against the door and kissed her.

She parted her lips without resistance. He liked the shape of her mouth and the softness of it, the spice of her tongue and the eager way she moved it against his. She tasted as sweet as she had that faraway day when he'd kissed her for the first time.

Back then, she'd belonged in that delicate room in her family's mansion, in her white muslin and perfume. Now her skin was pink with sunburn, her hair tangled by the wind. Her flowerlike face had changed to the face of a woman, with sharp chin and fine lines at the corners of her eyes. She was even more beautiful now, though she wouldn't believe that, either.

She made a soft noise in her throat and twined her

208

arms about his neck. She'd done that way back when, too. She always liked to pull him closer, as though to make sure he wouldn't leave before the kiss was over.

No fear of that.

"Christopher," she whispered.

"Not now," he growled softly.

"I just wanted to ask—"

"No." He nipped her lower lip.

"You don't know what I want to say."

He began the pleasurable task of slipping free the hooks on her bodice. "I have a good idea."

"I'll wager you do not."

Her eyes sparkled green and her voice was haughty.

"No?" He leaned his hand against the door, beside her head. "What will we wager? A kiss?" He stole a brief one. "Too late for that." He cupped her breast. "Your virtue? Too late for that, as well."

He saw the stubborn glint enter her eye. That was his Honoria, always ready for a fight. "If I win," she said clearly, "you will honor one request from me, without question, no matter what it is."

"All right," he said recklessly, his blood too hot to care. "And you'll honor one from me. No questions." He tilted her face upward. "No talking."

"Very well."

He pinned her against the door again. "So what were you going to ask?" Even if he had to endure endless questions about the marriage license, he'd just ensured himself a fine reward for her probing.

She cleared her throat, tried to look as prim as she could with her bodice half open. "May I steer the ship again tomorrow?"

He tried to hide his start but couldn't. Damn. "That was your question?"

"Yes." She smiled, triumphant. "Well?"

"You little vixen."

She gave him a pleased look. "I win."

"Yes, all right. What damn fool thing do you want me to do?" Knowing Honoria, she'd probably tell him to stand in the stern on one leg and sing Irish sea chanteys or something equally ridiculous.

"Answer my question first," she ordered.

"What question? Oh, taking the wheel. Yes, you will. You'd better. Your watch starts at ten."

Her brows shot upward. "My watch?"

"Young Carew will help you. He trains the new recruits."

Her chest rose against his. "Have I become one of the crew?"

"I don't have enough men to give you a free ride. Everyone works, everyone gets a share. That includes you."

"I see." She gave him an apprehensive look.

"You'll do fine. Carew will show you things you can do, even a Southern lady bred to give tea parties."

She gave a soft laugh. "Upper-class ladies don't give tea parties. That's for the *parvenu*."

He shook his head, mocking chagrin. "Damn, I knew I shouldn't have run away from finishing school."

She laughed again, her lips red and inviting.

"Tell me what my forfeit is," he said, steeling himself. "Get it over with."

Honoria fell suddenly silent. Her cheeks blossomed

pink. He waited for her to tell him to climb to the crow's nest and jump off.

She rose on her tiptoes and put her mouth to his ear. She whispered, he listened.

His eyes widened, and his loins stirred. *Oh, my sweet Honoria,* his mind beat. *No wonder I love you.*

Chapter Thirteen

Honoria felt Christopher's body tighten as she explained. She could not bring herself to say the words out loud, where she could hear them, but the muted whisper in his ear seemed to work.

He placed his hands on her shoulders, his eyes going almost a colorless gray. "You did not learn that at finishing school."

If he believed that, he had no idea what a dozen fifteen-year-old young ladies could find to talk about after the lights went out. But she hadn't, actually. "From Alexandra," she blurted. She flushed. She hadn't meant to say that.

He leaned to her ear. "Let me make sure I understand. My punishment is that you want me to . . ." He whispered one very enticing, and naughty, phrase.

Her face flamed. "I did not say *that*."

"You did. You just used different words. That is what you want?"

His steely gaze told her he was not going to let her say no. She did not want to in any case. "Yes."

He kissed the bridge of her nose. "You know, I should have dragged you away with me when I first met you. My life would have been so happy."

"You were a pirate," she said.

He shrugged. "You were a lady. It's worked before."

"You are still a pirate," she pointed out.

"But no lady made *that* suggestion. Brazen hussy."

She drew herself up. "Passion between a husband and wife is perfectly acceptable."

"Did Alexandra teach you that, too? I'm beginning to truly like Grayson Finley's wife."

"She was quite informative," Honoria admitted.

His voice grew low. "Someday, you can tell me everything you discussed. Right now, we can get to the business of unfastening your clothes." He continued to slip her bodice's clasps through their hooks.

"Are you certain the ship is not tossing too much?"

Christopher pulled open her bodice. "Smooth as glass on a fine summer night."

He skimmed the gown down her arms, dropped it to pool at her feet. He kissed her while he untied the ribbons of the chemise.

He lifted her closed fist, kissed her fingers. "Does it still hurt?"

"What?"

"Your hands were cramped. Are they better?"

She barely felt them. "Yes. No. I mean, I think so."

His lips were warm and dry. He unfolded her fingers, kissed them, then her palm. "You're strong. Did you know that?"

She swallowed. "I'm not, particularly."

"You'd never have survived me the first time if you weren't. Let alone married me. Or took the helm of my ship when I told you to, without question, without crying."

"I told you, I never cry. Besides, if I'd burst into tears, how could I have seen where to steer?"

He made a noise like a chuckle and bent to kiss her neck. She closed her eyes, sinking into the dark feeling of his mouth on her. He was bamboozling her again. And, as she'd suspected would happen, she did not care.

"I love sailing," she murmured. "My brother Paul and I used to climb all the way forward on James's ship and try to stand on the bow with our arms outstretched. It was like flying."

He snorted. "What a damn fool idea. I'm surprised you didn't break your neck."

"I know. We tore up James's rigging. He nearly killed us. Oh."

Christopher leaned to lick the warm place between her breasts. Her antics of long ago dissolved and floated away.

He kissed his way down to her abdomen, his mouth like fire, and finally sank to his knees. His breath stirred the curls at the join of her legs. Her feet, of their own accord, moved a little bit apart.

"Tell me about your brother," he said.

"James?" she cried, confused. Why on earth did he want to talk about James?

"No, the other one. The one who died."

"Paul? I don't want to talk about Paul right now. I want—"

"Yes, I know what you want. You told me." He kissed her where she ached. "I want to know about him."

"Why?"

"He's my rival."

Honoria stared down at the top of his head. Candlelight burnished his hair gold, but she saw a few white hairs mixed in.

"How can he possibly be your rival?"

Christopher's tongue flickered. She curled her still-aching hands, impossible heat flowing through her.

"You loved him," he said. "I want you to love me. So I want to know about him."

"It is not the same thing," she cried. Her body pulled her one way, her emotions the other. "He was my best friend. I loved you both, but in different ways. And you both left me."

The words rang in the tiny cabin.

Christopher eased to his feet, to her great disappointment. He put his hands on her arms. "I am here now. I came back for you, and I'm not leaving again. That's what I want you to understand."

"You came back for your stupid treasure map."

"Damn the treasure map. I don't need it. I remembered the numbers."

She stared. "I don't understand you. Why write them on the license, then?"

"Because I needed some way to tell Manda, and I didn't have anything else on hand. I didn't dare

215

record anything in my log, not with your brother breathing down my neck. Ardmore stole the logs anyway, so damn good thing I didn't. And I couldn't very well write Manda a note telling her *By the way, the gold is hidden at latitude X, longitude Y.* So I jotted it on the license. No one noticed me do that."

"What was the point?" Her body cried out for her to shut up, let him get on with what he'd been doing, but her thoughts whirled and wanted explanation. "Did you marry me so you could have a piece of paper on which to write a note?"

"No, you troublesome woman. I married you because I wanted to. The license just came in handy."

"But you knew you were going to be hanged."

"Yes. But when Manda came looking for me, she'd hear of the marriage and seek you out. She'd insist on you showing her the license. She'd see the numbers and know what they meant." He gave her a deprecating look. "I didn't realize you were going to keep our marriage a deep dark secret. I ought to have known."

Honoria put her hand on his shoulder, pushed him away. She felt silly standing there naked, glaring at him, but her indignation wouldn't let her stay silent. "You could simply have told me."

"The sister of James Ardmore? I couldn't risk you running straight to him and announcing you knew where I'd put the Mexican gold. It belongs to Manda, and Colby, and St. Cyr, and to the crew with me that day."

"It doesn't," she snapped. "You are bloody thieves."

He backed her against the door. The wood panel was cold on her bare skin. "We are pirates, Honoria.

We take treasure. It's what we do. We aren't the romantic stories in your pamphlets."

"Oh, I am more than aware of that."

He pressed his knee between hers, his rough breeches scratching her thighs. "You should write a pamphlet of your own."

"You mean one warning other women away from them?"

"One telling ladies how to give their pirates what they want."

She seethed, trying not to let his touch soothe her anger. "A guide to being a pirate wife? Let me see. . . . First, a woman must possess extraordinary patience and fortitude."

He smiled, eyes warming. "And resilience. Don't forget resilience."

"Yes, for the many times you throw your woman to the floor and ravish her."

"I think the bunk will do tonight."

He abruptly scooped her into his arms and tossed her there. She landed in the pile of quilts and bedding, and the real feather bed Diana had given her.

She wanted to seethe, to stay angry at him for deceiving her so. A small part of her told her that what he'd done had probably been reasonable under the circumstances. But her emotions wanted to rage.

Then he began to strip. As he slid his shirt and breeches from his body, her blood began to warm, and her anger began to slide away, no matter how desperately she held on to it.

His body was incredible, even with his ruined side. Strong thighs, narrow hips, ridged stomach, muscled arms. The Chinese dragon on his collarbone, with its curled tail, looked a bit smug.

She twisted a lock of hair through her fingers and wondered why sailing men liked to decorate their bodies with pictures from exotic ports they reached. Traveling ladies usually made do with a vase or cup painted with the name of the town.

Blast the man, he'd done it again. He'd distracted her from her very reasonable, justifiable anger.

He stepped to the bunk, ducking under the beam, and rested one knee on the quilts. "Open your legs," he said softly.

She did so without hesitation. Her thighs were already damp with female moisture.

He brushed a kiss to her lips. He kissed his way down her torso, pausing to swipe his tongue across her navel. He worked his way down her abdomen to the hair at the join of her thighs and farther, to her aching opening.

His breath ruffled her dark curls as he gently blew on them. He kissed the swelling nub there, then he slid his tongue into her cleft.

She could not stop the sharp cry that escaped her mouth. She grabbed the quilts, hands twisting. He began to explore her slowly, kissing her and licking her. He knew how to do incredible things with his tongue.

She'd asked him to do this, but she'd never dreamed what it would feel like. He skillfully touched his tongue to her folds, flicked over the nub above them that throbbed and tingled, dipped back inside her.

She called his name over and over in a hysteria of

longing. She told him that she wanted him, and many other things that would make her blush later.

Just as she thought her throat would go hoarse from her cries, he withdrew from her. She fell back to earth with a crash. She lay there, stunned, gasping for breath, feeling very wet and very wicked.

His smile was hot and evil. "I came back for you, my wife. I want it all back, my treasure, my crew, you. I won't stop until I have everything. Never forget that."

"You have me," she whispered.

"Damn right," he said.

Without preliminary, he climbed upon her, opened her thighs, and pushed his arousal into her needing body.

She screamed. He held her down, his hips rising as he thrust and thrust into her until his seed came.

He took himself out of her with the last of his strength and fell beside her, his legs tangling with hers. He lay there, breathing hard, eyes closing, his muscles still tense, like he'd just swum many miles and was happy to have made it to shore.

She brushed a wisp of hair from his face, wheat-gold on bronze. His lashes were the same color. They flickered as he looked at her again, gray eyes heavy. "Is my forfeit over?"

"What? Oh, the wager. Yes, yes, I think so."

He sent her a lazy smile. "Pity." He kissed her throat. "But that means I can now do what I want."

She swallowed, wondering if that meant rushing back on deck to see if his ship was being sailed correctly. "I suppose it does."

But he proceeded to prove that his thoughts were not on sailing.

What he did would have been downright sinful if she had not been married to him. Perhaps it still was. All she knew was that he began again the exact sequence of steps that had just driven her mad, this time with more creativity and still more enthusiasm. The things he asked her to do after that were just as naughty and possibly against the law.

He was gentle and tender, rough and playful. He hurt her and yet excited her. Stately Honoria, the alabaster statue, was crumbling like stone in an earthquake at his touch.

When they were finished, and Honoria was ready to curl up with him in oblivious slumber, he rose from the bed. The bunk was hot and tumbled with lovemaking, and his skin glistened with sweat.

He dragged on his clothes, kissed her gently. "Go to sleep," he said, and strolled out of the cabin, leaving a chill draft in his wake.

She lay back in the tangled bedding, too tired now for the anger that he'd so effectively diverted. She was a complete fool, and she had no idea what to do about it.

Christopher found Manda in the stern watching the horizon and the stars. Her teeth flashed in the lantern light as he approached. "Can you still walk?" she asked.

He leaned against the stern gunwale, eased his cramped muscles. "Barely." He could still feel the sensation of Honoria on him, not only her tightness and the kisses she showered on him, but also the bruises on his neck and scratches on his back wherever his shirt brushed them.

"You really like that girl, don't you?" Manda went on.

He shrugged, let her chortle. He felt no embarrassment about his feelings for Honoria.

They stood relatively alone, so he felt free to talk, though he kept his voice low. "I saw you kissing Henderson, Manda."

Her smile vanished. She pretended to concentrate on the pattern of Orion high above them. "I've kissed men before."

"Kiss him all you want. Just don't talk to him."

She glared at him almost as scathingly as Honoria could. "I wouldn't betray you—us—for a few kisses."

"I know. But falling in love changes the way you think. It makes men—women—do stupid things."

"I'm not in love with that bespectacled, prissy Englishman," Manda snorted, a bit too quickly, Christopher thought. He said nothing. She glared at the horizon. "Are you saying you are in love with your little wife?"

"I think so."

It didn't hurt to say it. They were just words. Words were just air.

His sister's look turned curious. "Why'd you marry her? I mean, the day before you were supposed to hang, you suddenly decide to get married?"

He shrugged again. He remembered the hot cell, smelling of damp and refuse, and then her, so pretty and clean, her eyes distressed, her soft lips whispering against his. A voice in the back of his mind had urged him not to let her go, not completely, not this time.

He'd put his grubby hands on her fine face and said, "Marry me, Honoria." For an instant, she'd stared at him like a startled dove, then her green eyes had grown determined and she'd said, incredibly, "Yes."

"I don't know," he finished slowly. "I suppose I just didn't want to die alone."

He expected another snort. His sister never had much room in her life for emotion.

But then, why should she? She'd never known her mother, and her father—their father—hadn't wanted her. Only Christopher had stood by her. He'd felt a bond between them, despite their differences in race and gender. Christopher had persuaded his father not to sell Manda, and he'd raised her himself, teaching her to be a sailor and a pirate.

Manda had always been strong, and not just physically. Her upright body, her quickness, her strength often made him forget that she could be as vulnerable as he was.

Manda fixed him with her skull-boring gaze. "I think I understand."

He knew she did. He did not have to doubt.

He thought about Honoria's worry about Manda's ordeal. He cleared his throat and groped his way along an unfamiliar phrase. "Do you want to talk about it?"

She blinked. "Talk about what?"

"You know, what you went through with Switton."

Her brows arched like blackbird's wings. "I don't

remember much now," she said. "And no, I don't want to talk about it. Why do you?"

"Honoria thought you'd need to discuss it. She likes everyone to talk about their feelings."

Manda stared at him like he'd gone insane. After a moment, her lips began twitching. She started to snicker, and then it became a full-blown laugh. It was derisive and at the same time affectionate, a woman amused by the misfortunes of her brother. "Chris, you poor thing."

Christopher folded his arms and let her laugh. "She makes up for it."

"I heard. I had to hang halfway into the water to drown out the noise."

He smiled, remembering what had caused the noise.

Manda laughed some more. "Lordy, look at you grinning." Her peals of laughter rang into the wind. Every so often they'd die off into chuckles, and then she'd repeat, "Talk about your feelings," and start snorting again.

Christopher just watched her, enjoying the fact that he was finally near to hear her laugh again.

The fine weather—few clouds, no storms—meant that as they sailed south, it turned sweltering hot. The men stripped down to breeches. The two sailors Christopher had recruited in Siam wore nothing but loincloths that covered their privates and not much else. Manda bound a strip of colorful cloth about her breasts and wore that and breeches, her brown skin shining in the sun.

223

Honoria took to wearing less and less under her lawn and muslin dresses. Christopher observed this delicious fact every time she came up on deck. At least the hot weather had some compensations.

Her nose turned bright red, then began to peel. Mrs. Colby kindly provided her with a cream, and Honoria went about with her nose slathered with the gray-green concoction. No one laughed at her, because the smelly, eucalyptus-scented sunburn cream made its rounds to all of them.

Christopher watched the blazing sun grow hotter, the clouds grow thinner and disappear. And finally, just as he'd feared, the wind died. The ship glided to a halt and the sails fell limp. No amount of tacking could find even a breeze.

He ordered the men to stand down, letting as many as possible rest below out of the sun, though it was just as sweltering in the forecastle and the cabins. Tempers ran high, and the water ran low.

Christopher had faced water shortage before. Most ships did. He immediately went to drastic rationing, and the routine fell into place. A cup a day to every man (or woman), less to a sick man. Two dozen lashes and curtailment of rations for stealing water or fighting for it. On some ships the penalty was death— if you died for stealing water, that much more would be available to the others. But Christopher needed all his crew alive.

"A sick man needs more water," Honoria tried to point out.

"A sick man sleeps in his hammock all day," Christopher countered. "While the others work in the heat. He gets less. Besides, if I announce that sick men get more water, half the crew will report ill in the morning."

Honoria looked unconvinced.

She was arguing because young Carew had fallen ill. He did not have plague, thank God, nor cholera or anything else that would render the *Starcross* a ghost ship. He simply had a fever from too much sun and overwork.

Honoria took it upon herself to look after him. She'd grown fond of Carew. He'd taught her how to steer the ship and how to tell when sails should be adjusted or when the wind changed dangerously—all without shouting at her. He'd been a patient teacher, and she'd been grateful. Now she'd become his most tender nurse, to Christopher's annoyance.

When Christopher remonstrated with her, Honoria changed in a heartbeat from enticing pirate's woman to stately Southern lady. "You have no compassion in you, Christopher. I am simply doing my duty to one less fortunate than I."

"He has the sniffles, not smallpox," Christopher snapped. "And your duty is to me."

She gave him a lofty look. "I know, you were robbed and butchered out in China or wherever. We feel very sorry for you." She stalked away and refused to talk to him the rest of the day.

He retaliated by making love to her that night until she was gasping for breath and too shaky to stand. Only then did he let her lie down.

It was a hell of a thing to be married to a wife who refused to grasp the idea of obedience. He guessed that in her fancy Charleston home she hadn't been denied anything. The pretty, only daughter of a wealthy family had commanded obedience, not given it.

Christopher wished she had learned it, and learned it forcibly. Because as the weather continued hot and still, and the sweating men stank, and the food turned sour, he caught Honoria giving extra water to her ill friend Mr. Carew.

Chapter Fourteen

Honoria had never seen Christopher as enraged as he was now. He faced her in the stern, stone-faced, but with eyes blazing fury.

Honoria held her head high. "I did not steal it. I gave him my ration. I can do as I like with it."

"No, you either drink it or pour it overboard."

"How ridiculous. Besides, ladies do not need as much water as men." She swallowed, her throat already parched. "Anyway, it brought down his fever."

Christopher's eyes sparkled dangerously. "I don't care if it made him dance a hornpipe. You need that water, Honoria. You can die of heatstroke faster than you know it."

She believed him. The heat pounded at them, and her thin dress was damp with perspiration. She wished she'd dare bare her torso, like Manda with her strip of cloth, but some things proper Honoria could not do.

"He needed the water," she repeated stubbornly.

Christopher glared at her. "Go below, and stay there. Carew can do without you for the afternoon."

She stamped away but threw the last word over her shoulder. "I know why you never want to talk about your feelings, Christopher Raine. You don't have any!"

That night, he proved her wrong. He took her to the stern again as the sun dipped into the horizon and the sky turned cool twilight blue.

He had certainly taken to ordering her about of late, Honoria thought, but it was far too hot to argue. Last night, he had not even made love to her; they had simply lain side by side, breathing the night air through the open window, exhausted from heat and thirst.

Instead of frenzied desire, she'd felt peace and languorousness, comfort in the feeling of his hard body next to hers. She'd lain awake and watched the moonlight travel across his bare torso, shadows outlining the ruin of his side as well as the perfection of his chest and shoulders.

Honoria was taken by the beauty of him now as he stood waiting for her, the dying light touching his tall body. He wore only breeches against the heat, and that was no bad thing.

He beckoned impatiently, so she left off her moonstruck staring and went to him.

He led her to the stern bench and sat her down, then he sat next to her, stretched out his long leg behind her, and pulled her back into the circle of his arms. He lifted a cup of water from the deck. Made of copper, the cup was corroded green around the top edge but moist with dew all over. Her dry mouth yearned for it.

Christopher held the cup to her lips. "Drink."

Honoria did not need the command. She opened her mouth, and he poured the cool liquid into it. Lovely, lovely water. Never mind that it tasted a bit musty and coppery.

She took a second, long swallow, savoring it all the way down. To think, at home she'd turn up her nose at such an offering, preferring lemonade with sugar and a bit of cinnamon. Here, musty, warm water seemed the purest heaven.

Christopher watched her drink, lashes shielding his eyes. She was surprised he'd procured an extra ration for her. Christopher was bent on following the rules, and made even harder rules for himself.

She took a third swallow before she realized. "This is your ration," she gasped.

"Yes, and I can do whatever I please with it."

She squirmed to face him. "You must drink it. I do not need it."

"Don't be stupid. Yes, you do."

"I am better now, really."

He gave her a narrow look. "I don't want a heroic wife, I want one with common sense. Lately you've been lacking any kind of sense. It must be the heat." The dryness rendered his voice even more broken.

"You're the one being heroic," she flashed.

"I'm not a hero," Christopher rumbled. "I'm a villain. And if you don't drink the water, I will do something even more villainous."

"What?" she asked, fascinated.

He gave her a look that made her shiver. "First, I might just hold your nose and dump the water down your throat."

"That would be foolish. You might spill it."

His scowl deepened. "Or I might toss you into the waves. You said you wanted to bathe."

"We all need to bathe," she said coldly. "Although I think being salt-encrusted might make it even worse."

"Then obey your husband and drink."

"You must drink, too," she said stubbornly. Her mouth did feel better, less swollen and dry. She was still thirsty, though.

He looked at her for a moment, his eyes quiet gray. Behind the ship, to the east, the sky was already dark. A pale moon hung over the horizon.

Christopher lifted the cup to his lips and drank. She traced the swallow down his throat, watched his Adam's apple move behind his tanned skin. He took another mouthful, and Honoria's own mouth quivered with envy.

He put his thumb under her chin, turned her face up to his, and kissed her. Water, lovely and soft, caressed her tongue. They shared the sip, then he broke away. They shared the next one, and the next. Christopher held the cup to her. "One left."

"You have it."

"Back to heroics, are you? Drink it, damn you."

Under his stern gaze, she did. Before she swallowed, she kissed him. He grinned, dipped his tongue in her mouth once more, then withdrew.

He settled her back against him, setting the empty

cup on the deck. The air had cooled, at least. Despite the hot days, the nights were chill. Honoria snuggled against Christopher's chest, already glad of his warmth. She slid her bare feet to the bench, nudged her toes along Christopher's calf.

If all her marriage could be like this, she thought, she could be happy. If marriage were nothing but soft caresses and comfort, interspersed with bouts of wild desire, she would consider herself well matched indeed.

She twined her fingers through her husband's, trailed her foot up and down his leg. At home in Charleston, gentlemen spent much time with their cronies at clubs, while ladies ran the household, sewed finery, and held fetes to raise money for various things. Pirates, as far as she knew, did not join gentlemen's clubs, Grayson Finley excepted. More likely, they spent time in port taverns where very low women circulated. Did pirate wives busy themselves with embroidery or the children while their pirate husbands clashed tankards of ale and sang bawdy songs in smelly portside taverns?

She had the feeling Mrs. Colby would object to her large husband dandling a low woman on his knee. Likely Mrs. Colby would march into the tavern herself and upend a tankard over Colby's curly head. She smiled a little at the image, while her heavy eyes drifted closed.

Through her drowsy lassitude, she heard Christopher's voice. "This life is hard for you."

True, she thought. She had calluses on her palms and her hair was dry and tangled. She very much needed a rosewater cream for her hands and a lavender rinse for her hair.

Christopher was speaking again. "We'll go to Charleston soon."

Would they? Charleston seemed very far away and unimportant. "Will we row there?" she asked.

Christopher bent to catch the words. He chuckled. "If we have to."

"I do not want to go." The words sighed from her lips.

"You belong there. You'll have feather beds and gardens and servants fetching you tea."

"I belong with you."

He was silent a long time. She opened her eyes. His face hung over hers, silhouetted against the fading twilight.

"You must have sunstroke," he said.

"It's dark," she pointed out.

He closed his arms around her, breathed into her hair. "I don't want to be the death of you, Honoria."

"I come from sturdy stock, Mr. Pirate. Look at my brother."

"Mmmph. That doesn't inspire confidence."

Thinking of James, as usual, brought a mixed wave of melancholy and anger. "James went a little mad with vengeance, I think, before he met Diana. Paul was, too. It changed him. And he never even got his revenge. He died before he could discover the identity of the man who had killed his wife. James had to finish it for him."

"I know," Christopher murmured.

"I suppose the story is all over the Atlantic." Last year, James had at last tracked down a pirate called Black Jack Mallory, who'd confessed to murdering Paul's wife and daughters. Diana had had much to do with that hunt.

Christopher said, "I know because I was the one who told Ardmore who killed your brother's wife."

In the silence of the night, against the muted speech of the men in the bow, against the soft lapping of waves on the hull, Honoria lay still for a full minute, not quite certain what she had just heard.

She sat up suddenly and gaped at him, her dry throat slow to find words. "*You* told him?"

"That was why he saved me from the hangman's noose. You didn't know?"

Honoria stared, a tight ache twisting inside her. "You knew?" Her voice rose. Sailors lifted their heads, looked their way. "All this time, you *knew*? Why didn't you tell me?"

He frowned. "I thought your brother did."

"Well, he did not. How did you know? Why did you keep it from us? How dare you!"

Her chest felt tight, her lassitude gone. Christopher watched her, his expression still. "I only learned the information by chance while I was looking for the *Rosa Bonita*," he said. "The man who told me didn't realize what he was revealing, or even what he knew. I put the pieces together, and told Ardmore about it when he arrested me."

She clenched her fists, cold in every limb. "You bargained for your life with it? *He* bargained with it?"

Tears of rage pricked her eyes. "You had to know what such information was to me. How could you have used it as a bargaining chip, you—you *pirate!*"

"I didn't bargain, Honoria," he said sternly. "I just told him. He never said a word, not even thank you. When you came to me in that cell, I had no idea he was going to save me."

Honoria faced him, breathing hard, fists pressed to her abdomen. Despite her rage, she believed him. It would be just like James not to tell Christopher he'd saved his life until after the deed was done. She could imagine her brother taking in Christopher's information, green eyes empty of everything, then walking away without a word.

"You didn't tell me," she went on. "You didn't tell me the name."

"At the time, I thought you'd leave all that to big brother, and I had other things to worry about. He never mentioned it?"

"No." She breathed heavily, surprised fire didn't shoot out of her mouth. "He never told me you knew about Black Jack Mallory, he never told me he'd set you free."

"I suppose he didn't want to scare away his prey."

"I am not his prey," Honoria snapped. "I am his sister."

The rising moon laced gold through his wheat-colored hair. "Right now, I feel very sorry for James Ardmore when you catch up to him."

"You still might have told me," she said, wanting to be angry with him. She couldn't reach James, but Christopher was right in front of her.

"When you walked into my cell, I had other things on my mind." He pulled her back down into his arms, his body warm even through her chill anger. "I wanted my final moments to be very good. I remember the last thing you said to me before you left. I was going to take it to my grave."

Honoria remembered, too. Her heart in her throat, still feeling his seed on her legs, she had said clearly, "I love you."

He wrapped his arms around her, stroked his palm across her belly. "I love you, too," he murmured.

"It isn't the same now."

His voice took a warning tone. "If you don't say another word, Honoria, I won't throw you overboard."

She drew breath for protest. His arms tightened. He was far stronger than she ever would be. "Not another word. Obey your husband."

"You are far too fond of saying that."

"I know." She felt him smile into her hair. "I enjoy it."

She subsided. She was too angry to drowse again, but she let herself succumb to his comfort. James certainly had much to answer for. He'd not known her passion for Christopher, so she might forgive him not telling her he'd saved Christopher's life, but she could not forgive James withholding anything concerning Paul. Anything.

James had known what she felt about Paul, and yet he'd decided that seeking the vengeance was his task alone. He'd not let her be any part of it.

She closed her eyes. Images of Paul came to her too vividly, even after all these years—his laughing eyes, crisp black hair that gleamed blue-black in the sunshine, his drawling voice as he teased the life out of her. They'd been partners in crime against big brother James, mocking him behind his back, standing in a united front against his fury.

It had been so long ago, and yet she still felt she could reach out her hand and he'd be there.

She'd watched him change in the space of a day from carefree young man to grieving, empty shell. They'd been together when they'd heard the news that his wife and children had been killed. Honoria had held Paul while he'd cried and cried. She'd cried, too, having loved the gentle brown-haired lady he'd been married to.

James learned of it and returned home, stone-faced and grim. When Paul had declared he would find the man who'd done this, whatever the cost, James had nodded in quiet agreement. Both James and Honoria had stood firmly behind Paul when he'd decided to turn pirate hunter, a decision that had ultimately led to his own death.

A delicate breeze ruffled the curls on her forehead, soothing her aching head. After Paul had died, James had shut Honoria out of his life, out of his grief, his vengeance—everything. He'd never understood that that was when Honoria had needed him the most.

The breeze strengthened. She closed her burning eyes and tried to put aside her hurt, trying to think only of the cool wind lifting the hair on her neck. . . .

Her eyes snapped open at the same time Christopher shoved her aside and leapt to his feet. The ship rocked heavily, the topsails of the foremast, always ready, catching the gust.

"Wind's up!" Christopher shouted, the strength in his voice touched with joy. "All hands, get those sails aloft, *now!*"

The ship exploded with happy activity. Sailors threw off blankets and boiled up from the hold. They whooped and laughed, scrambling up the masts.

Honoria held on to the bench and breathed the sweet wind. She closed her eyes, forced herself to focus on the heady relief of the gentle breeze, the movement of the ship as the sails filled again. Movement meant hope. They would not die here.

She opened her eyes. Christopher joined his men at the windlass, muscles on his bare back playing. Colby bent next to him, his deep baritone rumbling in a song, badly out of tune.

Manda was not with them. St. Cyr had taken the tiller, and Manda was not with him, either. Honoria's eyes narrowed as she scanned the deck. The lady was nowhere in sight.

In fact, she noticed that although the entire ship's complement was present, including Mrs. Colby, who tied lines like the best of them, Mr. Henderson and Manda Raine were notably and interestingly absent.

Chapter Fifteen

They ran before a fair wind the next three days, making fine time west and southwest. They still rationed water, but the rations increased as they drew closer to their destination.

Despite Christopher's revelation of James's perfidy, Honoria thought herself closer to happiness than she had been for many years. She awoke to sunshine and air and Christopher snoring, spent a companionable breakfast with Mrs. Colby in the galley, did her watch under the supervision of Carew, dined with Christopher and the other officers in his chart room, then leaned on the stern rail to study the stars until Christopher led her below to bed.

Then he'd remind her, with his mouth and hands and body, that he was her husband.

He refrained from talking about love and Charleston and choices. All fine with her. She wanted to enjoy the now, with him in the sunshine and freedom of the ship. Better to leave difficult decisions to another day.

She never had the chance for a talk with Manda, though she knew the young woman must need one. Christopher kept his sister constantly busy, and constantly away from Mr. Henderson. He, too, had noticed Manda's absence on deck when the wind had returned, though he'd said nothing.

Now, when Manda dined with them, Mr. Henderson was on watch and vice versa. If the pair ever appeared on deck together, Manda worked in the stern while Henderson was put to work in the bow.

Honoria tried to bring up the subject of Mr. Henderson and Manda several times with Christopher, but he only growled, and silenced her in interesting ways.

Christopher wanted his gold, and he focused all attention on that. The crew still did not know their true destination, although Honoria heard a few sailors murmur that their course was no longer right for Charleston. Still, they trusted their captain.

His tireless energy rather overwhelmed her at times. He'd done so much since being abandoned on the other side of the world. He'd found his crew, his officers, his sister, a new ship, and had scooped up his wife along the way. Now he wanted his gold, which would complete what he'd begun. He would let nothing stand in his way, not his sister's growing interest in Henderson, not his muttering crew, not his wife.

And certainly not the ship that was sighted behind them and to the north at the end of the fourth day.

* * *

They all piled on deck at the lookout's cry. St. Cyr watched in his quiet way, Colby muttered curses, Manda worriedly peered through her spyglass. Henderson leaned on the rail, not far away, spectacles glinting under the harsh sun.

Christopher knew damn well who followed them. Honoria, at his side, shaded her eyes and squinted against the glare. He watched her flush as she made out the outline of the ship. She knew, as well.

He said nothing until the lookout sang down from the top of the mainmast. "It's him, sir! It's the *Argonaut*."

"You sure?" Colby growled upward.

"He just unfurled the flag. Midnight with a gold slash."

"That is James, all right," Honoria muttered.

Colby raged. "Damn near the fastest ship in the seas. Why couldn't he leave us the hell alone?" He bent a sudden glare on Honoria.

Only St. Cyr kept his countenance straight. "Our ship is nearly as fast, Captain. Our modifications made it so. Do we run?"

Christopher watched the faraway sail for a long time. On that ship, no doubt, sailors were congratulating themselves on catching up to them. He imagined Ardmore standing on the deck, watching in his cold way. His wife perhaps stood by his side, her red hair shining in the sun.

"No," he said abruptly. "We don't run."

Colby stared. "Has the sun touched you?"

Christopher fixed him with a look. "Why should we

run? We sail in free waters, we haven't taken any ships, we're minding our own business."

"He will try to board us," St. Cyr pointed out.

"He is welcome to. One captain can request to speak to another. It's hospitable."

Colby's eyes narrowed. "What I'd like to know is, how did he find us?" He switched his brown-eyed gaze back to Honoria.

She lifted her chin. "Do not look at me, Mr. Colby. I did not see my brother before we left London, and Christopher never told me where we were going. James simply has the knack for turning up where he is not wanted."

Colby looked unconvinced.

"*I* told him," Christopher broke in.

All eyes turned to him. In the silence, a sail snapped and grew taut again. Colby asked, "You did, Captain?"

Christopher lifted his spyglass to study the outline of the ship heading their way. The *Argonaut* had much to admire, clean lines, low-riding hull, square mainmast, fore and aft jibs. He looked for a long time, letting tension build, before he answered.

"I showed his wife the marriage license. She doubtless figured out what the numbers meant and told Ardmore. She is an admiral's daughter, after all."

More stares. Mouths dropped open, countenances grew dismayed.

Manda was the first to realize what he'd done and why. She turned away, a faint twitch to her lips.

St. Cyr realized second. He turned back to the tiller, face relaxed. Colby still glared. Henderson asked quietly, "What numbers?"

241

Christopher lowered his spyglass. "Manda will tell you."

Manda jerked around. Henderson flushed.

Christopher did not give them time to shout at him, or let Colby splutter more questions. He ordered everyone back to work. Even his lovely wife. From the look in Honoria's eyes, she still raged about her brother's reticence to tell her things. Watching her walk away, back stiff, he decided that Ardmore would be safer if Christopher kept Honoria away from the cannon.

Honoria hoisted her knife, positioned her victim lengthwise, and brought the blade down sharply. *Chop!* She tossed its head into the pile and started on its body.

She slammed the knife again and again. Pieces flew, juices spurted. She stepped back when she was finished, panting.

"Well," Mrs. Colby said, "that's one carrot won't bother anybody again."

Honoria did not reply. She gathered up the pieces, added them to the pot, and selected another victim. This one was a bit shriveled from days at sea. No matter. She slammed down the knife, neatly decapitating it.

"Something on your mind, love?"

"Men!" Honoria snarled.

Mrs. Colby craned her head to look at the carrot. "Any man in particular?"

"All of them!"

The cook looked up from plucking the chicken that

would make tonight's meager stew, eyed the knife in Honoria's hand, and quickly looked away.

The knife went up and down. "My brother, my husband, all of them." Chop, chop, chop! She threw the pieces into the stew pot and eagerly grabbed another carrot.

"Tell me, Honoria," Mrs. Colby said, her voice deceptively calm. "When you're hacking like that, are you thinking of the whole man or just a certain bit of him?"

Honoria looked down at the carrot, long and firm and tapering. She hadn't thought of it, but perhaps there was a reason she'd chosen that particular vegetable. "I do not know," she said darkly. "It's only a carrot."

The cook hunkered over her chicken, back quivering.

"Just asking, love," Mrs. Colby said.

Honoria stood still, knife poised. "Am I a living, breathing human being?"

"Well, of course you are, dear."

The knife came down. "Then why is it that my brother and my husband believe that I should not act or think or feel without their permission? I should do nothing, say nothing, *think* nothing that they have not decided."

Mrs. Colby raised her shoulders in the universal woman's dismissal of the oddities of men. "It's their way, I'm afraid. The good Lord told them they were the masters, and they believed it. When you're first married, they test the waters, but after a while, they start to learn the way of things. You have to be patient with them."

Honoria viciously whacked the top off another carrot. "The whole of my life, I've been the perfect lady. I kept that house running for years. Did James ever thank me for it, ever even notice? No. And now, when I've done something for myself, he races after me to fetch me home like a disobedient schoolgirl. The one thing that marriage has done for me is to make me no longer have to answer to my brother. I am supposed to answer to my husband now, and my brother has no more say in the matter."

Mrs. Colby watched her for a time. "Are you worried Captain Raine will give you back? Don't worry, he won't let you go. He needs you."

"Ha."

Mrs. Colby smiled. "He does. I see the way he looks at you. He's a man what's found something good, and he won't let go of it quick."

Honoria shook her head. "He mentions love now and again. But I think he simply likes having someone he can order about. He treats Manda completely differently."

"Well, he and Manda have been together since they were tykes. Mr. Raine raised her himself." She resumed her more sedate chopping of turnips. "But a boy doesn't want much to do with a little girl, does he? So he treated her same as she was a brother, taught her what he would a boy. They're used to each other. Most likely, he doesn't know much what to make of you."

"I don't know what to make of him," Honoria said, jaw clenched.

"That's what happens when you're in love, dear."

Honoria sat on a stool, suddenly weary. "I am not in love." She looked up, worried. "Am I?"

"You wouldn't be so angry if you weren't. Nor would you blush when you talk about it."

Honoria laid down the knife, despondent. "There's no love left in me. I've used it all up, I think. I only have anger anymore."

Mrs. Colby smiled. Her face wrinkled up when she did that, laugh lines nearly hiding her warm eyes. Honoria could imagine her as a barmaid, always ready with a smile and a drop of ale. "You have young anger, and you've hurt like no girl should have hurt. Don't draw yourself up, Mrs. Raine; thirty is young still, you'll see."

"Thirty-one," Honoria said in a dull voice. She suddenly wished she hadn't had such a happy childhood. She'd been tricked into believing her adulthood would be just as happy.

Mrs. Colby smiled and subsided. Honoria knew the woman was placating her. Christopher was an arrogant, interfering man who thought women should do as he wished, and her brother was the same. Why women fell in love with them was beyond her.

She positioned another carrot, raised her knife, and viciously chopped her way down its long, full, hard length.

In another part of the ship, Manda Raine was drawing a similar conclusion about men.

245

Alden Henderson stood on the threshold of her cabin, blocking her exit and heating her blood. His broad shoulders filled the doorway, his hair glinted in the lantern light, and his gray eyes regarded her steadily. She knew his hair felt like silk, and that fact made her somehow even angrier.

The cabin was a mere compartment the length of her bunk. She had only enough room to stand, dress, and wash her face in the tiny washbasin and stow a trunk in which to keep a few personal items. There was not enough room for the two of them, and she felt that with every muscle of her body.

She supposed she could simply knock Henderson out of the way and step over his prostrate body. She just didn't want to.

"I understood from your brother that you would tell me what was going on," he was saying.

Manda folded her arms. The gesture closed herself in, made her feel more protected. "What he really meant was that I should use my womanly wiles to sway you to our side."

His brows, perfect lines of gold, drew together. "I doubt he said that, or meant it."

His lack of derision annoyed her for some reason. "Maybe not. What he meant is that you're a threat and I am supposed to keep you under control."

A puckered line appeared behind the nose band of his spectacles. "Why don't you tell me what it's all about, and then we'll talk about control."

She pressed her fists together, suddenly nervous. Manda Raine was never nervous. She assessed situations, she found ways out of them. Even when she'd been in a cage for that awful Switton, she hadn't worried very much. She'd get out somehow, and she knew it.

She'd never faced anyone like Alden Henderson. She did not want to fight him, although lately she'd supposed she might feel better if she just gave him a good punch.

He'd kissed her again just before the ship had caught the wind earlier today. They'd encountered each other in the chart room, and after some verbal sparring, he'd framed her face in his hands and kissed her, long and deep.

She'd forgotten everything around her, including the subtle signs that told her a wind had at last sprung up. She'd been late on deck, for the first time in her life, and Christopher had glared at her.

She realized that Henderson had shaken loose something inside her, and she neither understood the sensation nor knew how to respond.

"I imagine you let no one control you," she said abruptly. "You do as you please, go where you like, a spoiled English gentleman."

"And you drag the fact that I'm an Englishman into every conversation."

"Not English *man*," she corrected coldly. "English gentleman. Certain the whole world exists for your privilege."

The spark of rage in his gray eyes pleased her. She'd struck something.

"If that were true," he snapped, "why did I leave

my fine English home to hunt pirates? Life aboard James Ardmore's ship is not exactly soft."

She lifted one shoulder in a shrug. "You needed entertainment?"

"I needed a purpose, if you must know," he snarled. "I was supposed to be a clergyman."

She opened her eyes wide. "You?"

"Oh, yes. A respectable vicar with aspirations to a bishopric. I was promised a living by an earl—after the current vicar passed on, which he showed no sign of doing year after year after bloody year. I met James Ardmore by chance, and admired what he did."

"I see. So if you can't save souls, you will save bodies?"

"Something like that."

He said it with such detachment, like it was unimportant to him, a topic of conversation.

Manda had lived her life with two different types of men, the ones she could make fear her, and the ones she knew she could not and so avoided. She'd never met anyone like Henderson, who preferred talking to fighting. Yet she'd seen him fight at Lord Switton's. His punches had been neat and efficient, and he'd helped clear their way out of the garden without so much as bending his spectacles.

But he fought with words, and here Manda felt uncertainty for the first time in her life. She and Christopher had learned to communicate almost wordlessly. She tangled with Henderson and did not know what to do. Or say.

"Well?" Henderson said, his aristocratic brows arched. His hair had grown a bit longer in the past few weeks, and a pale lock of it fell across his forehead. "What is it Mr. Raine wants you to tell me?"

Manda let out a long sigh. Sometimes she wished the entire male sex would go lose themselves in a storm.

"He's after gold he was forced to leave behind. I'm betting James Ardmore is here to stop him."

Henderson stared at her for a few heartbeats. "The gold from the *Rosa Bonita*?" She nodded. He pursed his lips. "I remember. The Mexican gold bound for Napoleon that disappeared. Napoleon was livid."

"I am surprised your hero James Ardmore didn't force Christopher to tell him where he'd left it."

Henderson snorted. "I'm not. Ardmore doesn't give a damn about gold, and he certainly wouldn't give it to Napoleon, or even worse, the English. He's happy to keep it buried."

"Then why is he bothering Chris now?"

Henderson's gray eyes glinted. "Because he doesn't want your brother to have the gold, either. Raine's a pirate. James won't let a pirate win."

"And that pirate stole his sister."

Henderson gave a thoughtful nod. "You know, I honestly believe that if not for the gold, James would not bother to chase us. He and Honoria do not get along. At all. And that's an understatement."

"So I gathered."

She could not imagine having a brother she hated. She and Chris were friends and partners, the two of them against the world. They never shared their feelings or cried on each other's shoulders, but they both knew that the other would be there for them. Always.

"There, I've told you," she said, drawing into herself again.

She wished he'd go away. She didn't like light-haired men. She liked men with dark hair and skin and liquid dark eyes, not tall men who looked like colorless statues. His hair was so pale yellow it was nearly white, and his eyes were clear white-gray. The sun had turned his skin a golden hue, tanned rather than burnt.

His lips were thin, dry as silk. She knew that. Before she could stop herself, she leaned up to him, kissed him.

His arms came around her. He kissed with such poise, as though their angry words never existed. She brushed back the lock of his hair, reveling in the satin softness of it. He always tasted like he'd just drunk fine wine, though she knew they had none aboard.

He pulled her closer, hands snaking beneath her hair, cradling the nape of her neck.

If only they never talked, what a sweet affair she could have with this man. But he wouldn't keep quiet, and she couldn't.

His tongue flickered in her mouth and her blood warmed. In all her life, Manda Raine had never been afraid of anyone. But what trickled through her heart now made her very much afraid. And confused. She felt like a downy chick just hatched, one who stared at the big sky and wondered what it meant.

He eased away from her. His gaze, clear behind the glass of the spectacles, was remote. She closed her hands around his coat lapels, started to tug him gently into the cabin.

He remained firmly where he was and shook his head, his expression never changing.

Hurt flooded her, and confusion, like someone had just kicked the downy chick aside with an unkind boot. She snatched her hands away and bathed him in a glare.

He looked down at her a moment longer, then silently turned and walked away.

Manda Raine should have flooded him with scathing invectives or, at the very least, given him a roundhouse biff in the jaw. But she could only stand helplessly while he, a stuck-up Englishman, strode away like he didn't care one whit about her.

Manda turned and kicked her bunk. She kicked and kicked until her foot hurt.

When she stamped out of her cabin again, limping a little, she spied her sister-in-law standing in the passage, sympathy in her light green eyes.

"Do you want to talk?" Honoria asked her.

Manda's rage focused into one shout. "No! I don't want to talk—to anyone—ever again!"

She raced past Honoria and up the stairs. She knew she'd hurt Honoria's feelings, but she was past caring. Ignoring Henderson, and her brother, and everyone else, she took refuge in the shadows and busily worked the sails and ropes, things she knew would not confuse her and make her insides feel rubbed raw.

Christopher watched the *Argonaut* draw ever closer. For a day and a night, the other ship had chased them, gaining slowly. He knew that his men knew the *Starcross* could outrun Ardmore if Christopher

251

wanted to. They also knew that Christopher Raine never did anything without good reason. If Christopher wanted James Ardmore to catch them, then Ardmore catching them must be to their advantage. Or so they hoped.

By sunset of the second day, the *Argonaut* had drawn close enough to send a signal. Her gun ports were propped open, black holes of metal glinting in the sun's rays. Christopher resolutely kept his ports shut.

St. Cyr eyed the flags fluttering from the *Argonaut*'s forward rigging through his spyglass. Christopher stood next to him, hands on the rail, waiting.

"He wants to board," St. Cyr reported. "And meet with you."

Christopher gave a curt nod. Not surprising. Ardmore would want to confront Christopher face-to-face.

"Tell him he may come over," he said. "But only if he brings his wife."

St. Cyr looked at him straight-faced. "Do we have the flags for that?"

"Have a messenger row over and bring them back."

St. Cyr nodded, turned, gave orders to the tense, waiting crew.

"Begging your pardon, sir," Colby drawled, flexing his large hands. "But aren't we going to fight?"

Christopher looked at Honoria. The dying sun caught highlights in her sable-black hair and whipped her thin dress around her deliciously shapely limbs.

"No," he answered, holding her gaze. "We are not. We are going to give to James Ardmore exactly what he's come for."

Chapter Sixteen

"I'll not be going back with him, Christopher."

Honoria spoke quietly, but her eyes burned with furious anger. Christopher fixed part of his attention on her and part on the tiny sparks of light that moved toward them, lanterns on the gig that brought James Ardmore and his wife to the *Starcross*. He could see the glint of Diana Ardmore's bright red hair in the twilight.

Honoria pursued tartly, "Are you ordering me to go back with him?"

She wanted to argue. Christopher was not in the mood. "I'm giving you the choice."

Her fine brows arched. "Excellent. Then we know where we stand."

Her lips were pale pink in the half-dark. Christopher could not help but lean down and press a kiss to them.

Jennifer Ashley

Her mouth moved with the kiss, her desire never far away. He said he left the choice to her, but his heart didn't want him to. She might decide that returning to her house in Charleston, to baths scented with rosewater and servants bringing her things on trays, was best for her. Christopher needed to make her see that it wasn't.

The small boat bumped the ship. Christopher kept kissing Honoria until he felt certain that Ardmore had seen them.

The *Starcross* had a shallow stair built right into its hull, and the gig tied up next to it. St. Cyr let down ropes so those in the boat could pull themselves up. Christopher had ordered a harness made ready to hoist Mrs. Ardmore aboard, but she climbed after her husband, hands confident on the ropes.

At last Ardmore stood facing him on the deck. Christopher supposed that a meeting between admirals of rival navies must be similar to this. Tense politeness, exaggerated courtesy. All false. They wanted to fight, and pretended they didn't.

Ardmore had brought with him another officer, the small Irishman called Ian O'Malley. He also brought a barrel of water, which was hoisted aboard, the wood enticingly wet.

"Heard you'd run short," he said.

Christopher looked into eyes as cool as Honoria's. They resembled each other, the brother and sister, both with midnight-black hair and ice-green eyes. They also shared the arrogant curl to the mouth and the faint sarcasm beneath a polite Southern drawl.

"We were becalmed longer than I anticipated,"

Christopher replied. He made a brief bow to Diana. "Mrs. Ardmore. Pleased to see you again."

She nodded in return, her fine eyes revealing nothing.

The deck of the brigantine was crowded as usual, the masts, rigging, and windlasses taking most of the space, even though the windlass wheel was stowed when not in use. He and Ardmore stood close on the only open space, while Diana was separated from them by a protrusion from the deck below. Honoria had moved to the stern to watch, her expression mulish.

Ardmore shifted his frosty gaze to his sister, then back to Christopher. "I assume you invited Mrs. Ardmore with me so I wouldn't order my ship to open fire while I was here."

"True," Christopher admitted.

"What gives me the assurance you won't fire on the *Argonaut*?"

"My word." Christopher flicked his gaze to the distant ship. "I believe your son and stepdaughter are with you, am I right?" He turned to Diana, who nodded reluctantly. "I thought so. I am not barbaric enough to shoot innocent children."

"Kind of you," Ian O'Malley broke in. His eyes flashed in mirth. "Though the lass Isabeau isn't so innocent. She can climb halfway up to the fighting top soon as your back is turned."

Diana looked slightly pained. Christopher allowed himself a brief smile.

"You know why I'm here," Ardmore said, impatient. He looked pointedly at Honoria, who returned the gaze with the same belligerent expression.

The gusting wind tugged the tail of Christopher's hair. "If you want to speak to her, I have no objection."

Ardmore gave him a narrow look. "We've other things to talk about first. You want to go below, or discuss it in front of your men?"

"I trust my crew," Christopher returned. "But it might be safer for you if we went below."

Ardmore gave a nod. "I believe you. Diana, stay here with Honoria."

"Not likely," Diana retorted. "I don't trust either of you to keep things amicable, and I want to know what transpires. Therefore, I am going with you."

James raised his eyebrows at his wife, but he did not argue. It seemed to Christopher that he and Ardmore shared one thing in common: wives who had trouble with the vow of obedience.

"Whatever you like," Christopher said, and led the way to the stern.

In the end, Manda, Diana, Henderson, St. Cyr, and Honoria joined the two captains in the crowded chart room around the bare table. Ardmore had also brought a small cask of brandy with him. Henderson broached it and handed around cups.

The discussion that followed surprised no one. Ardmore knew that Christopher was going after the gold of the *Rosa Bonita* and had come to stop him. Christopher asked him how he planned to do so.

"Sink you," Ardmore said dryly. "I have room on the *Argonaut* for you and your crew. I'll take you to port, let you go. It took you a long time to find and outfit this ship. I imagine it will take you longer to acquire another."

Christopher studied the golden hue of the brandy, which blended into the copper cup. It was a sin to drink brandy out of such a vessel, but he hadn't laid in the crystal. Honoria would try to remedy that, of course, next port they reached.

"You'd have a fight," he said casually. "My men are itching for one. We'd not sit tamely and let you blow us out of the water."

James leaned forward, his eyes dark in the shadows. "I outgun you, I outman you, I can outrun you. You won't win a fight against the *Argonaut*."

Christopher shrugged, as though tension weren't crawling up and down his back. "You know, I've heard that privateer ships are prevailing against English frigates in the war between America and England. Ships with fewer guns."

"Yes," Ardmore agreed. "I am one of those prevailing. You won't stand against me. You fight, I sink you. You fight hard, there will be deaths on your hands."

Christopher drank brandy, set the cup down. Ardmore hadn't touched his. "You would be firing at a ship containing your own sister," he pointed out.

"I know that. Are you prepared to let her die for your Mexican gold?"

Christopher managed a smile. "You don't need to use Honoria as a hostage for my good behavior. We'll send the women and children out to sea before we fight."

"Or Honoria can return to the *Argonaut*," James said in a hard voice. "It is her choice. She can come with me, or stand by you while I sink you."

Honoria's voice lashed from the corner. "Don't you

dare talk about me like I'm not here, James Ardmore. Why do you want that gold, anyway? What would you do with it?"

James turned slowly to her. The icy fury between them could have frozen the air. "Give it to the American navy," he answered. "They need all the help they can get."

"Very patriotic of you," Honoria snapped. "How do you know the gold is still there? It's been four years. Some other pirate has no doubt stumbled upon it and snatched it up."

"That is a risk," Christopher said.

"One I am willing to take," Ardmore added.

"I have a much better idea, James," Honoria said coldly. "Why don't you go away? You are not wanted here. There have been no acts of piracy committed since I've been on this ship, so you've no need to be here. Go hunt pirates somewhere else."

Ardmore's voice went even quieter. "This isn't a game, Honoria."

"Of course it is! You are men. You make everything into a game. You are like cocks strutting around a barnyard, competing to see who can crow the loudest."

Diana spoke for the first time. "The comparison is apt."

"Ladies," Ardmore began in freezing tones.

"No, James, you will not shut us out," Honoria said. "We have as much at stake as do you. I am staying with Christopher. He is my husband. Sink us and be damned to you."

St. Cyr looked pained. Henderson had not said a

word. Manda looked angry enough to shoot Ardmore right there.

"I will do it, Honoria," Ardmore said. "Be certain you're willing to die for him."

Honoria flicked her gaze to Christopher. There was no undying devotion in her eyes, just flaming anger. "I will stay with my husband, James. I took a vow. Loyalty means something to me."

Ardmore gave her a cold look. "I suppose by that remark you mean it means nothing to me. You've always been wrong about that." He returned his hard gaze to Christopher. "If that was the gauntlet you've thrown down, then so be it. You go after the gold, I sink you."

Christopher traced the rim of his cup. "And if I tell you I have no intention of going after the gold, you'll follow me anyway, to make certain?"

"Yes," Ardmore said.

"Seems like a lot of trouble for you and your men."

Ardmore at last lifted his cup, sipped the brandy. "You are forgetting something. I know where the gold is. You sail off, I'll simply take the gold out myself."

Christopher let out a short laugh. "You know *approximately* where the gold is. That's a different thing from knowing exactly."

"Then you can lead me to it." Ardmore took another sip of brandy. "Or I can sink you, take you prisoner, and force you to tell me."

"You'll have a hell of a fight if you try," Manda told him, tight anger in her voice.

"That sounds fine," Ardmore said. "Your crew aren't the only ones spoiling for a fight."

"Well, you'll have one, James," Honoria spat.

Both Manda and Christopher's wife looked angry enough to crawl over the table and throttle Ardmore on the spot. Henderson regarded his captain just as belligerently as did Honoria and Manda. Only St. Cyr retained a neutral expression, sipped his brandy.

Christopher started to laugh. Low and sounding of rumbling gravel, he let his laugh gradually fill the room. Manda and Honoria stared at him, furious. Ardmore flicked him a cold glance.

"End of game, Ardmore," Christopher said. "There will be no fight, no sinking, no prisoners. If you want the damned gold, you can have it. I'll lead you there, take what you like." He stopped laughing, drained his cup, gestured with it at Ardmore. "In return, you'll agree to stay the hell out of my life."

"Christopher!" Honoria began.

Christopher ignored her. "I want my wife, my freedom, my ship. Anything else, I don't care about." He leaned forward. "You get the gold, I get my life."

Ardmore gave Honoria one long, measuring look. She returned the gaze, unrepentant.

He held out his hand to Christopher over the table. "Done," he said.

"Christopher," Honoria said from where she reclined on the bunk.

Her husband stopped in the act of untying his shirt. His muscles tensed, his gaze went watchful. "What?"

He'd not spoken to Honoria since the meeting in the chart room hours and hours before. James, on the other hand, had demanded to talk with her. He'd requested this of Christopher, if you please. Honoria had flat refused.

Diana had been distressed, but Honoria had taken her aside and explained her choice until Diana had understood. She'd not liked it, but she'd departed with James without further argument.

Mr. Henderson had gone back to the *Argonaut* with them. James had looked Henderson up and down and informed him he still had a job on the *Argonaut* if he wanted it. Honoria had thought for a moment that Henderson would tell James to go to the devil. Mr. Henderson had threatened to quit on him more than once.

This time, however, Henderson had nodded to James and climbed down into the waiting boat. He'd avoided looking at Manda. Manda had remained stubbornly at the tiller, refusing to watch them go.

Honoria sighed, wondering why Henderson had chosen to break Manda's heart. Probably because he was a man.

Christopher interrupted her thoughts. "What do you want to ask me, my wife?"

He slid his shirt from his body, muscles working. She lost herself in admiration a moment, then remembered what she was about.

"Do you love me?" she asked.

He laid the shirt carefully on the chair. "You know the answer."

She watched the sway of his wheat-blond braid as he leaned to tug off his boots. The single lantern shadowed the curve of his spine, the hollows at the small of his back.

261

Clad only in his breeches, he sat down on the bed. The quilts separated her from him, but his warmth touched her through them. She ran her gaze over the scarred, silver-white flesh where unknown villains had scraped his skin from his ribs.

"Perhaps I am asking the wrong question," she said.

His gray eyes were watchful. "What do you mean by that?"

"Christopher, why on earth did you agree to give James the gold?"

His brows went up. "That's an abrupt change of subject."

"Not really. Why did you?"

He shrugged. She traced the movement all the way across his shoulder blades. "Maybe because I don't give a damn about it."

"But it's gold!"

Christopher slanted her a smile. "Mercenary little thing, aren't you? You wanted me to use the gold to buy you pretty trinkets?"

"That is not what I meant. You struggled to hide it, you were arrested for it."

"That was a long time ago."

"Christopher!" She sat up straight. "The point is, you let James win."

His sun-colored brows tilted upward. "Did I?"

"Yes. Do not smile at me like you've done something clever. If you think you can mislead him or outrun him, you're wrong. He is right, he will find you and sink you. He will not much care whether I am aboard. He'll think it no more than I deserve."

Christopher rested his broad hands on the bunk on

either side of her. His breath soothed the curls at her forehead. "You smell nice," he murmured, aggravatingly not answering her. "Did you enjoy your bath?"

She nodded. James's gift had given them enough water to spare for a sponge bath. She'd tipped a little dried lavender in the bowl and reveled in brushing the scented water all over herself.

His eyes darkened. "I'm sorry I missed it."

Honoria began to be sorry, too. She could picture him drawing the dripping sponge across her naked body, tracing the path of the droplets first with his fingertips, then with his tongue.

A bead of perspiration rested on the hollow of his upper lip. She could lick it away . . .

She drew back, throat dry. "You are deliberately distracting me."

He feigned surprised. "Distracting you from what?"

"We were speaking of James, and why you gave in to him."

"Oh that. I thought we were finished."

"I still do not understand why you agreed."

The candlelight played warmth through his eyes, but behind the warmth lay a glint of something she could not identify.

"Do you find it so hard to believe that I am willing to give up the gold?" he asked.

"Yes."

He chuckled. "Because I'm a pirate? Who will do anything for a few pieces of silver? You read too many books."

"It is gold, not silver." She tried to give him a stern look. "What I do not believe is what you told James,

263

that you'd give up the treasure for me. That's why I asked if you loved me."

"What I said was I'd give it up for you and for my freedom," he corrected. "I think both those things are worth a pile of gold."

"How romantic of you," she said.

"No, practical. I'm not willing to die for a cave full of ingots. I have enough money. What I haven't had enough of is you."

"Manda and Mr. St. Cyr seemed to capitulate easily enough."

He gave her an exasperated look. "You aren't going to give this up, are you?"

"I simply want to understand."

"No you don't. You're angry because I didn't tell your brother to go to the devil." He pointed a finger at her. "You have a feud going with him, I don't."

"He arrested you and took away everything you had!"

Christopher rubbed his sinewy hand over his face. "Sweetheart, in my line of work, you learn a few simple rules. Stay alive, don't succumb to greed, and let go of past mistakes. I need to be alert at all times, which I can't be if I'm brooding about revenge or fixed on too big a prize."

"Like the Mexican gold."

"Like the Mexican gold. Not worth the effort."

She rested her chin on her knees. "You are still very forgiving," she remarked.

"I thought you understood. I *wanted* Ardmore to arrest me back then. I had three ships. I sent Manda and St. Cyr off in different directions and ran a little slower so your brother would pursue me, not them. It worked—Manda and St. Cyr got away."

She stared at him. He spoke in a matter-of-fact voice, dismissing a long chase through black waves, his ship sinking under him as James blasted cannon shot through it, his capture, being condemned to death. He'd been saved from the hangman by pure chance, then had to claw his way back to existence, braving murderers and God knew what else in his long journey home.

"You were ready to die for them," she whispered.

He shielded his gaze. "Of course I was. As they were for me."

The ache in her throat tightened. He spoke so casually about his willingness to sacrifice himself for his sister and his friends. Not many men would readily face death for anyone, let alone shrug and say "Oh well, it worked out for the best." It touched her and infuriated her at the same time.

"You let him catch you all those years ago," she said. "And you let him catch you now." She brushed her thumb over his cheekbone, gently forcing him to meet her gaze. "What are you protecting this time?"

He smiled, but his eyes hid whatever thoughts he didn't want her to see. "You, angel."

"Because you love me?"

"We've been through that."

"How do you know that you love me?"

His smile began to fade. "Honoria, don't you think we've talked about our feelings long enough?"

265

She frowned. "We haven't even begun to talk about our feelings."

He rolled his eyes. "Bloody hell. You mean there's more?"

"Of course there's more. You're avoiding the subject."

His strong body pressed her into the pillows. "You know I must love you. I haven't thrown you out the window like I did the bedding, no matter how many damn fool questions you ask me."

She held on to her courage. "That is not an answer."

He suddenly pounded fists into the thick quilts, his temper finally cracking. "Damn you, Honoria. *This* is why women drive men insane. You accuse us of avoiding your questions, then you never believe us when we do answer."

"I just want to know."

"All right." He held up his hands in defeat. "All right, I'll tell you how I know I love you." He leaned to her again, gray eyes hot. "I know because when I was half dead thousands of miles from home, you were all I could think about. I thought of you last thing before I went to sleep and the first thing when I woke up. I thought about the way you look only at me, like I alone exist." He smoothed the curls on her forehead. "I thought about how green your eyes were, and how sweet your lips taste. I thought about the lovely noises you make when I'm inside you."

He leaned even closer to her, resting his hands on the wall behind her. "I stayed alive to find you again. So I could look at you and taste you and feel you taking me into you. I stayed alive because of you." He pressed her down into the bed, his lips an inch from hers. "That is how I know I love you. So, for God's sake, stop asking questions and let me have my husbandly way with you."

Chapter Seventeen

She stared at him, lips parted, her heart beating hard. His breath still smelled of the brandy he'd drunk with James. His revelation stunned her, and yet at the same time gave her a wash of joy.

He'd thought of her, he'd worked his way back to her, he wanted her. She hadn't quite believed he'd returned for anything but the gold and his sister, but the hard light in his eyes now told her differently. He'd wanted everything, of course, as he'd told her before, but he truly wanted her.

"It isn't fair," she whispered.

He climbed onto the bed, ducking under the low ceiling. "I just gave up a fortune in gold to your brother. I am no longer interested in what's fair."

Before she could explain what she'd meant, he gathered up the nightdress and ripped it from her body.

She knelt there, shivering, while he tossed the garment away and looked her over with possessive eyes.

She wasn't certain what excited her more, Christopher slow and teasing, or Christopher abrupt and wild.

He wrapped her hair around his fists and pulled her to him. He did not bother to gentle his kiss. Christopher angry was dangerous, and yet he excited her. He held his strength in for her, and it was that tension, a volcano choosing not to explode, that made her heart beat hard and fast.

He pulled her legs out from under her and landed on top of her full length on the bunk.

No teasing this time. He yanked open his breeches, pressed her legs apart, and entered her, full and hard, without waiting to bring her to readiness first. No matter, she was already plenty wet. She held him with tight fingers as he drove and drove into her.

She shouted her climax just before he shouted his. He kept going, showing her indisputably that he was her husband and that she belonged to him.

After things quieted, he stayed inside her, kissing with lips gentled for her, the frenzy winding down. She basked in it, her body happy and tired.

Long after the moon had moved across the space of the window, Christopher eased out of her, tossed his breeches away, and dragged the quilts up over both of them.

She turned her head on the pillow, kissed him where he lay next to her. "Christopher," she whispered.

He made a growl low in his throat. "No more talking," he snapped, and then he fell asleep.

Or pretended to. The snore was a bit unconvincing.

* * *

The wind remained fresh, pushing the ships ever westward. Honoria scowled into the obliging breeze, wishing the sky would not remain so fair, the sea so annoyingly calm. A good storm could send them way off course, or perhaps separate the ships enough so that James would lose them in the dark.

Her fury at her brother had not abated. She longed to corner him and tell him exactly what she thought of him. But she would shout at him when *she* wanted to, not at James's pleasure.

She eyed the *Argonaut* sailing several ship lengths astern, a sleek, beautiful ship. Diana was there with her two children. Diana had softened James the tiniest bit, Honoria had to admit, but it would be a long time before Honoria could look upon James with anything other than shaking fury.

Honoria's own husband proved to be just as arrogant and irritating as her brother in the days that followed. If ever she tried to continue the conversation they'd begun about being in love, Christopher would stare at her as though he had no idea what she was talking about. Questions about what they would do after they led James to the gold were met with "I'm-too-busy-to-talk-to-you-now" answers.

Poor Manda also grumbled about men under her breath. After Henderson's departure, she remained in a towering fury and unapproachable by anyone, even Christopher. The sailors learned to give her a wide berth. Christopher endured her biting sarcasm with indifference. He either had a hide three feet thick, or he was used to her rages. Honoria, after her brief attempt to draw Manda into a woman-to-woman talk, decided to leave her alone. Clearly the lady did not want to discuss her troubles. It must run in the family.

They neared Christopher's hiding place without further adventure—except in private in their cabin. There Christopher introduced Honoria to worlds of pleasure she'd never known existed. When she and Christopher had first consummated their marriage four years before, she had thought she'd learned what it was to be with a man. But she now realized that their brief encounter in Christopher's cell had been just that, brief and succinct.

Christopher showed her how he could take his time, loving her in slow caresses, nearly bringing her to climax, then dragging her back to mere heart-pounding anticipation. He'd tease her for a long while before finally giving in to her pleas—usually with a satisfied chuckle—and taking her fully. Other nights, he came to her fast and furious until she screamed with joy.

He also taught her to pleasure him with her hands and mouth. She learned the heady joy of bringing him to readiness and even to climax before he could thrust inside her.

Her newfound skills made her feel just a little bit smug, especially whenever he seized her in his arms and kissed her like he could not stop himself. *My pirate husband,* she'd think. *You have been conquered.*

At least, in bed. Outside the bedroom, he never let her win anything.

* * *

They sighted the island three days after James had joined them. Rising out of the water in a series of cliffs, the small landmass spread its arms around a tiny cove too shallow for the ships.

Through the spyglass, Honoria saw thick green vegetation and thin silver streams of waterfalls pouring down cliffs. It reminded her a bit of Jamaica, which she'd visited with Paul years earlier, though this island was remote from that one.

"Plenty of fresh water," Christopher said. "We'll fill up." He slanted a glance at Honoria. "And my wife can have a bath."

"We all can," Honoria answered firmly. "And have our clothes washed. And not before time, too. You should order it, Christopher."

"Honoria," Christopher began in his warning tone.

"Well, I am mighty tired of smelling everyone," she continued. "I am beginning to be able to identify whoever stands behind me from his odor. If I am to remain on this ship, regular baths will have to become mandatory."

Christopher surveyed her with a cool gaze. "Are you trying to incite a mutiny?"

"Of course not. I am trying to preserve the final shreds of my sanity. And my sense of smell."

He studied her another moment, his face expressionless. Then he turned to his crew, cupped his hands around his mouth, and shouted. "New orders! Every man—and woman—on this ship reports to the springs for a bath. A full bath, with soap. Anyone

THE CARE & FEEDING OF PIRATES

shirking this duty gets ten lashes." He looked down at Honoria. "All right?"

She scowled. "You did not have to take me so literally."

The men muttered among themselves, some casting baleful glances at Honoria. One man shouted, "Shall we bring a mirror and primp?"

Another laughed. He sang out in a high falsetto, "Ooo, I'll bring me best perfume!"

More laughter. A few mimed patting curled hair; another, scrubbing himself all over with a brush.

"Get back to work," Christopher called to them, but he did not sound angry.

They went ashore in three small rowboats, two from the *Argonaut* and one from the *Starcross*. Christopher did not allow Honoria in the first landing, preferring, he said, to ensure that everything was safe.

"Pirates or smugglers might have set up camp here," he explained. "I haven't seen any smoke, but the island has many hidden valleys. And anyone ashore will have seen us approach."

James appeared to have the same idea. He rowed Diana over to the *Starcross* to wait with Honoria for their signal that it was safe for the ladies to come ashore.

It was Diana who fumed as James and the others rowed away. Honoria had thought Christopher's plan sensible, although she admitted a burning curiosity. If hostile pirates or smugglers had taken up residence on the island, it was best to let Christopher and James deal with them first.

Jennifer Ashley

She said as much to Diana. The tall woman hung over the rail, her hair loosened by the wind. "Oh, yes," Diana said waspishly. "But they get all the fun of it, don't they? By the time we reach the island, it will be crowded with sailors. And what if they meet *friendly* smugglers, who greet them with a huge barrel of rum? We shouldn't see them for a day or so in that case, and they certainly wouldn't remember to send for us."

Honoria laughed. "That is a bit far-fetched, Diana."

"Not really," Diana said darkly. "A band of pirates once tried to befriend James by offering him rum and a share of their take, as well as other—female—enticements."

Honoria raised her brows and spoke in her best Charleston-lady fashion. "Nonsense. I'm certain their bribes made James that much more determined to arrest them. And do not worry about female enticements. James does not like loose women."

At least, she did not think so. In the past, James had usually approached women because of some ulterior motive, such as vengeance or the need for information. He rarely chased a lady for the pure pleasure of it—the ladies of Charleston had found him maddeningly evasive. Now, of course, he was devoted entirely to Diana.

She turned back to the green expanse of the island and did not voice her other thought, *What about Christopher?* He was a charming rogue, and Honoria was not naive enough to think herself the only woman he'd ever had in his life. She'd not seen him for nine long years between their first meeting and

274

their second, and then, after their marriage, he'd disappeared for four years to lands far away. What he'd done during those intervals she could not imagine, and she did not really want to know.

Not really. Did she?

She bit her lip, craning to see the dwindling shapes of the boats as they neared the beach.

The landing party found the island pleasingly deserted. It had no name, lay off the main shipping routes, and boasted little but the fresh water that fell from cliff tops to gushing pools below. The trees here were not strong enough for masts, and the tiny harbor offered no protection from storms.

Christopher knew that pirates and other travelers rested here from time to time and replenished their water stores, but they found no sign that any had set up more than a very brief habitation. And no one had been here in a long while.

James Ardmore strode by Christopher's side as Christopher led him on the path that would take them to where he'd hidden the gold. Ardmore every so often would crane his neck to look up at the cliffs, then cast his gaze behind him. Christopher knew that Ardmore wondered whether Christopher's men would try some treachery, and he wondered the same about Ardmore's.

The summer day was fine and hot. Humid air pressed them under the junglelike trees and sweat trickled freely down Christopher's back. Ardmore wore a coat and no shirt beneath; his skin shone with perspiration.

The ascent was steep, following a faint trail, badly overgrown. The thick vegetation around them, the buzz of insect life, and the heat that poured down on them served to confuse direction. Manda and Ian O'Malley led the little party, cutting the path, the two captains climbing behind. Though Ardmore had brought him ashore in the first boatload, Henderson had remained below on the beach. That had been wise, Christopher thought. Manda had a knife.

"You see what I meant," Christopher said, gesturing to their surroundings. "Knowing approximately where the gold is doesn't mean knowing exactly."

"And you remember after four years?" Ardmore asked with much skepticism.

"I think so. But even if I don't remember, you win."

"Not if we don't find that gold. Or evidence that someone else made off with it. I wouldn't put it past you to lead me false, then wait until I'm gone and suddenly 'find' it."

Christopher drew his sleeve across his forehead. "That won't happen. You'd ambush me and follow me to make sure."

Ardmore gave a curt nod. "That's right."

"No man will ever accuse you of not being thorough, Ardmore."

Ardmore slowed, allowing O'Malley and Manda to surge ahead. Christopher slowed with him.

"It's interesting," Ardmore said in his slow drawl, "how willing you are to lead me to this treasure. Your crew, too."

"The gold's probably gone. It's been four years."

Ardmore's eyes narrowed. The canopy of leaves shadowed the two men like a dark green cave. "So you'll give me the Mexican gold if I leave you and my sister alone?"

Christopher nodded. Ahead, the sound of O'Malley's and Manda's voices and the ring of their knives against branches grew fainter.

"Maybe you don't believe Honoria is worth a shipload of gold," Christopher said. "But I do."

"How romantic of you."

"Honoria said much the same thing. But think about this, Ardmore. Would your own wife be worth it?"

Ardmore stilled. He was a man who could go utterly still, and under the trees, the breeze did not even touch the strands of his hair.

Christopher had not missed the way Ardmore looked at the beautiful, red-haired Diana. The times he'd met Ardmore before, first as a colleague, then as an enemy, Ardmore had cared for nothing and no one. That seemed to have changed.

From what Christopher knew about the man, Ardmore had been captured by pirates at a young age, and then turned pirate himself. Whatever had happened to him on that pirate vessel had scarred him. He'd become a pirate hunter after his brother's wife had been killed, joining his brother in his quest for vengeance.

Now the ice had thawed—a little. James Ardmore, the feared pirate hunter, now cared for something more than his fanatic pursuit of pirates.

"Yes," Ardmore said, words clipped. "Diana would be worth it."

"She'd be happy to know that." Christopher waved away a fly who thought his sweat was just what it needed. "Honoria is worth it to me."

"You love her," Ardmore said, still dubious.

"Yes," Christopher returned. "Don't you?"

Ardmore gave him a long look. For a time the two men studied each other, green eyes looking into cool gray, neither yielding.

At last Ardmore turned and resumed climbing.

Christopher watched the other man's back as they continued up the hill. James and Honoria shared a streak of obstinacy a mile wide.

By late afternoon, the climbers had reached a break in the trees. They stood on a cliff, a jut of rock that ran back into a deep crevice. Christopher peered across the narrow valley. Insects droned around him, birds and unseen reptiles rustled in the brush.

If he turned to his left, he could see the cove far below and the glittering water of open sea. A boat was just shipping its oars to land on the beach. Seamen scrambled over the side to pull it ashore. Christopher did not need his spyglass to see the flash of sun on one red head and one black. "Damn."

Ardmore snapped around. He raised his spyglass, stared through it at the landing boat. "Who gave that order?" he asked incredulously.

Christopher watched Henderson approach the boat and lift Honoria over the gunwale. "Which of them do you think it was? Yours or mine?"

Ardmore shot him a dark look. "Likely both." He

clapped his spyglass shut. "Do we go on or back? We can't reach the top and get down again before dark."

"Go back." Christopher gestured across the narrow valley to the next jutting cliff. "This is the wrong ridge. We should be on that one."

Manda, who had just come trotting back to them, stopped short, her black hair swinging. "What? You'd better be joking."

"I was here only once, four years ago, and I was in a hurry. We took the wrong path at the bottom."

Manda rolled her eyes, sat down on the grass. Her shirt was stained with sweat and green streaks. O'Malley also sank to his heels, looking slightly put out.

On the next cliff, a waterfall fell hundreds of feet to the valley below. Beneath it, Christopher knew, though he could not see from here, a series of pools fed into one another, then splashed over black rocks to empty into the sea. "It's there," he said.

Ardmore studied the waterfall, then looked back at Christopher. "It had better be."

"We'll go tomorrow," Christopher answered. "It's too late to get there tonight. We'll camp on shore, start early."

He turned away. Manda shot him a pained look, then levered herself to her feet and fell into step behind him.

Christopher hadn't missed the hard glance Ardmore had sent his direction. Ardmore didn't trust him; he expected Christopher to lead him astray or into ambush. Christopher honestly had gone the

Jennifer Ashley

wrong direction at the beginning, though he'd not announced his mistake until an hour after he'd realized it. Ardmore needed to be kept off guard.

He heard Ardmore and O'Malley speaking in low voices behind him. Christopher decided it a good idea that he and Manda alternate watches that night.

By the time they reached the cove again, the sun hung low above the horizon and the two women were nowhere to be seen.

280

Chapter Eighteen

St. Cyr volunteered the information. "Both Madame Ardmore and Madame Raine expressed the wish to bathe. They went to the pools. Mr. Henderson accompanied them."

"Henderson?" Ardmore growled. His tanned face darkened still further, and a murderous light entered his eyes.

"To keep them from coming to harm," St. Cyr finished. His countenance remained expressionless, but Christopher swore he saw the man's eyes twinkle.

Ardmore was already striding toward the path that led to the pools. Christopher jogged to catch up with him. Without speaking, the two men pushed their way through the undergrowth, boots sliding on the damp rocks.

The sound of thundering water drew nearer. Christopher saw evidence of the ladies' passing—broken branches and a piece of lavender lace from Honoria's gown.

Christopher knew by heart each dress Honoria wore, and how each one made her look. The cream-colored muslin hugged her hips deliciously, the coral one made her look like a ripe peach he wanted to bite. The light green dress pushed her breasts high and had little black buttons all down the front. He often amused himself imagining unbuttoning all those buttons.

What he liked best about his wife's dresses was removing them from her. She would have stripped the lavender one from her body by now, and be splashing in the clear pool. Water would bead on her lashes, trickle down her throat to the crevice between her breasts. She would lazily swim across the little pool, turning in the sunshine. She was waiting for him there, all sweet and wet, skin slick with water . . .

With Henderson standing guard over her. Christopher's footsteps quickened along with his pulse.

The cool spray from the waterfall beaded on the plants where the path narrowed and ended at a huge boulder. Mr. Henderson leaned against this rock, his gaze on the approaching men. Ardmore tried to peer past Henderson, but nothing could be seen beyond the boulder but more vegetation.

Christopher said dryly, "Noble of you to ensure the safety of the ladies, Henderson."

Henderson looked wooden. "Before you jump to conclusions, I am guarding the path. No one can get to the pools without climbing past me. Or would you prefer to let the sailors spy on your wives?"

The brush beyond the boulder moved, then Diana Ardmore climbed over the rock toward them. She was fully dressed with breeches and boots beneath her gown, as Christopher saw when she lifted the skirt to jump down. Henderson gallantly offered his hand, which she took with a grateful glance, before landing on the ground before her husband.

"James," she said, and smiled her dazzling smile. She must be the only person in the world ever happy to see James Ardmore. "Mr. Henderson has been gallantry itself," she continued, her blue eyes glowing. "So leave him alone, James."

"Mr. Henderson is always gallant," Ardmore drawled.

"Where is my wife?" Christopher asked her.

"She said she wanted to swim as long as she could."

Of course she would. Honoria had been nearly wild to submerge herself in a bath. Naturally, she would try to soak up as much water as she could in order to make up for lack of baths to come.

"You can go away now, Henderson," Christopher said.

Diana slipped her hand under Ardmore's arm and began steering him back the way they'd come. Henderson moved after them without a word. Christopher heard Diana asking about the gold before the noise of the water drowned out Ardmore's snarled reply.

Christopher climbed over the rock and pushed his way toward the pools. The waterfall thundered down about five hundred yards away, gushing water into rock-strewn rapids. The stream rushed down the hill, but at one place backed up into a little pond, where the current slowed and a bather could swim without danger.

In this pool, he found his wife.

She hadn't bound up her hair, only pulled it back, and the black tail floated on the water. Her body, white and sleek and graceful, gleamed in a slice of sunshine as she swam across the pool.

She did not see him at first. Christopher stood upon the bank, supporting himself on the branch of a tree. She was so lovely, perfect like the carving of a goddess that adorned a ship's prow. Her white breasts mounded up from the water, tapering to dark tips. A brush of black hair dusted the split of her thighs. She rolled over, revealing smooth, creamy buttocks before she dove under the surface.

When she came up again, she saw Christopher. She pushed her hair out of her eyes. The ends hung down, concealing her breasts. "Hello, Christopher. Did you find the gold?"

His throbbing arousal told him to rip off his clothes and dive in with her. "No. We'll look again tomorrow."

His seductress smiled. "I imagine James is wild with impatience."

Christopher nodded. "I think he wanted to row up to the beach, find a huge chest labeled *Mexican Gold*, and haul it away with him."

She laughed. She was delectable. The water lapped her hips and her dark fall of hair curled wildly in the damp.

There was nothing for it. He stripped off his shirt

and boots, and his breeches soon followed. Bare, he slid into the pool, ignoring the sudden bite of cold water.

She waited while he swam to her, her green eyes taking in his every movement. He surfaced in front of her, rising to his full height.

The buoyancy of the water let him easily lift her. He breathed in her scent, fresh and clean like the water itself. She wrapped her legs around him, pressing herself against his hardness without letting it slip inside. She rubbed him a little, whether consciously or unconsciously, the little wretch.

Her heat belayed the chill of the water. He closed his eyes and kissed her, dipping his tongue inside her. She kissed him back, tasting him to the corners of his mouth, like he'd taught her.

He'd taught her so many things since he'd first met her. She'd been an innocent girl who'd gasped with shock when their lips had first touched. He'd given her a vast helping of carnality in the daintily tiled room of her Charleston town house. She'd been surprised by that carnality, but not at all unhappy.

The sweet girl tasted just as sweet now. He let her finish playing in his mouth, then he tilted her head back and nibbled his way along her neck.

"Christopher," she whispered. Her eyes were heavy, languorous.

"Mmmm?"

"I still feel as though I'm on the ship. As though the land is going up and down."

"You will for a while, before you get used to being still."

"Then I'll go back on the ship and have to get used to that all over again."

He looked up, smiled. "I'll just have to make you go up and down all the time. Then you'll always be used to it."

She buried her face in his shoulder. "I'd like that."

"Would you, brazen hussy?"

"I like how you make me feel. Is that so wrong?"

"I have no objection." He stroked her hair, squeezing the water from it. "Be brazen with me all you want."

She lifted her head. A spirited spark danced in her eyes. "We are married, after all, Christopher."

"You were brazen with me before you married me," he reminded her.

"Because I was in love with you."

He had no intention of beginning another discussion about whether she loved him. He kissed her to stop her talking.

Her clinging, wet body was doing wonderful things to him, but he delayed the satisfaction of taking her. He so rarely got to simply hold her. He knew he'd sprung back into her life out of nowhere and probably scared the piss out of her. He'd not had time to build her confidence in him, and her trust.

"Don't stay with me because it's your duty, Honoria," he said softly. "I don't want that. Go home with your brother if all you want is duty. Be dutiful to him, and leave me alone."

She raised her head and looked at him, eyes quiet. "You always tell me I should obey you."

"That's different." The cold water was not calming

his erection the slightest bit. "I like ordering you about. Not that you ever listen."

Her lashes were wet little points. "I never obey without question. What if your orders make no sense?"

"You should trust your husband to know what's best."

She snorted. "You're such a *man*, Christopher."

He took her hand and rested it around his arousal. It throbbed even hotter, hardening to its fullest length. "I think you can feel that."

She blushed rosy red. He steadied his fingers on her wrist and then made himself let go. She could do as she pleased.

She squeezed a little, experimenting. His heart squeezed, too.

She went on, "I meant that a man cannot possibly know what's best for a woman."

He closed his eyes, giving in to sensations. "Manda obeys my orders without question."

"Manda is used to you. She has learned when to listen to you and when to ignore you."

"True."

Honoria snuggled closer, her fingers moving along the length of the shaft. He lost the thread of what she was saying. He heard only her voice, the low Southern tones that always drove him wild.

"I imagine I'll learn when to listen and when to tell you to go to the devil."

"Glad to hear it," he said, jaw tight. She squeezed so hard he felt almost like he was inside her. "You keep doing that, you can stay with me as long as you want."

Her light green eyes held flecks of emerald. "I don't want to go home with James."

"He thinks differently."

She clenched her hand in emphasis. It felt marvelous. "I don't care one whit what he thinks. I am legally married to you, and he can't drag me around anymore."

So she'd claimed the marriage so she could get away from her obnoxious older brother, had she? Oh, well, as long as she just kept—holding—on.

The sun was sinking fast. If they didn't leave now, they'd have to scramble over rocks in near darkness. He found it difficult to care. He cared only that his wife was a lovely armful, and that she'd just declared she'd stay with him through thick and thin whether she liked it or not.

She was an obstinate, proud woman who made his heart dance with delight. He breathed her fragrance, springwater and honey and some delectable spice. He could never get enough of her.

She not only made his heart dance. His arousal danced, too, oh sweet, sweet Honoria. Gasping, he firmly removed her fingers from his shaft. The water made her light, and it was so easy to lift her and fit her over him.

That was it, they *fit* well. Their bodies knew they'd been made for each other. Their thoughts and their conversations got in the way sometimes, but their bodies knew. That's why they'd never been able to keep their hands off each other whenever they met.

He'd waited too long. She was so lovely, so slippery, and so warm. He drove into her once, twice, before he spilled his seed. She cried out, her eyes heavy, and he kissed her.

"I love you," he said, voice raw. "I don't give a damn whether you believe me."

"I believe you," she whispered.

Chapter Nineteen

Christopher kept her on shore with him that night, wanting her nearby. He'd slept with her every night for two weeks, a habit he didn't want to break. They wrapped themselves in blankets before the fire, she spooning against him for warmth.

The air chilled as the sky darkened. The fires were small, because dry wood was scarce. The flames popped and snapped, but Christopher found the glare soothing, and his eyes closed.

The fire and Honoria were the only soothing things about that beach. Even as he lay still with his wife, he could sense the tension of the crews, his men and Ardmore's. Gold lay near, and no matter how much Christopher feigned nonchalance, his crew wanted it and resented Ardmore taking it. If Christopher's men did what they were told, everything would go well, but the possibility existed for someone to forget the plan and start fighting for the money.

That was the trouble with gold. They needed to find the cache—or not find it—soon. He did not want to lose half his crew to violence over a stash that no longer existed.

The only reason he allowed himself to drift to sleep was that Manda was awake and watching his back. For four years, he'd missed the comfort of knowing he had Manda behind him. He very much liked having that comfort again.

He closed his eyes, kissed Honoria's fragrant hair, and sought slumber.

Manda leaned against the longboat and crossed her booted ankles. She let her gaze drift from the sleeping form of her brother to the bespectacled face of Alden Henderson, who stood not far away with Ardmore's boat.

Her blood boiled. She wished the damned man had stayed aboard the *Argonaut,* because seeing him again had made her realize she'd fallen in love with him. Manda Raine had never done anything so stupid in her entire life.

He had only traveled aboard the *Starcross* until he could meet up with his captain again. She'd known that. So why had it hurt so much when he'd wordlessly climbed down into the gig and gone back to his own ship?

It shouldn't matter. It shouldn't affect her like this. She'd endured Switton treating her like a caged animal without breaking down, but one dandified Englishman's rejection had sent her into a world of heartache she'd never experienced.

Of course, when she'd lain in Switton's locked room or been taken to the garden in the cage, she'd always believed in the back of her mind that Christopher would rescue her. He'd helped her through every hardship in her life, and he would again. Even when the half-reasonable part of her mind knew that Christopher was dead and gone long ago, something inside her had told her he'd come for her.

And then, unbelievably, she'd looked through the bars of the cage and seen Christopher standing there looking back at her. She'd almost choked in astonishment. She had no idea how he'd done it, but he'd come for her. He'd defeated even death. He could do anything. She'd always known so.

In the realm of love, however, she knew he could not help her. Manda was on her own, and the thought terrified her.

But then, Christopher adored that Southern, black-haired wench, who was James Ardmore's sister of all people. She glanced back at Christopher, wrapped in his blankets, one muscled arm resting on his wife's hip, and suppressed a chuckle. Christopher had the fond thought that he had the upper hand in his marriage, but Manda knew he bloody well didn't. The little wench had wrapped him around her pretty fingers, and Christopher was happily letting himself be ensnared.

Manda returned her gaze to the shadowy form of Henderson and found him gone.

Her heart missed a beat. She scanned the beach but found no sign of him.

The ocean sighed across the sand, the foam luminescent. Moonlight silhouetted the bare masts of both ships standing well offshore. Too far for cannonballs to reach the island, Christopher had insisted. Sleeping forms mounded by the fire, dark blankets like huge mushrooms on the sand. A few men wandered restlessly just outside the firelight. They eyed one another, tension rife. She looked everywhere for a pale smudge of blond hair, the gleam of spectacles, and saw none.

She heard a noise behind her, the sound of a scuffle. She whirled, drawing her knife.

Beyond the jutting end of the longboat, two men struggled in the shallow water. One was small and wiry. The other had shed his coat, his linen shirtsleeves pale in the darkness. Light glinted off his knife and his gold spectacles.

Henderson fought hard and silently, fending off the other man's knife blows with his own. She stood, frozen, watching for what seemed a long time before she threw everything to the wind and rushed to Henderson's rescue.

She splashed into the water, dragged the wiry man away from Henderson, and put her knife to the attacker's throat. Henderson backed away, panting, his shirtsleeve stained red.

Manda realized that the man she held was Ian O'Malley, James Ardmore's second in command.

"What the hell?" she began.

O'Malley glared at Henderson. "You trumped-up English twit. Who the devil's side are you on?"

"You tell me," Henderson said, his voice taut with anger. "I see you sneaking up on the woman I love, ready to stick your knife into her. What do you expect me to do? Stand back and watch?"

"Oh, you love *her* now, do you?" O'Malley asked, incredulous. "That's a change, Mr. High-and-Mighty, too good for any but the highest ladies."

"Do not change the subject," Henderson said, tight-lipped.

Manda stared at Henderson, dazed, but she did not let O'Malley go or move her knife.

"Why were you trying to kill her?" Henderson went on.

"I never was."

"You were going at her with a knife, plague take you. On Ardmore's orders?"

"No." The voice of James Ardmore broke the stillness behind them. He strode out of the firelight, Christopher right behind him.

She recognized that Christopher was in a towering rage and just containing himself. Ardmore was icily calm.

Henderson quivered with anger. The look he turned on Ardmore would have made a lesser man quail. "What did you tell him to do?" he demanded.

Ardmore's green eyes flicked from one combatant to the other. Behind them, near the fire, Diana and Honoria stood together, watching.

"I told O'Malley to capture her," Ardmore said. "She would not have been harmed."

"*He* would have been," Manda snarled, jerking her chin at O'Malley. "If he'd gotten near me."

"A risk I was willing to take," Ardmore answered.

"Oh, thanks, me so compassionate captain," O'Malley said.

"Taking a hostage?" Christopher asked, his voice deadly quiet.

"To ensure your good behavior. You're up to something, Raine."

Christopher silently turned to him. Manda held her breath, wondering if Ardmore had just spoken his last words.

Then Christopher took a step back, raised his shoulders in a deliberate, controlled shrug. "Take her, then."

Manda gaped at him. Henderson glared. Even Ardmore stared in astonishment. Christopher said, "Manda, let O'Malley go."

He was up to something, all right. Manda thought she knew what, but it would be a while before she could get him alone and make him tell her.

She trusted him enough to obey him now, no matter what she privately thought. She eased her knife from O'Malley's throat and set him on his feet.

The Irishman gingerly touched his neck as though checking for damage. "Much obliged, me darling."

Christopher turned to Ardmore. "You want assurance against my behavior, this will do it. Everyone knows I wouldn't make any move that would cause Manda harm." He held the other man with a long gaze. "But I don't trust you, either, Ardmore. So I'd like a hostage, too. Your wife."

Ardmore went still. The waves boomed loud in the sudden silence, oblivious to the tension on shore. Ardmore and Christopher looked at each other, captain to captain, enemy to enemy. Manda held her breath.

"You already took my sister," Ardmore pointed out.

"Your sister doesn't like you," Christopher answered. "And I have the feeling you'd sacrifice her for some scheme of your own, if you had to."

Ardmore's mouth set in a thin line. "You'd be wrong."

Manda watched Ardmore debate whether to pit his wife's safety against the chance that one of his own men would not do something stupid. Manda knew Christopher would never harm Diana—he wasn't like that—but Ardmore did not know. To him, Christopher was just another pirate.

Diana herself broke the silence. "It's all right, James. I'll go."

"No," Ardmore said in a hard voice.

"It makes sense," his wife continued. "If you both have someone, it will keep the peace."

"Good," Christopher said. "She can stay on the *Starcross*. Mrs. Colby will look after her until we finish."

"I'll go with her," Honoria said quickly.

Christopher shook his head. "No, you won't. I want you where I can keep an eye on you."

Honoria glared at him but did not argue. Ardmore looked on in silent fury.

"This is better," Christopher said to him. "If Manda knows your innocent wife's life is at stake, she will not try to kill your crew and take over your ship." He looked pointedly at O'Malley, who still rubbed his neck.

Ardmore took a step closer to Christopher. "If Diana is harmed in any way, know that Manda Raine will die very painfully."

Christopher's look was just as quiet. "I know." He turned away. "Henderson, row these ladies to their respective ships. Make sure you take the right lady to the right one."

"Not Henderson," Ardmore snapped.

"Why not?"

"You heard him say he was in love with your sister. I don't trust him."

"Better still. If he's fond of Manda, he won't harm her, and he won't harm Mrs. Ardmore on principle. He's a true gentleman. And Manda *probably* won't kick his teeth in."

That was true, Manda thought. Probably not.

Ardmore at last conceded, though he was clearly unhappy. It was his own fault, Manda thought heatedly. He'd started it by sending O'Malley against her. She only worried that Christopher could not keep a firm eye on the man without her there.

Henderson helped Diana into the rowboat with exaggerated care, then he and Manda pushed it from the beach. The crews dispersed, excitement over. As she climbed over the gunwale, Manda heard a snatch of conversation behind her.

"It's good to see you care so much for someone," Christopher was saying. "I always thought you were a coldhearted bastard."

"I am a coldhearted bastard," Ardmore replied. "I just happen to love my wife."

The boat ran up a wave, and nothing more could be heard but the rush of the sea.

* * *

Henderson left Diana aboard the *Starcross,* in care of a bewildered Mrs. Colby. Diana was carefully polite when she said her good-byes. So was Henderson.

Henderson rowed himself and Manda toward the *Argonaut,* Manda at the tiller. The moon was so bright that it easily lit their path to the next ship. Warm yellow lanterns outlined the *Argonaut* from bow to stern, and moonlight bathed it in a chill white glow.

Henderson continued to pull the oars, oblivious to Manda's scrutiny, his muscles straining against his shirt. He managed to be graceful even at this menial task.

Where was she supposed to start? Saying "So you love me, do you?" sounded trite and hopeless. She should have asked Honoria how she went about talking about her feelings. Manda had never learned.

Henderson stopped rowing. He shipped the oars, sitting back to catch his breath. The moonlight turned the lenses of his spectacles opaque.

"We're not there, yet," Manda said testily.

"I know." He drew a breath. "But I think we need to clear up a few things."

"Talk about our feelings, you mean?"

Even in the dark she saw him flush. "You heard me say I was in love with you. Very well, where are the sarcastic comments? Where is your derisive banter?"

Her heart pounded. "If you love me so much, why did you go back to the *Argonaut*?"

He rested his strong arms on his thighs, regarded her quietly. "Because all my things are there. I have a silk waistcoat and some boots that—" He broke off.

"Never mind. I wanted to fetch them. I'm quit of Ardmore. I told him so."

Her throat ached. "You are?"

"I told him why, too." He smiled, such a handsome smile. "I fell for a warrior woman. Me, the proper English gentleman."

The waves slapped gently at the hull, the tiller bounced a little. She wished she could see his eyes. "Why didn't you tell me?"

"And have you spit in my face? I didn't mean to say it back there. It slipped out when I saw O'Malley with his knife."

Manda let go of the tiller. They weren't moving anymore, only drifting on the waves. She climbed over benches until she could sit facing him. "I don't want to spit in your face."

"Or kick me in it. I've seen you kick." His smile broadened. "You knocked a man out with your bare feet. I admire your technique. And your legs. You have beautiful legs, Manda."

She felt her face heat. "Never mind my legs." So why was she so absurdly pleased that he liked them? "I thought you'd like only prim and proper ladies, like Honoria."

"So did I. I think—" He broke off, staring out at the dark water. "I think in the past I tried to court ladies like Honoria and Alexandra precisely because they were unattainable. I did not truly want them. I believe what I want is a bit of wildness in my life." He looked back at her. The spectacles still obscured his eyes. "No, what I want is you. I knew that as soon as I saw you."

Manda leaned forward and snatched off the damned spectacles. His eyes were fixed on her, clear gray, pupils wide in the dark. She did not really want to hear about how he courted other ladies. "So what are you going to do about it?"

He sat up straight, put his hand on his heart. "I am going to ask you, dear lady, to marry me."

Her jaw dropped. "What?"

"As soon as we make the next port. I have money; I'll obtain the license. All I need is a bride."

He was serious. Her heart pounded until she felt queasy. But his eyes were so warm, his smile rueful and handsome.

The smile was not all that was handsome about Alden Henderson. His broad shoulders filled out his fine shirt, and she knew what it felt like to be held in his strong arms. She swallowed. "I'm the illegitimate daughter of a freed slave."

"Yes, my family will be shocked. But they will come to accept it; they are kind people. They've already become used to the idea that I am a pirate hunter shipping out with the fugitive James Ardmore."

She barely heard his words, delivered in his proper English gentleman's voice. "All right," she interrupted. "I'll marry you."

His smile warmed. "You've made me the happiest man in the world, my dear."

He put his hands on her shoulders, drew her to him. "I won't make you happy," she babbled. "I'm a pirate. You're a pirate hunter."

His eyes darkened. "I think that arrangement is

working out nicely." He kissed her lips, then lifted her onto his lap. "I love your legs, Manda," he murmured as he drew his hand along one. "And the rest of you, too."

She held on, sought his lips again. After a long time, she said, "The boat is drifting."

"Is it?" His breath was hot, his fingers heavenly. "I don't much care, do you?"

She didn't. They drifted a while longer before finally bumping against the *Argonaut*. They climbed aboard, ignoring the ribald remarks of Ardmore's men. Henderson led her below, where they found that his cabin was warm and his bunk just the right size.

In the morning Christopher, Ardmore, St. Cyr, and Ian O'Malley left the cove to trudge back up the ridge to search for the gold. Honoria stayed behind at the camp, eating hard biscuits and shriveled oranges, feeling worried and unhappy.

She knew why Christopher had allowed Manda to be made a hostage, and why he'd taken Diana as his own hostage. He did not want this expedition to turn into a battle. The crew of the *Starcross* must know that any move that put Manda in danger would be rewarded by the death of the perpetrator.

She knew how precious Manda was to Christopher, though he'd never, ever say such a thing out loud. But it was plain what they meant to each other, just by the looks they exchanged, by the easy way they spoke, even in disagreement, as though their words only finished thoughts they'd begun together. Honoria envied the easy fondness between them, something she would never have with her own brother and did not yet have with Christopher.

James, likewise, would do nothing to endanger Diana. James loved Diana with fierce intensity. No man would dare face James's wrath were something to happen to Diana.

But James did not understand what Honoria knew, that Christopher was truly a gentle man. Christopher might have a fierce growl, but whenever he touched Honoria, he restrained his strength so as not to hurt her. He mitigated his growls with caresses, he let her do as she pleased despite his claims to the contrary. Christopher intimidated those who did not know him, but those who did know him believed in him. Which was why she knew his men would do nothing to interfere with James or harm Diana unless Christopher gave a specific order.

Honoria idled about camp, took off her shoes and waded in the waves, scooped up shells, tried not to fret. She rubbed her nose with cream, put on a hat against the blazing ball of sun.

Just as that ball reached its zenith, the four men returned. They were dirty and tired, and grime creased lines on their faces.

Christopher looked smug, James cold, St. Cyr impassive as always, Ian O'Malley awestruck. They had found the Mexican gold.

Chapter Twenty

"Right where I left it," Christopher said.

Honoria watched the sunlight play on the planes of his face, which held a self-satisfied smirk at the moment. He seemed relaxed, as though pleased he'd be turning over all his gold to James. James seemed, if anything, the more tense of the pair.

The two crews assembled the ropes and winches and pulleys needed to haul away the gold. The cache lay in a cave near the top of the cliff, Christopher explained; the opening to it was a small hole beneath an outcropping. A short tunnel sloped from the entrance, then another hole dropped straight into the cave, which had been carved out of the cliff. The casks would have to be lifted out with ropes, then carried back down the hill.

With little reluctance, the crews of both ships agreed to be beasts of burden. The presence of the large amount of gold brought a quiet excitement to

303

the small group. Honoria could almost feel the treasure waiting in the little damp cave above, its presence almost palpable, like an entity, watching them.

Honoria insisted on trudging up the hill with the first party. Christopher, to her surprise, did not object.

Christopher and James had already removed the undergrowth and a half-dozen large, fungus-covered rocks from the entrance by the time Honoria reached it, panting. She squirmed forward to where the two men crouched, looking in. She peered around Christopher's well-muscled biceps and into a damp, rather smelly hole.

"If the casks were wood, they'd have rotted away by now," she observed.

Christopher turned his head. He scowled as though about to ask what she was doing there. She blissfully ignored him, went on looking down into the hole, in which they'd lowered a flickering lantern. She could see little but the circle of damp rock around the light.

"The casks are metal," Christopher said. "Tin and brass. Probably rusted and corroded by now, but still whole."

"Have you gone in yet?" Honoria asked.

"We need to widen the entrance," Christopher said, "Someone needs to go in and work on it from that side. Someone small."

All eyes turned to the Irishman, Ian O'Malley, who was the smallest man on either crew. He blanched. "Don't much like caves." He shuddered. "Did I mention that bloody English soldiers threw me in a hole like that once? For three months."

James and Christopher only looked at him. He turned whiter still.

"Don't make him," Honoria cried. "That's cruel. I'll go."

"No, you won't," Christopher and James said at the same time. One spoke in lightly accented English, one in a heated Southern drawl.

"Do you have another crewman smaller than I am? I'm not afraid to climb down there. And it can't be any worse than digging in my garden. The soil is loose and damp, not hard." She demonstrated, scooping a portion away with her fingers.

"Honoria," Christopher began, his voice a growl.

She met his gaze steadily. "Are you afraid it will cave in?"

"How the hell should I know? I was born and bred aboard a ship. That's not the point."

"No, the point is, I should obey you without question, is that it?"

"Yes."

"The vows never said that," Honoria retorted.

"Back to that argument, are you? The vows mean that your husband knows best, and so you should listen to him."

"I don't remember those words at all."

"I think you and I need to have a little talk."

"We have had them," she said softly. "We both know how they always end."

His eyes darkened. Was he recalling the time she'd slathered oil on his body in Alexandra's spare bedroom and the rather rough and tumble—and very slippery—lovemaking they'd had after that? Or the occasion a few nights ago, when he'd helped her undress and sponge off her body in their cabin? Things had gotten a bit wet and soapy, and Honoria's voice had been hoarse the next morning.

Christopher's own voice was a bit throaty when he said, "Don't play innocent with me, miss. You'll pay for it later."

"That is a risk I will have to take. And it's *Mrs.*"

His look turned dangerous, and her heart beat with excitement. She never thought verbal sparring with a man would be so satisfying. But then, the man was Christopher, who kissed like fire and touched her as she'd never been touched before.

To think, she'd once upon a time imagined she'd have a marriage to a courteous man who wore silk waistcoats and escorted her to balls. Foolish imaginings of a foolish girl. She believed now it had been no accident that she'd turned down every proposal after she'd met Christopher Raine.

A shadow fell over them. "If you two are finished with your interesting discussion," James Ardmore said, "I say let her down there. If she gets dirty and cries, it's her own fault."

The warmth in Honoria's body suddenly evaporated. She rose to her feet, every ounce of ladylikeness coming to the fore. "Really, James. It is most rude to listen to a private conversation."

Her brother gave her his most fearsome James Ardmore look. She gave him one right back.

Christopher cleared his throat. "I could give you both pistols and let you count off paces. But we don't have time. St. Cyr, get some ropes, the strongest you have. My wife wants to go exploring."

They rigged up a harness for her from stout ropes. Christopher held the lead rope himself, with St. Cyr to back him up. He would not let James touch it at all.

Honoria kissed Christopher on the lips, for luck and in gratitude, then put her feet into the hole and let them lower her.

It was not a very long way down. She thought the harness unnecessary, but Christopher insisted they be able to pull her out at a moment's notice. She knew, in her heart, that if it had been terribly dangerous, Christopher would never have given in. He'd simply have tied her up instead, and carried her back to the cove.

The cave had an earthy smell overlaid with the odor of rotting vegetation. Tree roots poked through the upper level around the opening, but the rest had been carved out from solid rock. A few lanterns had been lowered first—candle lamps, not oil—and the feeble flickers glistened on the water-damp walls. Moss and a red fungus grew in patches. The air felt marvelously cool after the blazing heat of the outdoors.

When her feet touched the ground, the lower edges of the tunnel were level with her eyes. She was to use the spade and pick they'd lowered to widen the opening so that larger men, like Christopher and James, could easily move in and out.

She ignored the pick and spade for now and turned to look around. The casks, brass and glinting in the candlelight, lined almost every inch of space in the cave. There must be forty or fifty of them, waiting to be discovered.

Honoria moved toward the nearest cask and touched its lid. The iron lock still rested in its hole, but the hasp had rusted through.

Christopher's voice bellowed through the hole. "Where are you going?"

"I want to look at the gold," she answered. She lifted one of the lanterns, shone it on the cask. The innocent brass glinted back at her. She carefully checked for spiders, then put her hand down and opened the lid.

The rusted hinge protested, but the lid fell back. The candlelight fell on rows and rows of glittering golden ingots.

Honoria caught her breath. The gold had not been minted but merely molded into the tiny bars for transportation. There had to be hundreds of the things. And at least forty casks filled this cave.

Napoleon must have been sickened to lose this much. The war in Spain was going badly for him; what he would not give to have this back! James would never give it to him, of course. James did not approve of tyrants. Excepting himself.

She suddenly understood the power that gold had. It was beautiful, the presence of it, weighty. Men murdered one another for it, adored it, hoarded it. And with it, they purchased women by buying them jewels and houses and clothes. Whoever possessed gold had power.

And Christopher was going to just give it away.

A strong tug on the harness brought her back to

herself. "Honoria, what are you doing?" her husband called.

Honoria dropped the lid back into place and made her way to the hole before Christopher could drag her there. "It's here," she panted up at him. "Really here. All of it."

"Thank you for the report," Christopher growled. "Now, start digging or I'll haul you up by your backside."

"Yes, dear," Honoria said, sarcasm dripping. She picked up the spade and began knocking damp earth away from the opening of the tunnel.

She heard Christopher chuckle. "I like this. My wife on the end of a tether."

"You would," Honoria said darkly.

After a half hour of tiring digging, the tunnel was wide enough to satisfy Christopher. Honoria lowered her aching arms as her husband slithered down into the tunnel and dropped to the floor. He still held the rope.

"Your face is dirty," he said. His eyes twinkled in the lantern light.

"I see no reason for you to be so happy," she said, rubbing her arms. "You are going to give away all this beautiful gold."

Christopher opened the cask she'd peered into. The reflection of the candlelight on the gold lit his face. He stared into the cask for a long, sober moment, then he banged the lid shut.

"Too much gold is a curse, my wife," he said. "I'll be glad to be rid of it." And he winked at her.

She gaped, stared at him. A sudden, deep suspicion stirred in her mind.

But she had no chance to ask him what he was up to, because James slithered down into the hole just behind them, and any secrets had to remain secret.

Not long later, Christopher's and James's men began the laborious process of lifting each cask from the hole. Only one could be moved at a time, because of the size of the tunnel and the fact that the casks, though small, were heavy.

They rigged a pulley system using the overhanging trees. Men below would bind a cask with ropes, and men above would haul it to the surface. Christopher made a makeshift sled of planks and ropes that would transport the gold to the cove. Three casks fit on the sled; one man could pull it while a second steadied and slowed it from behind.

The work was slow, and by late afternoon only half the casks had been taken down the hill. They tramped back with the last cask and camped again on the beach. James himself stood guard.

"I don't envy him," Christopher whispered into Honoria's ear as they lay snuggled together by the fire. "If the gold came to my ship, my men would at least know they got a share. His men get to watch him hand it over to the American navy."

Honoria felt some alarm. "Do you think he'll be in danger?" she asked over her shoulder. "Perhaps we should take Diana and her children with us until he makes the delivery."

Christopher kissed her temple. "No, my sweet. If

Ardmore can't command his men by now, no one can. He didn't get this far by allowing his crew to walk over him."

"I'd like to walk over him sometimes," she said between her teeth.

Christopher only laughed and rolled her over to kiss her.

She remembered that kiss, and the laughter in his eyes, for a long time to come.

They were awakened early in the morning by rain, which soon turned into a deluge. Sleepy men scrambled for the shelter of the trees, dragging blankets and clothes with them.

Honoria waited with them, panting and dripping, while James organized a few of his crew to row the casks of gold to the *Argonaut*. A little rain wouldn't hurt them, he said. Honoria wondered if he meant the gold bars or his crew.

They watched the boat slide to the *Argonaut* and back three times, until all the casks had been loaded onto the ship. By the time the boat returned after the last haul, the rain was pounding so hard the ships were obscured by the gray curtain of it.

The rain was less dense under the canopy of forest, and Christopher ordered them back up the hill to the tunnel.

Honoria insisted on being lowered back into the cave, where she'd be sheltered from the worst of the storm. Once inside, she squeezed out her rain-matted hair and watched Christopher.

He'd cast off his wet shirt and worked bare-torsoed, his muscles and sinews moving beneath his skin. She looked forward to returning to the *Starcross,* where she could lie with him in their bunk and touch those muscles to her heart's content.

After they had a proper bath, of course. The cave was muddy, and she longed for soap and clean water. Perhaps she and Christopher could bathe each other again . . .

She let her thoughts ramble down this delicious path as she moved the ropes on her waist so they would not chafe. Christopher had not let her down without the harness, which he'd tied off to a tree outside. She felt rather like a dog on a lead, but he made it clear that she either complied or went back to the cove.

At last, as the sky darkened outside, the final cask rested in position beneath the opening. Christopher sent the men who'd been helping him above, then turned to Honoria. "Up you go, sweetheart. The adventure is over."

"We did not have much adventure," Honoria said, coming to him. "I half expected to find that you'd buried a pirate alive down here so his ghost would guard the treasure."

Christopher gave her an incredulous look. "Why the devil would I do that?"

"Or set cunning traps to prevent others from reaching the gold. Like stakes coming out of the walls when they tripped on a rock."

He started to laugh. "Good God, Honoria, where do you come up with these things?"

"Books." She put her arms around him as he lifted her.

"I've only read two books in my life," he said, "and nothing like that ever happened in those."

She smiled and smoothed his sweat-dampened hair from his brow. "Maybe you'll be the hero in a book one day. One about all your adventures."

He shook his head, his grin crooked. "You're an amazing woman, my wife. Kiss me."

She complied. It was a warm, satisfying kiss, one she never wanted to stop.

"Up you go," he said.

Slightly disappointed, but knowing they could continue later, she allowed him to hoist her upward. Above them, a seaman began hauling on the rope.

When she was halfway up the tunnel, she heard the men outside begin to shout. James's voice thundered above theirs. Their cries were suddenly drowned by a roaring sound, as though all the rain that had fallen that day had decided to rush at them in one great wave.

Mud splattered her face, the droplets fast becoming splatters, then clods. They pelted down around her, turning to a steady fall of earth and mud pouring past her to Christopher, still waiting in the hole.

"It's caving in," James shouted above the noise. "Pull her out!"

The tunnel began to collapse in on itself. She watched in horror as it cascaded past her and down to her husband. "Christopher!" she screamed. "Grab my hand. James, pull us out!"

She felt Christopher's strong fingers close around her wrist, and then a deluge of water and mud fell right on her, filling her nose and mouth and ears, pounding her and threatening to carry her back down to the bottom. The harness around her tightened, and she was dragged upward, her body scraping the narrowing walls of the tunnel.

Christopher's hold on her wrist vanished. She spat grit from her mouth. "James, wait! Christopher, grab my hand!"

She felt his fingers scrabbling through mud, but she could not see him. A wall of earth rushed at her and at the same time she was yanked upward, hard. Her shrieks to stop were drowned by the crash of mud.

The earth parted above her, and James, white-faced, seized her beneath the arms and pulled her up and away from the hole.

"Wait," she sobbed. "Christopher is still down there."

James ignored her. He hauled her quickly to the tree to which she'd been tied and, with one stroke of his knife, freed her. She whirled, ready to run back to the tunnel, where men were already digging with hands and spades to reach Christopher.

There was another roar, and the digging men leapt back. St. Cyr swore loudly in French. James seized Honoria around the waist and ran.

Before Honoria's eyes, the entire hillside came down. Boulders, sapling trees, and torn roots, loosened by the mud and rain, tumbled down the hillside to cover the opening to the tunnel. The slide buried the ground around the opening and two of the casks that had not yet been moved to the sled.

They'd run about fifty feet before the mudslide stopped. Then, as suddenly as it had begun, it ceased. A few rocks and tree branches crackled and slid downward and then were still. The roar was replaced by deafening silence, except for the quiet sound of the abating rain.

Chapter Twenty-one

"Christopher!" Honoria screamed. She raced back to the tunnel, now blocked by boulders and scrub and broken debris. She began digging though it with her bare hands, trying to scrape away the layers and layers that buried her husband inside the cave.

She pounded and scraped until her fingers bled. Red streaks of her blood dripped from the boulders that shut her out.

A strong arm snaked about her waist and someone lifted her from the pile. It was James. Her muslin gown was plastered with black mud and slime, smeared with the blood from her hands. She batted at his arm in vain. He carried her away from the site and sat down with her on a fallen tree, she in his lap.

The sobs finally came, tears at last wetting her burning eyes. "We must dig him out. Please, James, get him out."

"Shh," he said into her hair. "They're digging, Honoria, as fast as they can."

She saw through blurred eyes that St. Cyr and O'Malley had organized the men with picks and shovels. She could scarce comprehend what they did; she only knew they did not do it fast enough. She had to go over there and dig him out herself.

She found herself dragged back to James, held firmly in his strong arms. "No. Let them work."

"They have to rescue him. I can't lose him."

"I know."

Honoria collapsed against him, shaking all over. He offered her no reassurance—not James, who'd watched their young brother die in his arms, who knew too much of the world to mislead her with false hope. She wished he'd try to comfort her with at least a few empty words. Her heart felt like lead.

This shock was worse, much worse, than when she'd thought she'd lost Christopher to the hangman. She'd barely known him then. She knew him now. She'd been married to him in every sense, slept in his bed, made turbulent love to him, argued with him, laughed with him, helped him, hindered him. He was her husband, much more now than when they'd simply signed a piece of paper.

"I can't lose him, James," she repeated brokenly.

James held her, rocking her slightly, as he'd done when she was a girl frightened by a storm. She'd always believed James strong enough to face anything, no matter how annoying he was. When their parents had died, even in her grief, she'd known she and Paul would be all right, because James was there to take care of them.

She had felt the same warmth and strength—and love—from Christopher.

She felt nothing now. She could only sit numbly in the circle of James's arm while his men dug and dug and uncovered nothing. The rain slackened, the lowering sun reached through torn clouds. And still the entrance to the tunnel remained stubbornly evasive, if it even existed anymore.

The sun sank completely and night came and the cold. Still they dug, to no avail.

Buried alive to guard the treasure. The thought sifted through Christopher's half-dazed mind. *What a wonderful idea, my wife.*

The mudslide had swept him from the tunnel's edge and across the cave and crashed him into the back wall. Sharp edges of rock cut his flesh, and water and mud covered him.

The tunnel had sealed itself, and the deluge subsided. The cave floor, covered with slime and water, at last settled. Christopher was left at the far end, dirty and wet and cold and walled off from escape.

His first coherent thoughts as he climbed to his feet were for Honoria. Thank God she'd been pulled out before the worst of it hit. Ardmore would have seen to that. Whatever Christopher thought of the man, he knew Ardmore would keep Honoria safe.

His second thought was *How the hell am I going to get out of here?*

At least six feet of debris, packed solid, blocked

him from the entrance. Who knew how many feet had fallen to cover the outside? The mud, still loose, came away easily in his hands, but he feared to shift too much, lest the whole pack give way and smash down on him. The picks and shovels and ropes had all been hauled outside before the slide began. The only things in the cave with him were a cask of gold, which now had a few tons of mud on top of it, and a lantern, which rested on a jut of rock in the far wall.

Incredibly, the candle was still lit. The lantern's panes had protected the flame inside from the huge rush of wind that had come with the mud. The candle burned merrily on, the flame tall and flickering, its light shimmering on the noisome muck on the floor.

Christopher stared at the light for a long time before he realized what it meant. The lantern's flickering told him that the cave had air from some source other than the entrance.

Of course, if he discovered the air came only from tiny slits in the ceiling far above, openings he'd never reach, he'd simply die of hunger and thirst here, instead of suffocating. Not a happy thought.

Then again, the air might come from somewhere accessible, which meant another way out.

He slipped and slid over to the lantern, lifted it from the rock, and began to explore.

What he found for his effort was a small hole, near the ground, opposite the entrance, now half blocked with mud. It might, when cleared, just admit the bulk of his body. A long shot, he thought. He might get some ways along and then get stuck.

But it was better than sitting here wondering

whether Ardmore and the others could dig him out. If Ardmore would even try. Christopher could imagine the pirate hunter dusting off his hands and murmuring "good riddance," then returning to the *Argonaut* with the gold and crossing another pirate off his list. He'd take Honoria with him, too.

The hole seemed the better effort. He scooped out the worst of the mud with his hands, shoved the lantern in, and crawled inside behind it.

He would get out, one way or another. He had to. He pictured Honoria, believing herself rid of an inconvenient husband, happily making ready to return home with her brother and Diana. Christopher would emerge, covered with dirt and mud, and say, "Hello, dear. Did you miss me?"

He wondered if she'd stare in dismay, or if her face would light up with her pretty smile. Either way, it did not matter. He was determined to make her love him, no matter what. Even if it took him every year of his life, even if he had to make love to her every night and argue with her every day, he would make her love him.

He loved her with every ounce of his strength.

He pushed his way along the tunnel, flat on his belly, shoving the lantern ahead of him. The light showed a long, low tube, just big enough to admit him. Dry rock jutted overhead, damp rock under him scraped his bare chest.

Christopher had been very close to death many times before, especially when struggling through China and Siam. He'd pushed through then, just as he pushed through this tunnel now. He'd pushed through by thinking of Honoria.

He'd imagined her green eyes, the feel of her skin, the taste of her mouth. He'd close his eyes and imagine himself kissing her, tasting his tongue against hers, feeling the softness of her lips as she kissed him back. She was his flame, guiding him through darkness.

She'd implied it wasn't fair of him to make her his flame. He'd not cared. They belonged together, Christopher Raine and Honoria Ardmore. That fact might annoy her, but she could not escape it. He would not let her escape it.

It took some time before Christopher realized he'd closed his eyes. He jerked alert, banging his head on the rocks above him. Cursing, he shoved the lantern along and kept crawling.

At one point, a small piece of rock stuck out, impeding him. He pounded it with his fist until it broke, then he dropped it behind him. He had to lie still a few minutes, wheezing from the small effort. The close air and the battering from the mudslide was taking its toll.

He jerked awake again. The candle had burned halfway down. He cursed out loud, making the harsh sound of his own voice wake him. He wondered why he'd drifted off, then realized that the candle flame had slackened and was beginning to burn blue. The air was thinning.

He'd have to go back. He prepared his aching muscles for the prospect.

No, a part of his mind said, he could not go back. *Never go back.* Hadn't he taught that to Manda? Never go back, always move forward.

Bloody hell. He woke up again. The candle had gone out. He was alone in blackness under a mountain.

He moved determinedly forward, pushing the lantern along. He had no way of lighting it again, even if any of the candle remained. *I don't want to die here*, his mind hummed. *I want to kiss Honoria one more time. She's worth kissing, any man would agree.*

She was worth doing other things with, as well. His loins swelled. He thought of her with her hair coming down, her head tilted back, her lips parting softly. She had true and unashamed desire, and she desired Christopher.

Whenever he'd mention this fact to her, she'd give him her prim look and tell him she was allowed to desire him—they were married, after all. But that was simply her excuse. She pretended she did only her duty, but she was a little liar. She wanted him. He chuckled.

He wanted to remember her all tousled with love-making, but the picture that came to him most vividly was that of her standing on the cove the day before, hands on hips, sunburn cream on her nose, informing him that of course she was coming up the hill with him to see the gold.

He hated himself for letting her in the cave at all. She might still have been in it when the mudslide started; she might even now be buried under all that rubble. Stupid. He should have sent her back to the ship and locked her up, threatening to flog her if she would not stay.

Honoria would not have believed him, of course. He wondered briefly what it must be like to have a wife who actually obeyed her husband. Probably bloody boring. He smiled.

Christopher jumped awake again. His breathing was labored. Damn it. He had to go back. There was air in the cave, probably from slits in the top of it after all. St. Cyr and Colby might succeed in digging him out. Eventually.

He pushed the lantern on a few more inches, crawling after it mindlessly. He pushed it again, and the lantern disappeared.

He stopped, uncertain what had just happened. He shook himself a little, in case he'd fallen asleep again.

Cautiously, he stretched out his arm. His fingers touched rock, and then nothing. A puff of cold air brushed his hand.

He inched forward as quickly as he could. He took hold of the lip of the hole, pulled his face over the opening, and breathed deeply of the faint air that wafted to him. He could hear water trickling somewhere far below. The rock was slippery with it.

He groped a little farther, trying to find the other side of the niche, to see if the tunnel continued beyond it. His body, tired and heavy, slipped. And then he fell. It was a silent fall; his throat was too parched to let him cry out.

He seemed to slide down a long tunnel, banging from rock to rock. With the last of his strength, he covered his face with his arms, trying to protect himself.

He tumbled down for a long, long time while his skin grew slick with blood. He futilely tried to stop his flight on ledges and rocks, but they cut his hands, evaded his grasp. After a while, he became so numb he scarcely felt the pummeling, and stopped trying.

The sloping tunnel abruptly ended, and he fell through empty air. Just when he decided he was dead, something freezing rose up and swallowed him whole.

Honoria's sobs had long since ceased. She sat alone, James's coat over her shoulders, staring at nothing. Night had fallen, but under the light of lanterns, the men still dug.

Without success. The black boulders that blocked the entrance would never budge. They'd either have to dig around them, which was proving impossible, or find another way in.

James's muscular form blocked the light. "Honoria," he said. He waited a moment for her to respond, then, when she didn't, continued, "We're going back to the cove."

Honoria shook her head without looking up. "I don't want to."

He sank down to rest on his heels. "You can't do anything here, Honoria. You need to get warm, and to sleep."

"I don't want to sleep."

"You need to," he repeated stubbornly. "In the morning, I'll take you back to the *Argonaut*."

Her head snapped up. "You're abandoning him."

James glanced briefly to where his men and Christopher's still labored. The lamplight made the hard planes of his face harder still. "They may eventually break through. But it might be too late."

He meant that Christopher might already be dead,

suffocated in the closed cave or buried by the debris. Honoria bowed her head.

She felt James's touch on her hair, surprisingly gentle. "It's best you come away with us, Honoria. On the *Argonaut*. Diana will look after you."

She shook her head. "Not yet."

James cupped her face, brushing her cheek with his thumb. "It's best we leave now. I don't want you to see—" He broke off. "We'll take you back home to Charleston. A few days sailing and we'll be there."

"It is not my home any longer. It's yours, and Diana's."

His usual growl softened. "Is that what you think? That's not true, Honoria. The Charleston house has always been your home. I can't imagine it without you in it."

"Like a piece of the furniture," she said dully.

He made a faint noise of exasperation. "No, like a lady who cares about it. I never worried about our home no matter how long I was away. I knew you were there, watching over it better than anyone else ever could. I knew I could always find rest there."

"So good of you to notice," Honoria muttered.

"Of course I noticed. Diana notices, too. I want you there, Honoria. I like knowing you are there."

She looked up, her temper stirring despite her despair. "And what do I know, James Ardmore? *You* knew I'd always be at home. What did I know about you? That you'd come home when you took the whim? Never mind that two, three years would pass before I saw you or had word from you? But that was fine. You knew I'd wait. After all, what choice did I have?"

His usual severe look returned. "You are upset. We need to go down."

"Of course I am upset! He is my husband. Do you know what that means?"

"I have some idea," James said dryly.

"No." She rose to her feet. Her legs shook, and hot pain shot through them. "You have no idea what it means to me. You do not know anything whatsoever about me."

He caught her as her knees buckled. "Damn it, Honoria, I'll put you over my shoulder and carry you if I have to."

She looked into eyes made dark by the lantern light. He cared, she sensed that, but he did not understand.

"I have to stay here," she grated. "I have to know."

He put his arms around her and gathered her to him, her older brother who so seldom showed her affection. "I promise, Honoria, the moment he's found, I'll tell you." He brushed back a lock of her hair. "But I think you already know."

In the pit of her stomach rested fear she did not want to name. "I hate you, you know, James."

"I am thoroughly aware of that."

Without letting her argue further, he led her down the hill. She collapsed very soon, and he had to carry her the rest of the way.

Somewhere beneath her numb grief, she cynically hoped that he hurt his back.

* * *

She did sleep, because James made her drink quite a bit of rum, which filled her with false lassitude. She lay on the blankets in soft sand, her head light. Cool air touched her face. The fire warmed her feet, the rum warmed her body, and treacherously she drifted into slumber.

She dreamed of Christopher. She remembered when she'd first seen him, when he'd been young and stunningly handsome and waiting in the garden room at home for her. He'd turned when she'd pattered in, then given her a long look and a slow grin. "Who do you belong to?" he'd asked.

Not the most auspicious of beginnings, but she'd only been able to stare in delight. Here was her idol, her fantasy, come to life. She'd stammered something and handed him the pamphlet that she wanted him to sign. He'd used it to tease a kiss from her.

She relived it in the dream. The playfulness had vanished at once. She'd found herself grabbing him and pulling him down to her. He'd slid his hand to the small of her back, dipped his tongue inside her mouth. She'd never had any idea a man would do such a thing. She certainly liked discovering it.

The kiss had swiftly turned frenzied. He'd scooped her against him, and she'd felt his very masculine hardness through her thin skirts.

After thoroughly kissing her, he'd lowered her to the floor, his gray eyes heavy with longing. Strong fingers had loosened her clothes, and then he'd touched her. He'd entered her only with his fingers, but he'd given her a taste of what it would be like for him to be inside her fully.

When it was over, he raised her to her feet, helped her straighten her clothes. He'd given her a quiet look, his arrogance gone. He'd taken her face in his hands, drawn his thumbs across her cheekbones. Just when she thought he'd tell her he loved her, he'd straightened up, shaken himself, deliberately winked and said, "Good to meet you, Miss Ardmore," and strolled away.

Nine years later, his devil-may-care bearing had all but gone. His swagger had vanished, but he'd given her the ghost of his cocky grin when she'd been admitted to the prison cell in the fort. He'd been condemned to death, but his strength had not dimmed.

As soon as the jailor had left them alone, he'd crushed her in his arms and kissed her without even saying hello.

"Honoria." She seemed to hear his voice cutting through her dreams, and yet part of it. "You are the best sight I could possibly see."

She'd touched his face, wondering that they'd come together again, and so sad that it would be for the last time. "I love you," she'd whispered.

They'd consummated their love that time, on the stone floor. Then she'd married him.

"Honoria," he'd said once they were man and wife. "I love you."

She seemed to hear him say it now, as though he knelt next to her and whispered it into her ear. But he was truly dead now, buried in the cave under a ton of rock. James had saved him from the hangman four years before, but James had not been able to save him today.

Honoria. The call was slightly more insistent and tinged with annoyance.

Gasping, she woke. Stars had spread out above her, the fire had died to a hot glow, and every man around her was asleep.

She sat up. Far out to sea, the ships rocked, lit by moonlight and starlight. The men on the beach slept, wrapped in blankets or sprawled on top of them. She alone was wakeful. Even James slept, a blanket around his shoulders, his back against the longboat.

Quietly Honoria shed her quilt and stood up. Her legs ached and her head hurt. Not bothering with her boots, she walked barefoot across the sand. It crumbled beneath her toes, soft and soothing.

Honoria. She heard her name again, as clear as the stars. She walked alone toward the path that led to the pools, moving numbly toward the voice that called to her. Automatically, she avoided roots in the path, stepped over rocks. Her feet would be cut and bruised later, but now she scarcely felt it.

She came to the large rock at the end of the path. She climbed over it without stopping. She pushed through undergrowth, her feet hurting now, and at long last reached the pool.

It lay still and clear, moonlight rendering it a silver sheet. She plunged her feet into the soothing water, sending ripples to the far side. She closed her eyes, letting the cool water ease her.

"Honoria."

She snapped her eyes open. He stood on the other side of the pool, moonlight playing on the muscles of his shoulders and chest and rendering his golden hair almost white. His breeches were wet and torn. But he walked toward her, through the water, his teasing grin on his face.

"You didn't think it could kill me, did you?" he asked.

She unfroze. She plunged through the water, heedless of her skirts, running to him, reaching for him. He caught her halfway across, lifted her into his arms.

She kissed his lips, his face, tears pouring down her cheeks. "Christopher," she said hoarsely. "I love you. I love you so much."

"I know, sweetheart. Always told you, didn't I?"

"You arrogant male," she said, smiling. She nuzzled his cheek. "I knew you wouldn't die."

"I couldn't, could I? With you to come back to?"

"You love me, don't you?" she whispered.

"With all my villainous heart."

She kissed the dragon tattoo that rested above his collarbone. The lines of it were silver, as though it glowed with inner fire. "Stay with me, Christopher. Forever. Please?"

He was silent. She raised her head, and her blood suddenly chilled. He still smiled, but his gray eyes held vast sadness. "I can't, angel."

"Why not? Why not, I love you."

He brushed her forehead with his lips. "I know. But I can't stay."

She clutched him, panicked. "No! Please stay with me. Don't leave me again." Tears streaked her face.

He kissed her, then held her tight. "You go back to sleep. In the morning, let your brother take care of you. He's a bastard, but he'll get you home. You'll be safe there."

She wrenched herself from him, fell to her feet in the water. "No. You are my husband. I belong with you. I love *you*."

He gave her another sad look, his gray eyes holding the light of the stars. "It doesn't always work that way, my wife. Good night." He chucked her under the chin, then turned his back and walked away.

She tried to run after him, but her sodden skirts tangled her legs and she couldn't manage a step. "Christopher!" she shrieked.

He continued to walk until he faded into the shadows under the rocks. He never once looked back.

Honoria's body jerked and she awoke. She was lying cocooned in a blanket on the cold sand of the cove. The sun was rising, men stirred, and James was talking quietly with one of his crew.

Chapter Twenty-two

Honoria pushed aside her blankets and slid her half-boots onto her feet. She rose and quickly but determinedly made her way toward the path that led to the pools.

She heard James, ever vigilant, call her name. She did not stop walking. Her heart beat heavily, not giving her much room for breathing. She was panting by the time she made the boulder at the end of the path.

The sunlight had not yet slid beneath the trees, and the air was cold and filled with mists. Damp coolness clung to her skin. Her feet, even in the boots, ached from the stones she trod on.

Her dream had been so vivid while she'd experienced it, but now she realized how unreal it had been. She'd felt neither the cold nor the exertion of the walk, nor had she smelled the decay of the damp undergrowth or stumbled over the sharp stones. But she'd heard her name so clearly, in his voice like broken gravel.

"Honoria!"

This shout came from behind her. James, irritated.

She scrambled over the boulder and continued to the pool, moving faster. The rational part of her mind knew she'd not find Christopher waiting for her, that he'd not walk to her wearing his grin and not much else. He had never called her name; she'd dreamed it. But she had to see. She had to know, for once and for all.

She pushed through the damp undergrowth. Flat leaves slapped her, spraying cold droplets over her face. Her feet slipped in mud.

She reached the pool just as the sun rose over the trees and spilled light into the clearing. The water rippled, fed from the currents beyond, something her dream had omitted. The sun, reflecting on the cliff face wet with falling water, dazzled her a moment.

Shading her eyes, she peered into the pool. Sunlight threaded its way into the corners. On the other side of the pool, in the cold shadows of the cliffs, a bulk of something floated.

She charged into the pool just as James, growling, crashed through the undergrowth behind her. Her skirts tangled her legs, as in her dream. This time, she dragged them up and out of the way. She heard James splash into the water, snarling at her to stop.

Honoria reached the shadows of the overhanging rocks. Christopher floated there, faceup, eyes closed.

His torso was raw with contusions, his breeches in bloody shreds.

Honoria grabbed him under the arms, began dragging him back into the sunlight. He was heavy, but she scarcely felt the strain.

James reached her. Without a word, he pushed her aside and pulled Christopher across the pool to the bank himself.

When they reached it, James hauled Christopher out of the water, dumped him on a space of muddy ground. Christopher's limbs were slack, his face pasty white. The dragon tattoo was stark black on his skin.

Honoria touched Christopher's throat, searching for a flutter of pulse. His skin was cold and clammy, and he lay so still. But at last, under her fingers, she felt a faint stirring, a feeble twitch that meant his heart still beat. She started crying. "James, he's alive."

Without answering, James flipped Christopher onto his stomach and pressed hard on Christopher's ribs. Water gushed from Christopher's mouth, but he made no other response.

A green snake slithered out of the undergrowth. It stopped and inspected Christopher's waterlogged boot with one jeweled eye.

James stood up, face grim. The snake slid hurriedly away. The leaves rustled. James pressed his booted foot on Christopher's back, forcing more water out.

Honoria felt Christopher jerk, and then suddenly he coughed. Honoria's heart beat hard with hope. Christopher's eyes half opened, then he turned his head and vomited up the rest of the water.

After a time, James gently turned him right side up.

Honoria gathered Christopher's head in her lap, brushed the sodden hair from his face. His eyelids fluttered again, then finally he opened his eyes.

Bloodshot and wild, his gaze flicked from her, smiling in pure joy, to James, who stood over him, tense and watching.

His voice was a croak, but Honoria made out the words. "Am I in heaven or hell?"

She leaned down, kissed him. "Be quiet, Christopher." Her tears fell on his lips. "I love you," she informed him. "You wonderful, arrogant, irritating man."

Christopher enjoyed lying on a blanket in the sand, washed by sunshine, letting Honoria wait on him hand and foot. Every so often, she'd stop what she was doing and kiss his cracked lips.

Every time she did it, he felt his limbs grow stronger.

He had no idea how he'd ended up in the pool. He must have fallen from the tunnel into one of the springs that backed up into the mountain. If he'd fallen down the waterfall itself, he would have died. He'd probably slid through a rock-carved tube that snaked rainwater into the spring, and the spring had been deep enough to cushion his fall. From there, unconscious, he could have floated down into the pool where Honoria found him.

She would not explain how she knew to look for him there; she would simply smile and kiss him. He decided to close his eyes and live with it.

When he next opened his eyes, a shadow hung over

his face. It did not belong to his beautiful wife. It belonged to his beautiful wife's brother.

Christopher sat up slowly and carefully. His chest was wrapped with bandages that Honoria had wound herself. He'd loved the feel of her small, firm hands on his body.

"Still here, are you?" Christopher asked Ardmore.

James's expression was granite-hard as usual. "We're leaving. We searched the rest of the island, just in case you forgot to tell us about more caches of gold. We found none. It seems you led me directly to the gold and gave it to me. Why?" His voice was quiet, smooth, waiting.

While Christopher had lain here this morning, half senseless, James had given the order to release Manda, so Christopher had courteously given the order to release Diana.

Had Diana and Manda gone meekly back to their respective ships, like the obedient ladies they were? No, they'd come charging to the island, demanding to know what had happened. Diana had at first flown into her husband's arms. Then, after expressing her wifely love and devotion, she'd let go, taken a step back, and started shouting at him.

Christopher had enjoyed the show. That is, until Manda approached and began shouting at *him*. What business did he have letting Ardmore lead him around by the nose and getting himself half killed? For a stupid little stack of gold that they didn't even need?

"I'm leading *him*," Christopher retorted. "The only person who leads me around is my wife, and that's not by the nose." He grinned as Manda rolled her eyes.

Manda had knelt next to him, then given him a belligerent stare with liquid black eyes and said, "I'm going to marry Henderson."

Christopher felt both amusement and a dart of sorrow. He'd just found Manda; he didn't want to let her go again, not so soon. "Are you sure that's what you want?"

She nodded, looking happy and miserable at the same time. "I love him." She gave Christopher a defiant look. "He's a good man in a fight."

He suppressed a laugh. "Well, in that case, you always have a place on my ship, you know that."

"I know. That's why we'll stay on the *Starcross*. Alden's a good navigator, even if he is fussy about his clothes. You'll need him."

Christopher let himself grin. As he lay here recovering from death, his emotions were running rampant. He reached for Manda, gathered her into his arms. Her black hair was soft under his hands, her cheek smooth against his.

"What are you doing?" she asked.

"Hugging you."

She awkwardly rested her arms on his neck. "We don't hug."

He squeezed her tight, kissed her cheek. "I promise I'll never do it again."

Manda broke away from him, gave him an incredulous look. "You've lost your mind."

"My beautiful wife saved my life today and told me she loved me. I'm pleased with everyone."

"Huh. I suppose I should enjoy it while I can."

Christopher gave her a friendly shove. "Go get the

ship ready to sail. We're leaving as soon as I can get rid of Ardmore."

They exchanged a long look, coconspirators once more. "Are we going where I think we are?" Manda asked.

"You'd know better than anyone."

"I'll have to tell Henderson, you know," she warned.

"I'd not have you keep anything from him. Tell him anything you want. Just wait until we're well away from here."

Her grin widened, and she winked. "Aye, Captain. See you on board."

She'd stood up, walked off with a long stride and buoyant bounce. Christopher's heart had lifted. It was good to be home.

Now he looked up at James Ardmore and answered his question. "I refuse to waste men and time trying to fight you. You want the damned gold so much, take it and go away."

Ardmore's lips compressed. "Are you paying me off so I'll leave you alone from now on? It won't work, Raine. You're still a pirate, and I'm a pirate hunter. Our debts to each other are paid, but we start again with a blank slate."

"Fine," Christopher answered, trying to look defeated. "But to tell the truth, I believe I'll retire from the pirate life. I'll take my wife and settle in some coastal town where I can smoke my pipe and bounce my children on my knee and regale them with tales of my exploits." He grinned. "I'll tell them stories about you, and they'll call you Uncle James."

Ardmore started a little, as though just realizing that Honoria's children would be related to him. The corners of his mouth moved slightly upward. "Sounds idyllic. I suppose Honoria will have me and Diana come round for Sunday dinners so we can be one big, happy family." He paused while both of them thought about this grim scenario.

"Was there something else?" Christopher asked.

Ardmore's eyes glinted with some hidden thought, as though he debated with himself whether to speak. "No. Except that I expect you and Honoria will live . . . what is the phrase?—happily ever after?"

They stared at each other for a moment. The glint became disquieting. It held a grudging respect, acknowledgment that Christopher had won this round.

In other words, the bloody man had deduced exactly what Christopher had done.

Christopher's pulse quickened. Ardmore was choosing, his look said, to let Christopher win. For Honoria's sake, perhaps, or the sake of children to come, or perhaps because Ardmore believed he was still paying his debts.

Before Christopher could speak, Ardmore gave him a lazy salute. "Until we meet again," he drawled. "Don't let Honoria drive you insane. She has peculiar notions about what carpets to walk on and what pillows you can't sleep on."

"Thank you for the warning." Christopher had already run into her notions about bedding and pillows. Painfully so, his backside reminded him.

"I'll say good-bye to her," Ardmore finished. "On my way out."

"She'll want to talk about her feelings," Christopher warned.

"I know." Ardmore gave him a curt nod, any friendliness leaving his eyes. "Good-bye, Captain Raine."

Christopher didn't have the strength to get to his feet, but he gave his rival a return salute. "Well met, Captain Ardmore."

Both men had come here trying to best the other, and neither had been defeated. They'd both won.

Without another word, James Ardmore marched off to face his last ordeal, a conversation with his sister.

Honoria ground her teeth as her argument with James wound down. They'd snarled and shouted at each other for the better part of an hour about all the things they'd shouted at each other about their entire lives: he having a cold heart; she doing whatever she wanted without telling him; James always staying so long from home; Honoria never making James feel welcome in his own house. They'd moved on to Honoria marrying Christopher without telling James, and James not telling Honoria how he'd found out who'd killed Paul's wife.

Honoria ran out of breath at the same time James did. He glared at her and closed his mouth in a grim line. She gave him a haughty glare back.

Diana, who'd watched, scowling, said, "Are you finished? For heaven's sake, James, we'll likely not see her again for a long while. You must do better than shouting at her."

"I told her she could return to Charleston with us,

with her husband." He bit off the last word as though it pained him. "She declined."

Honoria raised her brows high. "Live with you in the Charleston house? You and Christopher would be at each other's throats. Not what I'd call comfortable living."

"No," Diana agreed.

James frowned. "You will come home sometime, won't you? You won't forget where you were born and raised?"

"Well, of course not! I will return home quite often. That is, if I am welcome."

James met her frosty gaze with one of his own. "You'll be welcome. Why wouldn't you be?"

Diana rolled her eyes. She left them, gliding away to where Isabeau was supposed to be keeping baby Paul from eating sand.

After a moment of silence, Honoria said softly, "Why didn't you tell me how you found out who killed Paul's wife?"

James drew a sharp breath, his handsome face going hard again, then he blew out the breath and closed his eyes. "I was in a hurry. That's the only reason, I swear to you. I wanted to get right on the man's trail, and I didn't have time for anything else."

"And you didn't think I'd want to know what you'd discovered?"

"I didn't think anything," he said, green eyes going hard. "I just wanted to get him. I thought—" He sighed again. "For some reason I thought that if I came back and laid Mallory's dead body at your feet,

341

you'd be happy. You'd be proud of me. But of course, nothing worked out the way I thought."

It hadn't. She'd heard the full story from Diana.

"I've always been proud of you, James."

His brows shot up. "Have you?"

"Well, of course."

The stared at each other like two people who'd thought they'd known each other well but now were not so sure.

"I'm not proud of myself," he said lightly. "If I'd been there for Paul and his wife, they might be alive today."

Honoria touched his hand, for the first time having a glimmer of understanding of what her cold, older brother had gone through. "You can't ever know that."

His eyes darkened. "Oh, I know it. But I'm learning to live with it."

They were silent a moment. The men around them shouted and joked, seamen happy the task was over and they could get back to normal. A longboat left the beach, half a dozen men leaping into it in unison.

Honoria said softly, "I wonder what Paul would have thought about me marrying Christopher."

James snorted. "Marrying a pirate?" A deprecating look crossed his face, then he stopped, letting it go. "He'd have been glad you were happy."

She believed him. For all his teasing, Paul had been generous-hearted. "He would have been glad you found Diana," she said.

"Yes."

They fell into awkward silence again. The wind

darted around them, stirred up sand where Diana laughed merrily at the antics of the two children at her feet.

She and James watched them for a time. Then James said, "Well, good-bye, then."

"Good-bye."

She gazed at his tall, tanned body, his flyaway black hair, the green eyes that missed nothing. His wife, Diana, loved him so well, and Honoria, as a girl, had admired him. Now they stood staring at each other, feeling the distance between them. She sensed he regretted their distance; she knew she did.

"James," she said sadly.

He opened his arms. She came into them for a long, tight embrace. He hadn't embraced her in a very long while.

"Thank you for saving Christopher," she whispered. "You could have let him die. You didn't."

He tilted her chin back. "I saw what it did to you when you thought him lost. I didn't want to watch you hurting. I want you to be happy, believe it or not." He smiled his rare, slow smile. "Besides, if I'd let him die, you'd never have let me hear the end of it."

"Certainly not." Her voice rang with conviction.

The smile widened. "Good-bye, Honoria." He bent, pressed a brief kiss to her lips, then turned and walked away to his wife.

Honoria's heart ached to see him go, but the parting held promise. She and her brother might just have bridged a tiny gap in the chasm that separated them. It was something, at least.

* * *

The *Argonaut* sailed away with James and Diana, their children, Ian O'Malley, and a hold full of Mexican gold. Honoria shaded her eyes and watched from the stern as the *Argonaut* grew smaller and smaller.

Christopher steered the *Starcross* determinedly in the other direction. Manda stood near him. Henderson leaned against the gunwale nearby, checking a timepiece, the sun glinting from his spectacles.

Honoria's heart was full as the other ship disappeared over the horizon. She'd nearly wept again when parting from Diana and the children, but she knew they'd all visit soon. There would be Christmases and birthdays and midsummer, and any other occasion that gave her an excuse to go home. She'd bring Christopher and see the children, and one day she'd bring children of her own. They'd be a family, just as she and James and Paul and their mother and father had been a family once upon a time.

"Honoria," Christopher said, breaking through her thoughts. "Stop daydreaming and take the wheel."

He stood with one hand lightly on it, his stance impatient.

She heaved a sigh, lifted her skirts, and climbed forward. When she reached the wheel, he relinquished it without further word and strolled away down the deck with Manda.

Honoria scowled at Christopher's fine and straight back. "I know why you are captain, Christopher."

He glanced at her over his shoulder. His gray eyes were clear, warm, and watchful. "Because I was elected."

"No, because you enjoy ordering everyone about."

344

She held the wheel steadily, remembering how Carew had taught her to not grip it too tightly. "Would you mind telling me where I am supposed to point the ship?"

Christopher fixed his attention on his sister. "Manda?"

Her dark eyes roamed the horizon, her black hair fighting the tail she'd pulled it into. "Thirty degrees south-southeast."

Honoria moved the wheel. Mr. Carew had also taught her how to line up the bow to the compass points.

"St. Cyr?" Christopher glanced at his third in command, who watched impassively while the crew hoisted a sail up the forward jib.

"It is correct, I think," St. Cyr answered.

Honoria looked at Christopher in sudden suspicion. "What is correct?"

Christopher's handsome face remained serious, but his eyes twinkled. "The location of the Mexican gold."

"But—" Confusion crept over her. "You gave the gold to James. I saw it in the casks." She frowned. "It was real gold, wasn't it? If you tried to trick him, that was foolish. He'd know if the gold wasn't real."

His lips curved into the smile of a devil who's gotten away with something. "Don't worry, my love, we gave your brother plenty of genuine gold from the *Rosa Bonita*. But the *Rosa Bonita* was a huge ship."

Manda was smirking. St. Cyr, stoic as usual, let nothing show on his face, but his eyes betrayed amusement.

"Explain to me what you mean, Christopher Raine," Honoria said severely.

He rested one booted foot on a bench beside him. The stance stretched his breeches enticingly over his well-muscled legs. "Very well, my wife, I'll tell you a story. Once upon a time, I had three ships. The *Saracen*, commanded by me, a ship commanded by Manda, and one commanded by St. Cyr. The *Rosa Bonita* was loaded with gold and far too slow and conspicuous for us to sail ourselves. So we each filled our holds with as much gold as we could carry and sailed off in three different directions. James Ardmore caught only me."

Honoria stared at him, openmouthed. Behind her Henderson barked a laugh. "Good Lord, Raine."

"So there is more gold?" Honoria squeaked.

"Plenty more where that came from. We just need to fetch it."

"But—" She spluttered, fury rising. "My brother is no fool. He'll have thought of that. He'll simply follow us to the other stashes."

Christopher's gaze drifted to the horizon over which the *Argonaut* had vanished. "No. I don't believe he will."

"How can you know that? He's treacherous and tricky, and has the habit of turning up where he's not wanted. I should know."

"He will not follow us, Honoria."

She opened her mouth to argue further, than snapped it closed. "You made another deal with him, didn't you, Christopher?"

Christopher's eyes were warm and full of good humor. "Let's say that Ardmore and I understand each other, villain to villain."

"Well, Diana and I both agree that you are a pair of villains," she said darkly.

Her face was warm from sun and temper, and her heart beat hard. It felt good to be angry with him, felt good to have him here before her, whole and strong, to be angry with. She wanted to storm and rage and rail and swear, if only for the joy of having him stand there and look at her like that. His eyes told her he loved her and thought her beautiful.

"Honoria," he said, cutting off her diatribe. "I have a better idea. Leave your post to Manda and go below."

Honoria glared at him. "There is no sense in my going below, Captain. You need all the men you have above."

Christopher's brow quirked. "That was not an order from the captain. That was an order from your husband. The husband you vowed to obey, remember?"

"To obey when he is reasonable."

The deep spark in his eyes made her the slightest bit nervous. She clutched the wheel and glared at him over it.

"Manda," he said in commanding tone. "Take the wheel." Then he came for Honoria.

Christopher carried her down to the cabin over his shoulder, letting her squeal and protest all she liked. He slammed the door and tossed her onto the bunk.

She squirmed there like a bug on its back, her skirt tangled in her shapely legs. Her eyes, full of fury, sparked with wild green light.

"That was hardly dignified," she said, struggling to sit up. "What must the crew think?"

"They think I am madly in love with you." He pushed her back down into the quilts. "They don't blame me for celebrating the fact that I'm still alive."

The reminder of his ordeal in the cave filled her eyes with flattering worry. "Christopher, I thought I'd lost you."

He stretched out beside her, gathering her into him and resting his hand on her very shapely hip. "I thought I'd lost me, too." He paused. "Now that we're alone, tell me how you knew to find me in the pool. You couldn't have seen me fall."

She stopped squirming, which was a pity, because her backside had rubbed against the front of his breeches most fetchingly. She looked at him, her eyes luminescent in the cabin's shadows. "I dreamed of you. You stood in the pool and laughed at me for being so worried. And then you left me."

He let his fingers drift across the curve of her waist as he thought about this. "Hmm."

"Did you dream of me?" she asked. "Perhaps we met wherever we go when we have dreams."

A smile tugged at his mouth. "The very practical Miss Honoria Ardmore believes that? I didn't dream of you. At least not like that."

Her brow quirked. "Like what, then?"

"Like I did when I was in Asia. I pictured your beautiful face." He touched it. "Your extremely sensual body." He ran his hand from her soft breast to her hip. "Your lips." He brushed his finger across them. "How your eyes light up when you scold me."

He grinned. "I knew I had to see you one more time, even to hear you shout at me."

Her eyes grew wet. "I thought I'd never see you again."

Christopher soothed her brow with his lips. "But you found me in time. We Raines are hard to kill."

As he'd hoped, her sad look turned to a glare. "Raines are bloody arrogant, too."

"What language. You're turning into a pirate, my wife."

"I most certainly am not."

He kissed her eyelids. Her lashes tickled his lips. "The words I want to hear again are the ones you said to me when you dragged me from the pool. Let me see, what were they?"

She scowled, brows moving beneath his kiss. "You know perfectly well what I said."

"I want to hear it again. I command it, as your captain and your husband."

Honoria lay still. She stared at the whitewashed boards above them for a long time, her eyes unmoving. He waited. He had all the patience in the world, he could show her that.

At last, her lips parted. "I said 'I love you.'"

He bent closer. "What was that? I didn't quite hear."

"You heard me, Christopher," she said between her teeth.

"You barely moved your lips." He turned her to face him. "I want to hear it loud and clear, my wife."

The glare from her eyes could have lit the room. She threw off his hand and sat up straight, nearly cracking her head on the beam.

"I said, I love you Christopher Raine!" she shouted.

"Ah, yes, that was it." He traced her soft, round cheek. "I love you, too, Honoria."

"Damn your hide."

"It's already been damned," Christopher said dryly. Most of the skin had come off his hide in the tunnel and during the fall. Healing was painful.

She became instantly solicitous. "Are you all right? Do you need me to rewrap the bandages?"

As much as he knew he'd enjoy feeling her hands on his body, he shook his head. He pulled her back against him. "I'm already feeling better. Just lie with me awhile."

She lay back down. She threaded her fingers through his, pulled his arm around her waist. Bright sun on the water reflected on the low white beams of the cabin. "Christopher?"

"Mmm?" he murmured, breathing the scent of her hair.

"What are we going to do with all that gold?"

He chuckled. "I'll buy you a fancy house and a fancy carriage and fancy dresses. You'll live like a princess."

"I'm rather enjoying running about your ship in old muslin gowns."

He let his hand rest on her breast. Beneath her gown, she wore only a thin shirt to keep herself showing too much. He liked her without stays, without binding, without anything to keep him out. "I'm enjoying it, too," he murmured.

"It was kind of you to reconcile with James."

"He is my brother-in-law now, unfortunately. Best to keep harmony within the family, don't you think?"

She turned her head, smiled an intoxicating smile that took his breath away. "Thank you, Christopher. I so love Diana, I would hate to never see her again. I will put up with James for her."

"You love your reprobate brother, don't you?"

She looked thoughtful. "I do, I suppose, underneath it all. James is simply not very good at showing affection. Neither am I, I think."

His warm feelings of love began to mix with darker feelings of wanting. "You're just fine at showing affection. At least to me."

Her look turned serious. "That is lust. It is not the same thing."

"Let love and lust blend together, and see how it makes you feel."

She stared at him as though she'd never thought of such a thing. Then her gaze took on a faraway look and a small smile tugged the corners of her mouth.

He began to smile back. He'd been filled up with love for her for so many years, but that had been for a mere image of her. He'd remembered her first as a sweet, pretty girl, then as an enticing, beautiful woman.

Since returning for her, he'd learned she was both of these and more. She was sensual, funny, aggravating, haughty, pleasing, caring, proud, and beautiful. She was his wife in all senses of the word, and he loved her.

The look she fixed on him now made his blood heat. "What are you thinking?" he asked her.

Jennifer Ashley

She didn't answer. She pushed him onto his back, touched the buttons of his breeches.

"Vixen," he said.

Her smile widened. She popped open the first button and then the next. His arousal tumbled from the opening, confined too long.

Honoria caught it in her hand. Dark sensations trickled up his spine and made his heart beat hard and fast.

She teased him, oh she teased him. For the better part of an hour, she teased him with her fingers and her lips and her tongue. He lay back, an invalid, and let her have her way with him.

Just when he thought he could stand it no longer, she slid her leg over his torso and lowered herself onto him. He slid right inside; she was slippery and inviting.

Her green eyes opened wide, starry in the afternoon stillness. "You are right, Christopher. It's much better when it's mixed with love." She gasped, her frenzy beginning to take her. "I love you so much, Christopher."

"I love you, my wife," he said, meaning every word.

"I want you, too." She closed her eyes tight. "Please, Christopher. I want you."

"I wouldn't have it any other way," he said, then he gathered her to him and finished it.

Epilogue

They found the Mexican gold right where Manda had hidden it. They loaded it and sailed off to seek out the rest.

They found that, too, and divided the spoils. Each man—and woman—got an equal share, and the captain, because he was the captain, got two.

Christopher gave the *Starcross* to Manda. She sailed off to find a place in which to marry her Mr. Henderson. Mr. Henderson had shaken his hand, given Honoria a good-bye kiss on the cheek, then slid his arm around Manda's waist and walked away with her. His spectacles had never looked so shiny.

Christopher watched them go with some sorrow, but he was glad that his sister had found a taste of the happiness that Christopher had. And she'd be back. She and Christopher still shared a bond that nothing could break.

Christopher took Honoria to a coastal Carolina

town not far from Charleston and bought her a fancy house and a fancy carriage and fancy gowns.

They lived near an isolated beach and took endless walks up and down the warm sand—and used the stretch of sun-warmed sand for other activities as well. At last he did get to see her run, leaving her dress behind, while he pursued her with his blood hot in his veins.

The first child they had was a little girl, followed by a boy and another girl. Christopher taught them all how to sail a pirate ship, how to find and board a prize, how to sell the booty. He held them on his knees while he told them tales of his adventures, and they clamored for him to take them to sea so they could have adventures of their own.

Honoria Raine wrote a book about her own adventures. In it she explained to young ladies what they could expect from any pirates with whom they might find themselves involved. She recorded what pirates liked and disliked, how they behaved, the words they used and what they meant, what kind of ships they sailed, and the kinds of treasure they preferred. She described what pirates expected from their wives, and why their orders should not always be obeyed.

Honoria had conferred with Christopher on the title, and they decided to call it *The Care and Feeding of Pirates.*

The little book sold thousands of copies up and down the coast and as far away as England. It was read by the ladies in London who enjoyed Alexandra's soirees, and smuggled into young ladies' finishing schools in Charleston.

Diana and Alexandra each made sure to acquire a copy.

Christopher read bits out to her as they lazed on the beach, their children playing in the sand not far away. Then he held the book over his head and told her he'd give it back for a kiss.

"That's how all this started," Honoria said, smiling her pretty smile.

"I know," Christopher said. He studied the sheen of her dark hair, the lovely coolness of her green eyes, the tiny lines around her mouth now much given to laughter. "I'm smart enough to know a good plan when I see it."

She laughed then, and kissed him, his fine Southern lady, and he fell in love with her all over again.

THE PIRATE HUNTER
JENNIFER ASHLEY

Widowed by an officer in the English navy, Diana Worthing is tired of self-important men. Then the legendary James Ardmore has the gall to abduct her, to demand information. A champion to some and a villain to others, the rogue sails the high seas, ruthlessly hunting down pirates. And he claims Diana's father was the key to justice.

When she refuses to tell him what she knows, James retaliates with passionate kisses and seductive caresses. The most potent weapons of all, though, are his honorable intentions, for they make Diana forget reason. They make her long to believe she's finally found a man she can trust, a man worth loving—a true hero who could rescue her marooned heart.

The Pirate
Next Door

JENNIFER ASHLEY

What is a proper English lady to do when a pirate moves next door? Add the newly titled viscount to her list of possible suitors? Take his wildly eccentric young daughter under her wing? Let the outlandish rogue kiss her with wild abandon?

As everyday etiquette offers no guidance, Alexandra Alastair simply sets aside her tea and follows her instincts—whether that involves rescuing her new neighbor from hanging, fending off pirate hunters, plotting against aristocratic spies, or succumbing to a little passionate plundering. Forget propriety! No challenge is too great and no pleasure too wicked, for Grayson Finley promises the adventure of a lifetime.
